THE WORLD'S CLASSICS

TILL EULENSPIEGEL

HIS ADVENTURES

PAUL OPPENHEIMER is a professor of comparative medi-
eval literature and English at The City College of New
York (CUNY). He has taught in the Department of
German at University College London, and in Germany,
as the recipient of a Fulbright senior scholar teaching award.
A widely published translator and critic, his publications
include two volumes of poetry, *Before a Battle and Other
Poems* and *Beyond the Furies: new poems*, as well as a study
of the origins of the sonnet, *The Birth of the Modern Mind:
Self, Consciousness, and the Invention of the Sonnet*.

Title page woodcut by Hans Baldung Grien from Johannes Grüninger's 1515 edition of Eulenspiegel's adventures.

THE WORLD'S CLASSICS

Till Eulenspiegel
HIS ADVENTURES

Translated with an Introduction
and Notes by
PAUL OPPENHEIMER

Oxford   New York
OXFORD UNIVERSITY PRESS
1995

Oxford University Press, Walton Street, Oxford OX2 6DP
Oxford   New York
Athens   Auckland   Bangkok   Bombay
Calcutta   Cape Town   Dar es Salaam   Delhi
Florence   Hong Kong   Istanbul   Karachi
Kuala Lumpur   Madras   Madrid   Melbourne
Mexico City   Nairobi   Paris   Singapore
Taipei   Tokyo   Toronto
and associated companies in
Berlin   Ibadan

Oxford is a trade mark of Oxford University Press

First published as a World's Classics paperback 1995

British Library Cataloguing in Publication Data
Data available

Library of Congress Cataloging in Publication Data
Eulenspiegel (Satire). English
Till Eulenspiegel : his adventures / translated, with an
introduction and notes by Paul Oppenheimer.
p.   cm. — (The World's Classics)
Includes bibliographical references.
I. Oppenheimer, Paul.   II. Title.   III. Series.
PT941.E8E5 1995   833'.3 — dc20   94–11778
ISBN 0–19–282343–4

1 3 5 7 9 10 8 6 4 2

Typeset by CentraCet Limited, Cambridge
Printed in Great Britain by
BPC Paperbacks Ltd.
Aylesbury, Bucks

For Julie and Ben

ACKNOWLEDGEMENTS

I am grateful to many colleagues at The City College of New York, University College London, and Garland Publishing for advice and assistance, as well as to the staffs of The British Library, The Library of The City College, The New York Public Library, and the library of Princeton University, from whose copy of the Schröder facsimile of the Grüninger edition of 1515 the woodcuts for this edition were reproduced. I wish to acknowledge, too, the corrections offered on very early versions of this book by the late W. T. H. Jackson and Howard Schless, both of Columbia University. The wealth of contributions from other scholars is, I trust, either implied or indicated in the text and bibliography. I am, finally, most grateful to Andras Hamori and Francesca Simpson Pedler, whose friendship and constant stream of good suggestions have enabled me to make this a better book than it otherwise would have been.

New York, London, 1994   P.O.

CONTENTS

CONTENTS

INTRODUCTION

Europe's most famous jester is himself the creation of a jester. His book is in many ways itself a jest. Whether the author is Hermann Bote (ca. 1467–ca. 1520), as certain investigators of these tales lately wish to maintain, burying his name as a mangled acronym in his text, or someone else whose surname begins with N., as the author announces in his Foreword, it seems clear that he is busy on a well appointed medieval-Renaissance stage in acting out elaborate charades before his audience. His inconsistencies thus become his calculated consistency. His humility becomes a special sort of bravado. His disdain of hypocrisy belies his obvious enjoyment of it. His highest personal value is no doubt his invisibility. In this, his curious reticence about himself, he matches the curious invisibility of his jester-hero.

Till Eulenspiegel is both spectacularly famous and paradoxically unknown. Regarded with delight as Germany's, if not much of the world's, jester *par excellence* for the past five hundred years, he has suffered the frustrating indignity, over the last two centuries, of being reduced to infantile proportions as the childish hero of a children's book. If every German is weaned on Eulenspiegel's adventures, so to speak, and believes that he knows who Eulenspiegel is, he has probably not read his adventures in their original, highly scatological forms at all, but instead run into one of their numerous bland adaptations. The satire too has been censored, or so toned down, that its native hue of sophistication, an adult and often merciless instrument, has been sicklied o'er with the pale cast of mortification. Lately this situation has been changing, perhaps because in the new social climate of Western cultures prudishness itself is readily regarded as an impropriety. Wolfgang Lindow's impressive re-editing of the earliest complete edition of Eulenspiegel's adventures, that of 1515, in 1966, opened a green and fruitful period in Eulenspiegel scholarship. His efforts were succeeded, in 1969, by an event even more remarkable. Peter Honegger, a Swiss jurist and Eulenspiegel enthusiast, announced the discovery of a lost fragment of either the first or second edition of the Eulenspiegel stories, published in Strassburg in 1510–11. Ingenious detective work, done on the basis of this discovery, prompted Honegger to declare, in 1971, that the entire book had been written by Hermann Bote, a Low Saxon author of repute, who had concealed his name in an acrostic among his penultimate six Late Middle High German chapters, possibly because he feared reprisals from scurrilous local officials. The book could thus no longer be regarded as anonymous. Nor was it, as quite a few scholars had believed, a *Volksmund* product, a 'communal effort' over decades to link in picaresque fashion the elements of a popular or 'people's' legend reaching back to 1350, the year of the 'real' Eulenspiegel's supposed death. The legend, which certainly existed, and which sustains an amazing vitality to this day, had been supplied with an organic unity by a single writer.

With this said, it must be added that Honegger's ideas are both intriguing and problematic. The reader new to Eulenspiegel's adventures, however, should understand that despite this, Honegger's discovery as well as his ideas led to an explosion of scholarly and critical interest over the next eighteen years, a veritable flood of fresh articles and books. This flood continues unabated. There may in fact be no area of *Germanistik* that has experienced so rapid and fascinating a recent expansion, or with such constructive results. The expansion is appropriate and long overdue. The importance of the subject demands it. The truth is that Till Eulenspiegel — the Eulenspiegel of this book — occupies a position of secret happiness in the German soul. It is a position, as well, of impudent glory. It rivals — not in grandeur but in magic, influence, and mystery — the positions of King Arthur in the soul of England and the Roland of *La chanson de Roland* in the soul of France. Like these legendary figures, Eulenspiegel exerts a magnetism that has been felt not only by many subsequent authors writing in German and other European languages, but also by composers and artists, including brilliant ones such as Hans Baldung Grien, who was a friend of Albrecht Dürer and who made a number of the woodcuts for the earliest editions (these are reproduced here and are discussed below). Eulenspiegel's attraction for millions has also expressed itself in even more obvious signs of public self-perception. As of 1983, at last count, at least twenty-one public statues, carvings, painted figurines affixed to houses, plaques, and other *Denkmäler*, some of them quite recent, in Germany, Flanders, and Holland commemorated Eulenspiegel's exploits. The jester whom Germans always felt to be far more than a jester—who was, and is, an actor, thief, liar, prankster, devil, saint, sadist, philanthropist, and, more than these, an early and interesting linguistic philosopher—still mesmerizes and enchants. The fact, therefore, that this new, full, and collated translation of the editions of 1515, 1519, and recently discovered fragments is the first complete one done into English in several centuries must be seen as rather astonishing. As becomes clear to the most casual reader of Eulenspiegel's adventures, the absence of an English version has shuttered a lucid window through which to view ordinary life in the later Middle Ages and the Renaissance. The absence has also prevented an encounter with one of the most original and compelling authors to have written in Late Middle High German.

Whoever composed, compiled, and wrote these tales, and in the process created the complex jester who survives today, lived in a pre-national Germany during the Age of Christian Humanism. This historical context, which is also political, economic, social, philosophical, and to some extent religious, needs to be recognized. The grand German castles, fortresses, and palaces—ten thousand of them in German-speaking duchies at the start of the sixteenth century—must in fact be reimagined, not in their present ruins but in their previous magnificence. The stones still sang of a dying knightly splendour. The crossbow, with its steel-tipped missiles, remained a ubiquitous obsolescent weapon. Artillery, a creature of the feral European battlefields for over two centuries by 1500, roared against the awkward clashings of obsolescent armour. Cavalry horses, to be sure, would continue to mass, glitter in their protective steel casings, and charge until the invention of the tank, and beyond, some four centuries later. At a time when printing books with moveable type was a spreading novelty, new coal and iron mines in Saxony and Bohemia lured thousands of worker-colonists from across Europe. Cities such as Strassburg, together with the growing urban communities of the German south, formed a nexus of trade, banking, and a more sophisticated cultural life than elsewhere in Germany. In Strassburg alone, where Eulenspiegel's adventures were first published by the prolific publisher Johannes Grüninger, at least eighteen publishers produced dozens of books per year by the end of the fifteenth century, on an array of subjects that included the classics, collections of *fabliaux*, and beer-making.

The intellectual climate consisted of revolutionary storms and arid frigidity. The quest of the new, often inspired by the rediscovery of the old, encountered a gelid rejection. The dismissal of Church Latin and medieval scholasticism—as is reflected in N.'s remark in his Foreword to the tales, 'I am, I'm sorry to say, unfamiliar with written Latin and am a simple layman'—is part of the humanist author's typical pose as an advocate of the vernacular. Where today a classical education is viewed as broadening, fifteenth-century humanists, opposed to mere catechistical uses of Latin, often saw it as constricting. 'Ciceronianism,' as this sort of learning was called, was mere slavish imitation, albeit one condemned by writers who had certainly studied their Ovid and Virgil. The tolerance of the new Renaissance art and humanistic scholarship in one district matched the fierce repression of both in the next. At the same time, the loose and often squabbling confederation of German princes under the Holy Roman Emperor Maximillian I (1493–1519) permitted the flowering of an inquisitive literature, humanist in character, whose intellectual vigour, satire, and bitter assaults on priestly corruption helped to stimulate the coming Reformation. Conrad Celtis (1459–1508) produced a popular erotic poetry full of physical images and candour. Ulrich von Hutten (1488–1523) wrote anti-clerical diatribes whose teasing satirical tone contributed to the rebellions among German knights in 1522. Johann Reuchlin (in 1506) published a book, *On the Rudiments of Hebrew*, in which he argued that Hebrew was the only proper language for Christian theology. His bizarre position led him to reject anti-Semitic theologians on the one hand, and Martin Luther on the other. Rudolf Agricola (1443–85), probably the first major German humanist, though he was born in Holland, wrote a life of Petrarch, a textbook on logic (in which he sought to make logic the basis of grammar), and the *Mensa philosophica*, at least one of whose witticisms, found in the adventures of Till Eulenspiegel, suggests that the author of the Eulenspiegel stories was familiar with Agricola's work (see the note on Tale 57). In the darkened recesses of the great German and Austrian cathedrals, among the rich new altarpieces lit by candles and by sunlight distilled through windows of medieval and Renaissance stained glass, the Church seemed to await, in mistrustful patience, the waves of popular disgust soon to rise against it. A lush choral music could nonetheless be heard in the cathedrals, as well as in the town and city streets outside. Sacred and secular polyphonic songs, by Hofhaimer, Finck, Isaac, and Senfl, have survived in two major *Liederbücher*. Part-singing was most favoured, and many of the songs reveal influences of the medieval *cantus firmus* technique and the *Minnesänger*, often in a melodic line whose 'Germanness' is distinguishable less as a smoothness — a quality more typical of Dutch and French compositions — than as an awkward, alien intensity. Wandering professional musicians, plying their trade in the large market places and on feast days, made intricate use of the transverse flute, so called because when played it was held across the face. This instrument had been invented in Germany in the twelfth century. While its manufacture had spread to other countries, it retained a special popularity in Renaissance Germany.

In such an atmosphere, mixing scepticism, entrepreneurial daring, technological and aesthetic innovation, fierce liberalism, and fierce conservatism, jest-books, or *Schwankbücher*, found a ready audience. To judge from the popularity of jest-books such as Eulenspiegel's, nearly everyone who could read was prepared to laugh at everyone else. Nationalism, in the modern sense of national consciousness or even nation-worship, was hardly an impediment to national jeering. Nationalism did not exist, any more than did Germany as a nation. Christianity itself, as an institution, invited contradictory responses. An early German example of the jest-book genre is *Der Pfaffe Amis*, a rhymed *Volksbuch* of the thirteenth century, and one of the sources of the Eulenspiegel stories. More influential on the medieval-Renaissance tradition of these books, though, is Poggio's *Facetiae* (1438–52), which is another possible source (for Tale 26). Gian Francesco Poggio Bracciolini was born on Feb. 11, 1380, in Terranuova, and died on Oct. 30, 1459, in Florence. He spent much of his life in making scholarly discoveries. He found, for instance, 'lost' manuscripts of Quintilian, Cicero, and Lucretius (his *De rerum natura*) in monastic libraries at Cluny, St Gallen, and Cologne. As the inventor of 'humanist' script, which later served as the basis of roman type fonts, he became secretary to Pope Boniface IX. Poggio's obscene and scatological *facetiae* certainly broaden the range of what becomes an international humanist tradition of *Schwankliteratur*, or 'fool's literature' in the widest sense. This tradition, influenced by folktales and medieval *fabliaux*, includes *Das Narrenschiff* of Sebastian Brant (published in 1494, with illustrations by Albrecht Dürer; translated into English in 1509 as *The Ship of Folys of the Worlde*, by Alexander Barclay), Thomas Murner's poem *Die Narrenbeschwörung* (1512), and Erasmus' *In Praise of Folly* (in Latin, 1509). Eulenspiegel's book and its author belong squarely in this quixotic stream of humanist satirical writing. The international spread of the jest-book genre — its indifference to mere territorial passions — is in fact crucial to understanding it, and to understanding Eulenspiegel and his literary creator as well. Local details, especially in the Eulenspiegel stories, are often sketchy, though valuable as cultural indices. They emphasize, rather than detract from, the author's ambitions to mock and satirize the pretentiousness of mankind generally. The foreign settings of some of Eulenspiegel's adventures complement this fact. So too does the author's concern with the great themes of his Renaissance-humanist as well as his (later) Reformation contemporaries — Martin Luther, Castiglione, Machiavelli, and Rabelais, as well as Erasmus. Luther's passion for a Christianity purified of corruption shows in traces here and there, as do Castiglione's perception that cultures without rules of civilized behaviour cannot survive, Machiavelli's exposure of the mechanics of political power, Rabelais' ridicule of megalomania and fatuous language, and Erasmus' fascination with folly born of greed. The achievements of Luther, Rabelais, and particularly Erasmus exhibit precisely that delight in philology — an international study by definition — which lies at the centre of the Eulenspiegel stories and which is typical of humanist scholars. The Renaissance *homo universalis* was in fact first a philologist and second an artist and encyclopedist. In a pre-Copernican universe in which God was still regarded as an abstraction, a word or *verbum* (a concept derived from the beginning of the Gospel of St John, 'The Word was God'), this philological *Wanderlust* was not in the least surprising. Beyond these typically internationalist concerns of the humanists, the author of the Eulenspiegel stories shares another, perhaps personal quality with them and other Renaissance thinkers: his contradictions. Like Rabelais, he combines vulgarity with sensitivity. Like Machiavelli, he mixes elegance and (as in Machiavelli's comedies) poor taste. Like Benvenuto Cellini (1500–71), he displays violence and sympathy. Like Poggio, he marries eloquence and scatology. The author of the Eulenspiegel stories also makes no effort to resolve his contradictions, or those of his hero, into some sort of unctuous ideology. In this too he resembles Machiavelli, Cellini, Rabelais, and Erasmus — or for that matter, Hamlet. If he never offers anything resembling their larger visions, he certainly seems bent on suffusing his work with a mischievous genius of individualism and independence. These contradictions are likewise apparent in the character of another humanist contemporary who may supply an explicit link between the author of Eulenspiegel's adventures and humanist satire: Willibald Pirckheimer. Pirckheimer (1470–1530), a wealthy Nuremberg physician, was a widower who lived with several mistresses in succession and the bastard children he had by them. He was a classicist of note. He corresponded with Erasmus. He was a friend of Albrecht Dürer, whose most famous assistant, Hans Baldung Grien, created (as already noted) a number of the woodcuts for the first editions of Till Eulenspiegel's adventures.

In the Foreword to the tales, which is the only part of the book written in the first person singular, the author tells us these facts about himself: that his initial is 'N.'; that he is writing in the year 1500; that he has been asked to 'compile' [zesammenbringen] these 'accounts and tales' by various people who would have been 'pretty grateful' to him for doing so; that he lacks sufficient 'intelligence and understanding' for the job; that he believes, or strongly suggests that he does, in God; and that he does not know how to write Latin. He also makes his ambition clear: 'to create a happy feeling in hard times, so my readers may experience good, pleasant entertainment and fun'. His work will, if successful, give the greatest pleasure to people who are lonely in winter, when the 'hours grow short'. This information is skimpy enough, and while reading the tales tells a good deal about the author's interests, it reveals nearly nothing about him biographically. The peculiar quarrels among scholars over the author's identity have, at least until recently (and even here the results are questionable), added little to the information about him.

The puzzle here has to do with unity — is the book indeed by a single author? — as well as with the original sources of many tales and the possibility that, if there is a single author or compiler, he may be Hermann Bote. On the issue of unity, the evidence now seems sound enough. Consistently, the style makes an unusual division between the types of language used in its paragraphs of description and conversation. Virtually no figures of speech appear in any of the descriptive paragraphs, though there are occasional similes, while numerous figures of speech, including especially hyperboles, abound in the passages of conversation. This fact reflects both the author's and the hero's own fascination with language, something to be taken up below. Of equal importance is the book's presentation of an unusual 'excremental vision' of mankind. The word 'shit' appears in more than fifteen tales, and excrement is referred to in many of the rest. The excremental context is invariably satirical, and excrement becomes a mocking weapon that exposes pomposity. What is curious, however, is not so much the repeated theme of excrement as the absence of sex. At least thirty-three tales have prior sources,

but in collections that mingle excrement jests with sexual ones: *Die Geschicht des Pfarrers vom Kalenberg*, *Die Geschicht des Pfaffe Amis*, Poggio's *Facetiae*, *Le cento novelle antiche*, anecdotes by Morlini and Heinrich Babel, *Les repues franches*, and the prose romance *Wigoleis vom Rade*. By eliminating sex (though there is a bare, implausible hint of it in Tale 38) the author of the Eulenspiegel stories, unlike Chaucer but somewhat in the manner of Swift in *Gulliver's Travels*, stresses a sour merriment indeed.

While this type of evidence certainly indicates a single hand, none of it proves the case for Hermann Bote, which as yet remains unestablished. The 'acrostic' of Bote's name in the book's final chapters, as discovered by Honegger, is incomplete. It may not be an acrostic at all. The 'misarrangement' of many of the stories, claimed by various scholars, may or may not exist (in translating I have adhered to the order of the tales in the editions of 1515 and 1519, which is duplicated in an almost complete edition of 1510–11, discovered in 1975 by Bernd Ulrich Hucker). Stylistic resemblances, also often insisted upon between Bote's considerable *œuvre* and the Eulenspiegel stories, consist mainly of adages and popular sayings. Even N.'s Foreword, with its exhortation to his readers to rewrite and improve his work, repeats literary conventions commonplace through much of Europe since the thirteenth century. As a result, modern readers are probably forced to content themselves with the remarkable literary character, Till Eulenspiegel, invented by a still unknown writer and thinker, who most likely came from Brunswick and who may, or may not, be Hermann Bote. To this it may be added that the author's initial, N., is probably not an initial at all and may merely mean unknown or unknowable.

Till Eulenspiegel is one of the most scandalous characters, and one of the queerest fish, in the history of German fiction. Even his name, which means 'owl glass' or 'owl mirror' or 'wise mirror' or, metaphorically, 'wise reflection', but which also had more sinister meanings in the sixteenth century, has provoked controversy among scholars who question whether his name has any meanings at all. He is a creature, and largely literary creation, of infinite contradictions and skirmishing paradoxes. He died, or so the last chapter of his adventures announces, in 1350, but it is a puzzle whether he ever lived. He practises, or so he says in Tale 30, the telling of the 'truth', but his definition of 'truth' is odd, and by any usual standards he must be judged a liar. His incessant need to expose human gullibility, superstitious fears, and naïve frailties—this, if anything, is the theme of his life—has so horrified translators and adaptors of his tales that they have consistently mistranslated, misadapted, misrepresented, and mischristened them, subjecting them to a prudishness that would no doubt have made Eulenspiegel and his sixteenth-century audience laugh with derision. Estimates of his intentions also differ. He has been regarded as an avenger of peasants, a representative of the oppressed, a romantic loser, a rebel, a nihilist, a callous judge of humanity, an embodiment of German motherwit, a critic of language, a good-for-nothing, a cataloguer of Low German humour, a symbol of Satan, a parasite, an incarnation of the 'cold spirit' of materialism, an enlightened explorer of the 'I–Thou' relationship, a traitor to humanity, a cynic, and a representative of a new age, or modern times. The discrepancies indicate his tenacious and complex vitality. If many of these views seem absurd and divorced from what the tales actually say, revealing little about Eulenspiegel himself, they at least show a good deal about the hallucinations of private enthusiasms flimsily disguised as literary criticism. In fact Eulenspiegel's import, as a contradictory character with clever ideas about the world, has been frequently, though not always, overlooked. Far from being a 'representative' or 'symbol' of this or that fad or trend of the moment, or from being simply a fool, clown, rogue, and example of the medieval literary type of the buffoon and rascal, he is, as the tales in fact demonstrate and as will be discussed shortly, a protean and original philosopher of language.

Startlingly, and with the connection so far unnoticed, the literary Till Eulenspiegel is also a vagabond and explorer of sorts, and steps onto the public stage in a Renaissance society full of vagabonds and fascinated with explorers. This social context is vital to illuminating his refreshing paradoxes, various facts about his name, and humanist aspects of his character, such as his passionate interest in language. Vagabonds and wayfarers were well known in Europe since at least the eighth century, when Charlemagne issued an edict against 'magones et cogciones qui sine omni lege vagabundi vadunt' [peddlers and hucksters who wander about lawlessly as vagabonds], tricking and deceiving people right and left. Undeterred by Charlemagne's attitude, vagabondage increased hugely. By 1250, it was an organized way of life. By 1400, it had become an established, if risky, profession of sorts, especially east of the Rhine, with masses of itinerants, many of them rogues, knaves, thieves, and mendicant frairs, as well as quack doctors and idle mercenary soldiers, flooding the roads. Eulenspiegel clearly belongs among this company of potential Bardolfs, Falstaffs, and Lords of Misrule, in Thomas Nashe's famous phrase. In tale after tale (see, for instance, Tales 15, 16, 36, and 65), Eulenspiegel appears as a tramp and vagabond, as a type that would have been easily visible and familiar to N.'s audience, defeating the harshness of incessant penury and the fierce cold of winter with a native predatory shrewdness.

He is a type of explorer too, not only of places and countries but of groups and classes of people, and this aspect of his nature must be seen in the light of a growing German and European enchantment with explorers generally, and especially with explorers of the New World. His Continental adventures complement their American adventures. His ridicule of the mundane matches their worship of the fantastic. His wanderings and practical jokes mirror in reverse their visits among alien tribes and their efforts at economic exploitation. By 1500, printed broadsides, sold in major German cities such as Brunswick and Augsburg and serving as the newspapers and magazines of their day, depicted the unusual and often fanciful customs of Brazilian indians, their 'many' wives, their devotion to magic, their 'purity', and their 'simplicity' (anticipating Rousseau's conception of 'natural' and unspoiled man two and a half centuries later). The illustrations accompanying these broadsides were big and colourful, the captions lengthy. The broadsides sold right alongside others that depicted and recounted *facetiae* such as those in *Till*

Eulenspiegel. Popular enthusiasm for the two ran in tandem, as if the muses of history and comedy, Clio and Thalia, shared a new frontier.

   Much of N.'s method can be seen in his combining qualities of the vagabond and explorer in the Eulenspiegel that he creates out of the materials of folklore. His method is to synthesize. In fact he synthesizes several contemporary types, the court jester, the clown, the medieval-Renaissance vaga-bond, the Renaissance explorer, the actor, and the rogue, with those other two familiar humanist interests, satire and philol-ogy. The result, N.'s achievement, is a complex and vibrant enigma. Even the hero's original name, Ulenspiegel, seems to show this method at work. It appears to be a fortuitous synthesis of meanings, leading early scholarship to be con-cerned with the question of the 'real' Ulenspiegel (with the name spelled in confusingly different ways). While this ques-tion may never be completely resolved, it is obvious, on the basis of the many intermingled sources of Eulenspiegel's exploits that even should this be the case, the Eulenspiegel who survives is primarily a literary creation (see also the note on Tale 1). The problem here is that the author never seems to connect the possible meanings of his hero's name with his character. On the other hand, in Tale 40, for instance, we find: 'Now, Eulenspiegel had this custom whenever he did some mischief where he was unknown: he took chalk or coal and drew an owl and a mirror over the door, and underneath wrote, in Latin, *Hic fuit*.' It may thus be true that the stories supply no explicit connection between the character of the hero and his name, but this description, which clearly links his name with his customary behaviour, indicates (a) that Eulenspiegel himself sees his name as meaningful, and recog-nizably so, and (b) that his audience also knew what his name meant and expected him to behave mischievously. Two other points should also be made. The first is that Tale 94 describes Eulenspiegel's gravestone as having an owl and a mirror carved into it; the second, a signal of a widespread view surely, is that two contemporary woodcuts, of Eulenspiegel himself, on the title page, and of his gravestone, also show the owl and the mirror. What, then, did his name mean? The answer is that it fairly glowed with meanings for N.'s audience, these ranging from the socially cutting to the mythic to the scatological to the bloodthirsty. The 'mirror book' (in Latin, *speculum*; in German, *Spiegel*) was extremely popular in the late Middle ages and into the Renaissance. Such books sought to 'mirror' various activities and classes, such as confessions and wives, and usually overflowed with sententious ethical and moral instruction. Whether *Eulenspiegel* belongs in this tradition has always been a matter of dispute, chiefly because 'Ulenspiegel' is also an identifiable family name (see the note to Tale 1), though it is probably not the hero's, and because the name can also be understood as 'Ul'n speghel', a command or invitation to 'wipe one's arse', in contemporary hunter's jargon (from 'ulen', to sweep or wipe clean, and 'spiegel', arse or behind). Beyond this lies the metaphorical idea of the owl in Eulenspiegel's day. According to the *Etymologicum Teutonicae Linguae* of Cornelius Kilianus (1598) the Dutch 'wl', which is the source of 'ul' or 'ulen', was a symbol of the 'homo stolidus et improbus', or the stupid and evil or wicked man. The book, and the hero's name, may thus at least be understood as the 'mirror of the stupid and wicked', together with the less delicate image of arse-wiping or cleaning implicit in it. The owl in the Middle Ages was also regarded as the 'devil's bird', a perhaps appropriate symbol for a sometimes diabolical-seeming hero who turns all sorts of conventional values and morals upside down. The owl image, a conventional symbol of lost wisdom, may indicate enlightenment as well. The ancient 'owl of Minerva', goddess of crafts, became in fact a symbol of the new craft of book publishing. 'Ulenspiegel' or 'Eulenspiegel' may have pointed to the book as a 'mirror of wise enlightenment', in which readers, seeing their stupidity and evil reflected in Eulenspiegel's adventures, were to be led into a new and better condition. To this it must be added that the text itself never actually says or suggests anything of the sort.

What this wealth of meanings clearly reveals is what any reader at once realizes, that Eulenspiegel is far more than a mischief-maker, far more than a supremely entertaining practical joker. Goethe's one recorded statement about him is quite

to the point: 'Eulenspiegel: alle Hauptspässe des Buches beru-
hen darauf, dass alle Menschen figürlich sprechen und Eulenspiegel es eigentlich nimmt [Eulenspiegel: all the chief jests of
the book depend on this: that everybody speaks figuratively
and Eulenspiegel takes it literally]. Goethe's statement applies
directly to about half the tales in the book and in many of the
rest it is clear that figurative speech and Eulenspiegel's
interpretation of it influence the action. He wins a barrel of
beer from a priest who fails to shit, as he promises, in exactly
the middle of his church (Tale 12); he bakes owls and long-
tailed monkeys for a baker who jokingly tells him to bake
them (Tale 19); he presents a soapy sausage to a priest who
wants to eat till his mouth 'simply foams' (Tale 37); he breaks
through the roof of the house of a smith who tells him to get
up and out of his house (Tale 39); he cuts animals out of the
leather of a shoemaker who tells him to cut 'large and small',
like those the swineherd runs out of town (Tale 42); he brews
a dog called Hops instead of hops (Tale 46); he leaves his shit
in a wool-weaver's dining room when the wool-weaver tells
him to put it 'where no one will have it' (Tale 50); and so on.
When the response to his typical behaviour is a foul-faced
explosion, his mild reply is that he has only done what he was
asked to do. As has been suggested, Eulenspiegel is enthralled
with two cudgeling features of human relations: their need for
the sort of figurative language that amounts to dishonesty, and
their frequent collapse into violence when 'the facts', or any
truth at all, come to light. He is a jester and mythical buffoon
on a crusade against evasiveness and confusion.

  What should also be noted about Eulenspiegel (in contrast
to the sources of his adventures, such as *Pfaffe Amis* and
Pfaffe vom Kalenberg) is that, far from simply playing tricks
on the naïve, innocent, and gullible, he very often sets out to
deceive the dishonest, harsh, cruel, stupid, conceited, obnox-
ious, boring, and pretentious. There is little of the strutting
fop in N.'s hero, and nothing of the pavonine aristocrat. It is
usually hypocrisy and inhumanity that N. and Eulenspiegel
wish to debase, never the arrogance of wealth. Eulenspiegel
thus moves through what often seems a pitiless world, in
which his own ethics and compassion appear all the more

wondrous for their rarity, like green oases among murderous dark dunes. If his behaviour is generally sadistic, it is also, in this sense, moral. A full exposure to his adventures offers the choice pleasure, unobtainable in life but possible in art, of seeing wrongs perfectly righted and punishments perfectly suited to crimes. He frequently, as well, displays an interest in justice, as in Tale 70, when he twice comes to the rescue of some blind men while baffling and duping a greedy innkeeper and a duplicitous priest (stock characters whom N.'s audience would automatically have suspected of treachery in any case). Eulenspiegel is, however, interested in a special sort of justice. He has in mind not a legalistic idea of compensation, but justice as a child's passion for symmetry, logic, and retribution would like them to be, and as an unfair world only rarely allows them to be. Where more pliant people are satisfied with approximations of justice, Eulenspiegel advocates a fierce, literal precision. He is an eccentric mathematician of human reality, believing as much in the possible absolute perfection of the human world as a mathematician must believe in the absolute truth of the infinitesimal calculus. Eulenspiegel's near obsession with this sort of justice, like his devotion to 'truth' and to telling the truth, gathers with an erratic, accelerating force through tale after tale, impressing the reader eventually with the realization that his is a career with a definite intellectual dimension. This dimension, it turns out, and at a time when German itself was rapidly maturing into a modern sinewy expressiveness, is not only ethical but linguistic and even philosophical. Eulenspiegel is thus revealed as an explorer not only of groups of people but also of the effects of ordinary colloquial speech. He is apparently fascinated with the idea that vast numbers of injustices, along with misunderstandings, disputes, and struggles, result from errors in speech, as well as from the nature of language itself. In these senses, Eulenspiegel steps before his audience as both a humanist and a modern linguistic philosopher. His passion is to explore the mechanisms of psychological and what may here be termed assertional language. He yearns for information that can be trusted.

The trouble, from Eulenspiegel's point of view, is that the reality of most speech, and most literature, is psychological rather than informational. It is more concerned to recreate and reveal recognizable states of mind than to communicate 'facts'. In doing so, such speech adds to 'the stock of available reality', in Richard Blackmur's phrase, with the emphasis here falling on the word 'available' and on the idea that 'reality' becomes available only when endowed with language. 'A rose is a rose is a rose', for example, neither makes, nor intends to make, a statement about roses. It is not informational. Neither is it meaningless. Rather it is what may be called psychological and in a broader sense assertional. It depicts perfectly a state of mind, one that mocks logic and perception, and that does so through an unexpected exaggeration or extension; in other words, simply by asserting itself. It thus lets us look at a sort of stop-frame photograph of logic and perception. In valuable ways, it also sets us free to examine logic and ourselves. Its surprising repetition becomes an ambushing delight. Most of what we call conversation and imaginative literature is assertional in this way. It is more concerned to reveal or 'photograph' complex states of mind than to disclose the outside world. Swift's *Gulliver's Travels*, Lear's raging that seems to induce an actual tempest, and Dante's circles of hell are each logically absurd if they are considered as offering logical or true propositions about conditions in the physical world. Their intentions, however, are not to offer logical propositions, but to depict states of mind and states of internal conflict.

The language of imaginative literature, and of most speech, is indeed only seldom the language of factual propositions. Beyond this, it may be argued that sentences which contain propositional or purely factual truth are unlikely also to contain emotional 'truth', or to produce an emotional impact. The two categories appear in most cases to be mutually exclusive. This is why art and a good deal of conversation are deliberate nonsense and lying in the conventional sense, and also why art must remain so. Art's exposure of how to perceive and feel the world seems to result from its asserting conditions out of an emotional and psychological realm rather than proposing them out of the inanimate or even social world. Where science organizes what is speechless, art explores whoever is articulate. The artist (and most people probably attempt to become artists in at least their conversational lives) is more concerned with a statement's being right than with its being true. A revealing mirror of some recognizable psychology, and this blithely presented or asserted, is what counts.

It is precisely this revealing mirror that Eulenspiegel rejects and shatters wherever he finds it. In all of those tales in which he reacts literally to metaphors or hyperboles or emotional phrases, he seems deliberately to disregard the psychological and assertional qualities of the language addressed to him. In chapters in which he seeks to impose a perfect 'justice' on someone who has treated him harshly, he often exposes the innocent cruelty of the psychological and assertional language which we all speak and cannot do without. A single example may illustrate what is meant by this. In Tale 50, Eulenspiegel becomes a wool-weaver's apprentice, and does his work absurdly, as is his habit. The wool-weaver tells him sarcastically, 'If you want to beat the wool that way, you could just as well do it sitting down on the roof instead of standing up here on this ladder'. So Eulenspiegel climbs onto the roof and beats the wool up there. When the wool-weaver catches him on the roof, he remarks, again with obvious sarcasm, 'If you want to beat wool, beat it. If you want to fool around, fool around. Climb off the roof and shit in the wool basket'. So Eulenspiegel shits in the wool basket. But the point is that when Eulenspiegel takes the wool-weaver's 'instructions' literally, he ignores their assertional content. The purpose of the wool-weaver's statements is clearly to ridicule and to assert the state of mind of ridicule. It is hardly to inform or instruct. The wool-weaver, who is here using the assertional and psychological language of the artist, though admittedly in a rather shallow way, is himself ridiculed by someone who refuses to recognize the possibility of such language, and who in fact treats all language as if it were 'propositional', informational, and logical. It is also clear that Eulenspiegel acts as he does deliberately, rather than whimsically or petulantly. His cunning and intelligence are scarcely in question.

What then is to be concluded, if not that Eulenspiegel is deeply fascinated with language? His usual rejection of assertional and psychological speech simply emphasizes his avid sensitivity to it. Clearly, too, the conflicts in many of Eulenspiegel's tales arise because of nonsensical, or psychological, or purely assertional phrases. Is there, however, except in exclusively logical realms of thought, such as mathematics, any alternative to such language? Would not any alternative be finally less essential to us personally than its psychological and assertional opposite? This dilemma is incapable of a satisfactory resolution, except the provisional resolution of continuously remaining sensitive to its existence. That is what Eulenspiegel manages to be. A great deal of Eulenspiegel's life is spent in revealing the nature of the linguistic trap in which everyone thrives, fails, flourishes, struggles, and often thrashes about. His life also reveals ways of becoming free within this trap, through his frequent enthusiasm for justice, and through his apparent conviction that many of the fictional, or linguistic, confusions of life can be made to vanish, or turn into pleasures, if only they are met with clear, humour-filled thinking. His is a linguistic philosophy like a running midnight brook that flashes at the moon here and there, as its waters trick between strange, thick trees.

Woodcuts illustrating books were still a bright new invention in 1510. There is evidence that both artists and the public regarded them with awe. If one was wealthy and could buy what one pleased, one would have been familiar with the dazzling colour illuminations of medieval manuscripts, the Dutch tradition of which reached its apex in a series of posh, elegant books produced in the fifteenth century, coincidental with the invention of moveable type. The developing literate classes, who bought the first printed books with woodcuts, knew little, it may be assumed, of their colourful predecessors. Most of the new buyers and readers were not rich. A black and white illustration, printed on a portable world of pages, was therefore, in addition to its aesthetic qualities, an object of intense, novel, and miraculous pleasure. If people today can carry about with them, in tiny electronic boxes, the ghostly voices and moving image-ghosts of singers, dancers, and actors, the Renaissance audience for printed books, with their woodcuts, could suddenly pocket an entire universe, reduced to squiggly lines, human forms, and white space made voluptuous and plastic by a gifted use of black ink.

The virtual inventor of the illustrative woodcut was Albrecht Dürer (1471–1528). To be sure, he was not the very first to work in a medium that began to look recognizably more and more modern as early as the 1470s. Fine woodcuts illustrating books, by Schongauer and Israhel van Meckenem, were already announcing an interest of artists, as opposed to mere craftsmen, in what would soon mature into a startling new art form. Their influence, however, except on fellow artists such as Dürer himself, remained spotty and scant. An older conservatism prevailed. At the end of the fifteenth century, most illustrations for printed books were votive and practical, in the sense that they were mostly of the how-to variety, showing the intricacies of tools, wells, machines, and catapults. As a result, the decorative initial letter, an import into printed books from the illuminated capital letters of medieval manuscripts, gleamed on the new printed pages with an isolated, ebony grandeur. The problem, and one quickly solved by Dürer and his successors, was a universal artistic obedience. If the art that accompanied most illuminated manuscripts was not always interlaced with the text, still it almost always obeyed the text. The sensibility of the artist simply surrendered. The aesthetically eccentric bowed to the literary. The details of text and miniatures, usually corresponding exactly, or intended to do so, collaborated on an illuminated page that, with its designs, colours, and human figures, became, like the universe of medieval theologians, a single harmonious language, waiting to be read by all who knew the allegorical style of the Word, or *verbum* of God. If the books produced in the climate of this repressive attitude toward artists were often thrilling, they were so in the nervous, expectant sense in which prison-literature and concentration-camp art may also be thrilling. Against all odds, and in spite of imperious strictures, an individual artist's temperament has managed to express its vision and to blossom.

Dürer almost singlehandedly swept aside all questions of surrender. What had been merely a buoyant aesthetic game for Schongauer, that of making pictures for the amazing printed books, became for Dürer a billowing mission. His ambition was to illustrate the books rather than to illuminate their texts. For the first time, the artist would forge ahead with stylish abandon. He would set sail on his own, across seas and in directions scarcely or not at all revealed among the words. Impelled by this novel concept, writes Panofsky in his biography of Dürer, 'his prints set a new standard of graphic perfection for more than a century, and served as models for countless other prints'. An unexpected outcome of Dürer's rebellion, as can be seen in his own illustrated volumes, was that the pictures, whether woodcuts or etchings, often took precedence over the text altogether. His woodcuts, especially, became commentaries and assertions in their own right, a natural enough step in his case, if only because the chief catalyst of his adventurousness was humanism, the iconoclastic, testing outlook which, through his friends Erasmus and Pirckheimer, guided his entire career.

It is a matter of pure speculation whether Dürer did any of the woodcuts for *Till Eulenspiegel*, all of which are unsigned. The possibility cannot simply be dismissed. Not only was Dürer's relationship with Johannes Grüninger, the first publisher of the Eulenspiegel stories, probably professional as well as personal, but also Dürer's interest in the tales is well documented. What is more, nine of the woodcuts for the earliest editions have been shown to be by Dürer's pupil, Hans Baldung Grien: the woodcut for the title-page (which bears his characteristic vine leaf motif) and those for Tales 1, 5, 6, 8, 10, 11, 12, and 22. Baldung Grien thus remains the only identified artist, among perhaps four or five, who worked on Grüninger's editions. Behind him, as in a five-hundred-year-old twilight, may perhaps be discerned the ghostly influence of his friend and teacher, Albrecht Dürer.

The woodcuts themselves present their own grab-bag of puzzles, beauties, and revealing interpretations of the tales. Six woodcuts are repeated, with those for Tales 16, 36, 45, 49, 53, and 59 turning up again in Tales 51, 66, 81, 54, 77, and 60, respectively. The woodcut for Tale 20 also appears in Grüninger's earlier volume of Horace, published in 1498. The edition of 1519 substitutes different cuts for Tales 16, 44, 56, and 57. 67 woodcuts are accompanied by side-bar motifs, of which 63 are architectural designs and the remainder human figures. The side-bar woodcuts differ considerably from one another, with no clear pattern apparent in their differences. The larger, or chapter, woodcuts, though, almost invariably depict Eulenspiegel himself at the very moment when he plays his prank in the tale that they illustrate, and are clearly meant to catch him in the act.

Interestingly, none of the depictions of Eulenspiegel shows him in jester's costume. He nearly always appears in late fifteenth-century riding clothes, in garments so simple, so lacking in the sumptuous and gaudy, as to seem anonymous. The meanings of his plainness of dress will perhaps by now be obvious. On the one hand, he is not merely a jester; or more precisely, the role of jester is only one of the roles that he plays. On the other hand, he is obviously an actor. His simplicity of dress, exhibited over and over in the woodcuts (here slightly reduced in size), points to the fact that one of Eulenspiegel's chief activities is play-acting. Where Pfaffe Amis and Pfaffe vom Kalenberg almost always play themselves, Eulenspiegel (in more than thirty-six tales) either acts a part or pretends to be someone he is not. On various occasions he plays page-boy, barber's boy, painter, scholar, wandering monk, salesman of religious relics, cleaner of pelts, Abbess' scribe, dying man, blacksmith's boy, shoemaker's apprentice, brewer's apprentice, furrier's apprentice, tanner, carpenter, optician, cook, horse dealer, and sacristan. He deeply enjoys role-playing for its own sake. His role-playing is an instrument of revelation and an escape. Acting allows him to expose human pretensions and to be free. The rogue is hidden.

The woodcuts thus highlight the theatrical aspect of his nature. Certainly he operates on many levels of psychology, and of theatre, and this is no doubt one of the many reasons that he has been so well liked by his German audience. If he plays the devil, he also plays the philosopher of language; if he delights in clowning, deceiving, and provoking, he also not infrequently delights in setting matters straight between people. The final pleasure of Till Eulenspiegel seems in fact to lie in his fearless tearing at the masks of others, in his exposure of their egotism. He exposes it through language that means what it says, through behaviour that refuses to be diplomatic, and often (as mentioned earlier) through an aggressive, satirical use of human excrement. Eulenspiegel's aim, if he believes that any aim is worth anything at all, is thus to humble, charm, and entertain us by showing us that we are all linguistically and emotionally clumsy animals, animals that always fall on their faces and begin to babble when they aspire to become gods.

SELECT BIBLIOGRAPHY

Texts

ANON., *Ein kurzweilig lesen von Dyl/Ulenspiegel gebore uss dem land zu Brunsswick. Wie/er sein leben volbracht hatt. xcvi seiner geschichten*. Anon. text. Brit. Lib. cat. no.: C 57 C. 23 (Strassburg: Johannes Grieninger, 1515).

HONEGER, PETER, 'Faksimile wiedergabe des Fragmentes S1510/11 aus der Offizin des Johann Grüninger zu Strassburg', in *Ulenspiegel: Ein Beitrag zur Druckgeschichte und zu Verfasserfrage* (Neumünster: Karl Wachholtz Verlag, 1973).

LAPPENBERG, J. M. (ed.), *Dr Thomas Murners Ulenspiegel* (Leipzig: T. O. Weigel, 1854). [Earliest important investigation of Eulenspiegel sources, though the ascription of authorship to Murner is no longer accepted.]

LINDOW, WOLFGANG (ed.), *Ein kurtzweilig Lesen von Dil Ulenspiegel* (Stuttgart: Reclam, 1966).

SCHRÖDER, EDWARD (ed.), *Ein kurzweilig lesen von Dyl/Ulenspiegel gebore uss dem land zu Brunsswick. Wie/er sein leben volbracht hatt. xcvi seiner geschichten*. Photographic facsimile (Leipzig: Inselverlag, 1911).

Secondary Works

BOLLENBECK, GEORGE, *Till Eulenspiegel, der dauerhafte Schwankenheld: Zum Verhältnis von Produktions- und Reproduktionsgeschichte* (Stuttgart: Metzler, 1985).

CHANCE, JANE (ed.), *The Mythographic Art: Classical Fable and the Rise of the Vernacular in Early France and England* (Gainsville, Fla.: Florida University Press, 1990).

CHUTE, MARCHETTE, *Ben Jonson of Westminster* (New York: Dutton, 1953).

HUCKER, BERND ULRICH, 'Eine neuentdeckte Erstausgabe des Eulenspiegels von 1510/11', *Philobiblon*, 20/2 (June 1976), 78 f.

KINNEY, ARTHUR F. (ed.), *Rogues, Vagabonds, and Sturdy Beggars: A New Gallery of Tudor and Early Stuart Rogue Literature* (Boston: University of Mass. Press, 1990).

SICHTERMANN, SIEGFRIED H. (ed.), *Till Eulenspiegel: Vollständige Ausgabe des Textes von Hermann Bote* (2nd edn., Frankfurt am Main: Insel Verlag, 1981).

THOMPSON, STITH, *The Folktale* (New York: Holt, Rinehart and Winston, 1946).

WELSFORD, ENID, *The Fool: His Social and Literary History* (New York: Farrar & Rinehart, 1936).

WUNDERLICH, WERNER (ed.), *Eulenspiegel-Interpretationen: Der Schalk im Spiegel der Forschung 1807–1977* (Munich: Wilhelm Fink, 1979).

CONTENTS OF *TILL EULENSPIEGEL*

TILL EULENSPIEGEL

His Adventures

FOREWORD

In the year 1500 after Christ's birth, as one reckons, I, N., have been asked by various people to collect (for their sake) these accounts and tales and to show how in times gone by a clever, foxy and roguish son of a farmer was born in the Duchy of Brunswick and named Till Eulenspiegel — the sorts of things he dreamed up and did in foreign and German-speaking countries.

For this (my trouble and work) they would have been pretty grateful. I replied that I would be willing to do it, and more, but did not know how to finish anything like it with intelligence and understanding. So I made them a lot of excuses, with an amicable request to let me off from writing about Eulenspiegel (the things he did in various countries, which might have annoyed them), but they showed no willingness to agree with me. So according to my slight understanding, I have committed myself and taken the thing on, with God's help (without which nothing can be done), have started off with diligence, and would like to beg everyone's pardon so my narration puts no one in a bad mood or embarrasses anyone. That would be far from my desire.

My only ambition is to create a happy feeling in hard times, so my readers and listeners may experience good, pleasant entertainment and fun. Also there is in this my rather plain writing no art or elegance, because I am, I'm sorry to say, unfamiliar with written Latin and am a simple layman. My writing will best merit reading (providing that the reading of the usual masses not be interfered with) as the mice bite under the benches, and the hours grow short, and the baked pear tastes good with the new wine.

So I ask everybody: wherever my writing about Eulenspiegel seems either too long or too short, that he improve it. I do not wish to merit mere disapproval.

So much for my foreword. I now present Till Eulenspiegel's birth, along with various fables of Father Amis and Father vom Kalenberg.

1. *How Till Eulenspiegel was born, how he was baptized three times in one day, and who his godparents were.*

Eulenspiegel was born near a forest called the Elm, in the district of Saxony, in the village of Kneitlingen. His father was named Claus Eulenspiegel and his mother Anna Wibeken. Well, when she had recovered from childbirth, they sent the child to Ampleben, to the village, for baptism, and had it named Till Eulenspiegel — with 'Till' after a citizen of Ampleben who became his godfather. Now, Ampleben is the castle that was destroyed as a wicked thieves' castle by Magdeburg, with the help of other principalities, somewhat more than fifty years ago. The church and the village nearby were now in the charge of the worthy Abbot Arnolf Pfaffenmeier of St Ägidien.

When Eulenspiegel was baptized and they were ready to carry the child back to Kneitlingen, the godmother who was carrying him decided to cross a narrow bridge that lies between Kneitlingen and Ampleben. Well, they had drunk too many beers after the child's baptism, for the custom there is that one bring the child into the tavern after the baptism and have a good time toasting it (the child's father is supposed to pay for this). Well, the godmother fell into the water and muddied herself and the child so completely that the child almost suffocated. So the other women helped his godmother out with the child, went home to the village, washed the child in a kettle, and made it neat and clean again. Thus was Eulenspiegel baptized three times in one day: once at his baptism, once in that puddle, and once in the kettle with warm water.

2. *How all the farmers and their wives complained about the young Eulenspiegel, saying he was a rogue and scoundrel; and how he rode behind his father on a horse, quietly letting the people behind him see his arse.*

As soon as Eulenspiegel was old enough to walk and stand, he played lots of games with the young children. Like a monkey, he tumbled about and lay around on pillows and in the grass till he was three years old. Then he began to apply himself to all sorts of mischief, so all the neighbours complained together to Eulenspiegel that his son Till Eulenspiegel was a rascal. Well, the father went to his son and said, 'Why are our neighbours saying that you're a rogue?'

Eulenspiegel said, 'Dear father, I do absolutely nothing to no one. That I'll easily prove to you. Go mount your own horse, and I'll sit behind you and, keeping quiet, ride with you through the lanes. They'll still lie about me and say what they please. Take note of it.'

His father did so, hoisting his son behind him on his horse. Eulenspiegel now lifted his behind with its hole, let all the people look into his arse, and sat back down. So the neighbours and their wives pointed at him, and said, 'Fie on you. See what a rogue he is.'

So Eulenspiegel said, 'Listen, father, you see well enough that I keep quiet and do nothing to anyone. Even so, the people say I'm a rogue.'

So the father tried the thing again, seating Eulenspiegel, his dear son, before him on the horse. Eulenspiegel now sat still, but he opened his mouth widely, grinned at the farmers, and stuck out his tongue. This time the people ran over and said, 'Look here. He's a little rascal.'

His father then said, 'You were clearly born in an unlucky hour. You sit still, keep silent and do nothing to anybody. Even so, the people say you're a rascal.'

So the father left that place with him, and moved his household into the district of Magdeburg on the Saale — the river — from where Eulenspiegel's mother had come. Well soon afterwards, old Claus Eulenspiegel died, so the mother took care of her son. Well, his mother was poor, and Eulenspiegel had no desire to learn any trade. He grew to be sixteen years old there, amusing himself, and learning lots of ridiculous tricks.

3. *How Claus Eulenspiegel moved away from Kneitlingen to the Saale, the river, where his mother was born, where he died; and how his son Till learned to walk the tightrope.*

Eulenspiegel's mother lived in a house, and its courtyard led down to the river called the Saale. Well, Eulenspiegel began to walk the tightrope, doing so on the lattice-work of the house, because he did not want his mother to see it. She tolerated no foolishness from him when he played on that rope, and threatened to beat him for it. Once she found him on the rope, got a large club, and tried to shove him off it — so he ran away from her, out through a window, running up to sit on the roof where she could not get at him.

This held him till he got a little older. Then he began performing on the rope again, stretching it across the Saale, from the back of his mother's house to a house opposite. Well, lots of young and old people, observing the rope on which Eulenspiegel was going to perform, came over, eager to see him walk across it, for they were quite curious what sort of rare trick he might demonstrate or what sort of incredible jest he might pull off.

Well, when Eulenspiegel was sitting on his rope, with his performance at its best—for his mother was indoors and unable to do much about it—she crept up secretly anyhow, back in the house, to the lattice-work to which the rope was tied, and sliced the rope in two, so Eulenspiegel, her son, fell into the river, amid much derision, taking quite a bath in the Saale. The farmers also roared with laughter, and the young boys yelled at him, 'Heh-heh, have a good bath,' and so on. 'You've been asking for a bath for quite a while.'

This annoyed Eulenspiegel a good deal, so he paid no attention to the water, only to the mocking and screaming of the boys—and considered how he might get even with them and pay them back for this. In the meantime he washed himself off as best he could.

4. How Eulenspiegel relieved the boys of 200 pairs of shoes, over which they fought, making young and old tear their hair over them.

A short time after this, Eulenspiegel decided to avenge the hurt and mockery he had at his ducking. He stretched the rope out from another house, over the Saale, and let the people know he planned to walk the rope. The crowd, young and old, soon collected.

Eulenspiegel then told the boys that each one should give him his left shoe: he planned to show them a fine trick on the rope with their shoes. The boys believed this, thinking it all true. The old men did too.

So the boys started taking off their shoes and giving them to Eulenspiegel. Well, there were almost two equal piles from those boys; that is, twice sixty: half the shoes went to him. So he tied them onto a string, climbing with it onto the rope. When he was on the rope, and had the shoes with him on it, the old men and boys gazed up at him, for they thought he intended to do something extraordinary up there; and the

boys became a bit worried, as they wanted their shoes back
again.

Well, Eulenspiegel sat on his rope, making his preparations.
Then he yelled down from the rope, 'Everybody look out,
and everybody hunt for his own shoe again.' Then he sliced
the string in two, tossing all the shoes from the rope to the
ground, with one shoe tumbling over the other. The boys and
old men rushed right over to them. Well, one found his shoe
here, another there. And the one said, 'This shoe is mine.' The
other said, 'You're lying. It's mine.' So they grabbed one
another by the hair and began pummeling each other. One lay
underneath, another on top; the one screamed, the other wept,
the third laughed. This went on till the old men got into the
face-slapping too, pulling each other's hair.

Well, Eulenspiegel was sitting on the rope, laughing and
calling down, 'Heh-heh! Now look for your shoes, the way I
had to finish my bathing yesterday.' Then he ran off his rope
and left the boys and old men to themselves.

After that—because of the shoes—he dared not approach

those boys or the old men but stayed at home with his mother and mended Helmstädt shoes. This made his mother happy enough, and she thought he might still turn out all right. But she did not know that he had now made even more of a fool of himself — so he dared not come out of the house, and so on.

5. *How Eulenspiegel's mother tried to convince him to learn a trade — with which she meant to help him.*

Well, Eulenspiegel's mother was delighted that her son was so quiet. But she criticized him for not wishing to learn a trade. As he stayed silent, his mother continued to admonish him.

Finally Eulenspiegel said, 'Dear mother, anything a man decides on will take care of him all his life.'

So his mother said, 'I certainly have my doubts about that. I've had no bread in my house for two weeks.'

Eulenspiegel said, 'That has nothing to do with my statement. But a poor person who has nothing to eat should fast decently for Saint Nicholas, and if he has something, then he'll eat by Saint Martin's Eve. And that's how we'll eat too.'

6. *How Eulenspiegel cheated a baker out of a sack of bread at Stassfurt, in the city, and brought it home to his mother.*

'Dear God, help me!' thought Eulenspiegel. 'How can I satisfy my mother? Where can I possibly find bread for her house?'

Thus he went out of the village where his mother lived, toward the city of Stassfurt. There he noticed a rich baker's establishment, went into the baker's house, and asked whether he would send his master ten shillings' worth of rye and white bread. Eulenspiegel then named the Lord of some place, and went on to say that his master was at Stassfurt, in the same city, naming an inn at which he was staying. The baker was supposed to send a boy with him to the inn, where he would give him the money.

The baker agreed to this.

Now, Eulenspiegel had a sack with a hidden hole, and he let the baker count the bread into this sack. The baker also sent a boy with Eulenspiegel to pick up the money. But when Eulenspiegel had got a crossbow's shot from the baker's house, he let one white loaf drop out of the open hole into the mud. Eulenspiegel at once set down his sack, saying to the boy, 'Oh, I couldn't bring this dirty bread to my master. Quick—run home with it and bring me another loaf. I'll wait for you here.'

The boy ran back to get another loaf—while Eulenspiegel took off, going to the outer city, to a house. A cart from his village was standing there, on which he placed his sack. He walked on beside it, and so was led to his mother's house.

Well, when the baker's boy returned, Eulenspiegel had vanished with the bread, so the boy raced back to tell the baker. The baker quickly got over to the inn Eulenspiegel had named to him. There he found no one, and realized he had been tricked.

Eulenspiegel returned home, bringing the bread to his mother, and saying, 'Look at these! Now, eat them while they last—and fast with Saint Nicholas when they're gone.'

7. *How Eulenspiegel ate the breakfast bread, or rolls, with other boys, how he was made to overeat, and was beaten into doing so.*

Now, there was a custom in the village where Eulenspiegel lived with his mother: whenever a householder slaughtered a pig, his neighbour's children went to his house, there eating a soup or broth called the breakfast bread.

A farmer was living in that district, in that same village, a man who was extremely stingy with his food but who still dared not refuse the children their breakfast bread. So he thought up a scheme to make them sick of breakfast bread — and sliced the fatty rind of the bread into a milk-jug.

When the children arrived, boys and girls, with Eulenspiegel along as well, he let them in and closed the door. Then he poured out his soup, or breakfast bread. Now, there were a lot more of these pulpy pieces than the children wanted to finish eating. But whenever one walked away from eating and was 'full', the householder rushed over with a whip and beat him about the thighs — so everybody had to overeat. This householder was well apprised of Eulenspiegel's trickiness, so he watched him. Whenever he beat one of the others about the thighs, he beat Eulenspiegel even harder. He kept this up till they had been forced to eat all the pulpy pieces and breakfast bread.

Now, this pleased the children as well as grass might a dog, so afterwards none of them had any desire to go to that stingy man's house to eat breakfast bread or butcher's soup anymore.

8. *How Eulenspiegel made the stingy householder's chickens play tug-of-war over bait.*

The next day, when the man was going out, Eulenspiegel met him.

The man said, 'Dear Eulenspiegel, when would you like to come over for some breakfast bread?'

And Eulenspiegel said, 'When your chickens play tug-of-war over bait — four to a bit of bread.'

But the man said, 'Well, if that's your idea, you'll be a long time coming.'

Eulenspiegel replied, 'But what if I come before it's fatty-soup-time again?' And with that he walked off by himself.

Well, Eulenspiegel kept an eye out till he got his chance and the man's chickens went feeding along the lane. Eulenspiegel had twenty or more strings with him, and tied each, two by two, in the middle. He fastened a bit of bread onto the end of each one, took the strings, and laid them down hidden, with just the bits of bread exposed. Well, the chickens pecked here and there, and gulped down the bits of bread, getting the ends of the strings into their throats. They could not swallow them, though, because another chicken was tugging at the other end. Each one dragged on the next, neither swallowing the string nor able to get it out of his throat, because of the size of the pieces of bread. More than two hundred chickens stood about there, each one choking opposite the other, playing tug-of-war over bait.

9. *How Eulenspiegel crawled into a beehive; how two men came by night, intending to steal it; and how he made them tear each other's hair and let the beehive drop.*

It once happened that Eulenspiegel went with his mother to the dedication of a church in a village. Well, Eulenspiegel drank till he became drunk, so he went off to look for a place to sleep pleasantly and also be free of trouble from anybody else.

He soon found a pile of honey standing behind the place in the courtyard, and nearby were lying many empty beehives. So he crawled into an empty hive next to the honey, thinking he would sleep a little. But he slept from noon straight through to midnight. Well, his mother thought he had gone home, because she could not find him anywhere.

Now, during that same night two thieves came along, planning to swipe a beehive. 'I've always heard the beehive that's heaviest is best.' So they lifted the baskets and hives, one after the other, and arrived at the hive in which Eulenspiegel was lying (that was heaviest), and said, 'Here's the best beehive.' They hoisted it onto their necks and carried it off.

Meanwhile Eulenspiegel awoke and realized what they were about. Well, it was quite dark, so the one man could barely see the other, and Eulenspiegel reached out of the hive and grabbed the first man by the hair, giving him a good yank. At that he became furious with the man behind him, thinking he had pulled him by the hair, and started swearing at him. The man behind him said, 'You're dreaming or falling asleep. How could I grab you by the hair? I can hardly hold this beehive in my hands.'

Eulenspiegel laughed and thought, 'This game'll turn out all right.' And he waited until they had gone the length of a field. Then he gave the man behind a good yank on his hair also, making him wince. This man now got just as angry, and said, 'I'm walking and carrying enough to break my neck, and you're saying that I'm grabbing you by the hair. But you're grabbing me by the hair, enough to tear my scalp.'

The first man said, 'You're lying in your throat. How could I grab you by the hair? I can hardly see the road before me. Also, I know you just grabbed me by the hair.'

They walked on like this with the beehive, bellowing as if they were about to fight with each other. Not long afterwards, when their quarreling was most violent, Eulenspiegel yanked the first man again, making his head bang against the beehive. This fellow now got so angry that he let the beehive fall and then hit the man in the darkness behind him—in the head with his fists. The man behind also let go of the beehive, and plunged into the hair of the man ahead, and they tumbled over each other. Well, the one lost the other, not seeing where he was—and they lost themselves in the darkness, leaving the beehive lying there.

Well, Eulenspiegel peered out of the basket. Then, seeing it was still dark, he slept again, and stayed lying in there till it became bright day. Then he crawled out of the beehive, but had no idea where he was. So he followed a road till he came to a castle. There he hired himself out as a page-boy.

10. *How Eulenspiegel became a page-boy; and how his squire taught him that whenever he found the plant hemp, he should shit on it; so he shitted on mustard, thinking hemp and mustard were the same thing.*

Soon afterwards Eulenspiegel approached a country squire at a castle, pretending he was a page-boy. Well, presently he had to ride over open country with his squire. Now, along the paths stood hemp, which is called, in the area of Saxony where Eulenspiegel was at the time, 'henep'.

So his squire said, as Eulenspiegel was leading his horse for him, 'Do you see that plant standing there? That's called "henep".'

Eulenspiegel said, 'I see it all right.'

So his squire said, 'Wherever you find it, shit on it. The reason is that with that plant we tie up and take care of those who, without serving a proper Lord, support themselves from the saddle—with the fibre that's spun from those plants.'

Eulenspiegel said, 'Sure, that's a good thing to do.'

The courtier or squire rode here and there with Eulenspiegel, into many cities, and helped to rob, steal, and pilfer, as was his habit. But one day it chanced that they were at home and at rest. Well, when it was getting toward mealtime, Eulenspiegel went into the kitchen. There the cook told the boy, 'Go down to the cellar. An earthen jug or pot is standing there, with senep (as in the Saxon speech) in it. Bring that up to me.'

Eulenspiegel said, 'Yes,' but had never in his life seen any senep, or mustard. So when he found the mustard jug in the cellar, he thought to himself, 'What does the cook want with this? I suppose he wants to tie me up with it.' Then he thought a bit further, 'My squire's told me that whenever I find a plant like this I ought to shit on it.' So he crouched over the jug, filled it up, and brought it to the cook.

What happened? The cook suspected nothing, quickly prepared the mustard in the little dish, and sent it to the table. The squire and his guest dipped into the mustard—but it had a rather awful taste. The cook was sent for and asked what sort of mustard he had made. The cook tasted the mustard too, spat it out, and said, 'This mustard tastes as if it had been shitted on.'

Eulenspiegel started laughing. His squire said, 'How dare you laugh so casually? Do you imagine we can't taste what it is? If you don't believe it, come and taste this mustard too.'

Eulenspiegel said, 'I certainly won't eat it. Don't you remember what you told me in open country on the road?— If I see that plant, I'm supposed to shit on it? You take care of thieves that way, by hanging and throttling them? Well, when the cook sent me to the cellar for the senep, I followed your orders.'

The squire immediately said, 'You worthless scoundrel, this is the absolute end of you! The plant I showed you is called henep or hemp — and the one the cook asked to be brought is called senep or mustard. You've done this out of sheer spite.'

And he grabbed a club and tried to smack him. But Eulenspiegel was smart enough: he raced out of the castle and never returned.

11. *How Eulenspiegel hired himself out to a priest; and how he ate his roast chickens off the spit.*

In the district of Brunswick lies a village, in the Bishopric of Magdeburg, called Büddenstedt. Eulenspiegel arrived at the priest's house there. The priest hired him as a servant. But he did not know him. So he told him he should have happy days and pleasant service with him, eating and drinking the best — as well as his maid — and all he would be asked to do he could do with half-time work.

Eulenspiegel said 'Yes' to this (he intended to stick close to its meaning); then he saw that the priest's maid had only one eye.

Well, the priest's maid presently took up two chickens and stuck them on the spit to roast. She told Eulenspiegel to sit down and roast them. Eulenspiegel was agreeable and turned the chickens round. But when they were almost roasted, he thought, 'The priest definitely said, when he hired me, that I'd eat and drink as well as he and his maid — and that appears to be nonsense as far as these chickens are concerned. If that's the case, the priest's words won't be true, and I won't get to eat any of these chickens. I ought to be clever enough to make him keep his word.' So he snapped one off the spit and ate it without bread.

Well, when it was getting on to mealtime, the priest's maid (who was one-eyed) came over to the fire, meaning to baste the chickens. But she saw just one chicken on the spit, and said to Eulenspiegel, 'Well, there were two chickens. Where's the one chicken gone?'

Eulenspiegel said, 'Woman, open your other eye too — then you'll see both chickens.'

Now, when he poked fun at the woman that way for her one eye, she became extremely angry, and furious, with Eulenspiegel. She ran to the priest and told him how his splendid servant had mocked her for her one eye, how she had put two chickens on the spit, and how when she looked in on him to see how he was roasting them, she had found just one chicken.

The priest went over to the fire in the kitchen and said to Eulenspiegel, 'Why're you making fun of my maid? Besides, I see very well that there's just one chicken stuck on the spit, and there were definitely two of them.'

Eulenspiegel said, 'Yes, there were definitely two of them.'

The priest said, 'Well, where's the other chicken.'

Eulenspiegel said, 'It's stuck there all right. Open both your eyes and you'll see perfectly well that one chicken's stuck on that spit. I said so to your maid, but she got angry.'

Well, the priest began to laugh, and he said, 'My maid can't open both eyes. She's got just one.'

Eulenspiegel said, 'You're saying that; I'm not saying it.'

The priest said, 'Let's forget it. But it's still a fact that one chicken's gone.'

Eulenspiegel said, 'Yes, one's gone and the other's still stuck there. I've eaten the other, since you promised earlier I was supposed to eat and drink as well as you and your maid. Well, it made me sad that you might be regarded as having lied — that you might be regarded as having eaten both chickens so there'd have been none of it for me. So you'd not be a liar in what you said, I ate one chicken.'

Well, the priest accepted that, and said, 'My dear servant, that's one roast I didn't get. But from now on, act according to the wishes of my maid, as she sees fit.'

Eulenspiegel said, 'Yes, dear Father, just as you've told me.'

So after that, whatever the maid told Eulenspiegel to do, he half-did. If he were to fetch a bucketful of water, he brought one half-full; and if he were to fetch two logs for the fire, he brought one; were he to give the bull two bundles of hay, he gave it just one — and so on with a lot of things, till she realized that he was doing this to irritate her. She decided to say nothing to him, however, and complained about him to the priest.

So the priest told Eulenspiegel, 'Dear servant, my maid's complaining about you. Now, I've absolutely ordered you to do everything she wants.'

Eulenspiegel said, 'Yes, sir. I've also not done anything other than what you've told me to. You told me I could do your business with half-time work, but your maid ought to see well with both eyes. She sees, though, with only one eye, and sees only half. Therefore, I did half-work.'

Well, the priest started laughing. But his maid became increasingly irate, and said, 'Father, if you plan to keep this fool and rogue as a servant any longer' — she planned to leave him.

So the priest, against his will, had to give Eulenspiegel

notice. But he helped the farmers in choir-singing, since the sexton or sacristan of the same village had recently died. Then afterwards, because the farmers could not make do without a sexton, the priest came to an agreement with the farmers to take on Eulenspiegel.

12. *How Eulenspiegel became the sexton in the village of Büddenstedt, and how the priest shitted in his church and Eulenspiegel won a barrel of beer.*

When Eulenspiegel became a sexton in that village, he could sing out, as was proper for a sacristan. So the priest was now properly supplied with a sacristan.

One day the priest was standing before his altar, dressing himself and preparing to say mass. Eulenspiegel stood behind him, arranging the priest's vestment decently. The priest now let loose so enormous a fart that it thundered through the church.

Eulenspeigel at once said, 'Sir, what's this stuff? Is this how you serve Our Lord, with this sort of incense smoke, here before His altar?'

The priest replied, 'What're you talking about? This church is mine right enough. I've even got the right to shit in the middle of this church.'

Eulenspiegel said, 'It will cost either you or me a barrel of beer, if you do it.'

'All right,' he said. 'It's a bet.'

So they bet with one another. The priest said, 'You think I'm not daring enough?' And he turned round and shitted a really large pile in the church. Whereupon he said, 'Look, my dear sacristan, I've won the barrel of beer.'

Eulenspiegel said, 'No, Father. First we've got to measure accurately whether it's in the middle of the church, as we agreed.'

Eulenspiegel measured it. It was far from the middle of the church. So Eulenspiegel won the barrel of beer.

But the maid was outraged. She said, 'You won't let that cunning servant go till he brings you into utter disgrace.'

13. *How Eulenspiegel played a trick during Easter matins that led the priest and his maid to tear the hair of their farmers and go to war with them.*

When it was nearly Easter the priest told Eulenspiegel, his sacristan, 'It's a custom here that at Easter, during the night, the farmers always put on an Easter play, "How Our Lord Rises From His Tomb".' Well, he had to help with it. It was only right that the sacristan arrange and direct it.

Eulenspiegel thought, 'How can the play of the Marys possibly be set up with these farmers?' So he told the priest, 'Now, there's obviously no farmer here who's educated. You'll have to lend me your maid. She can read and write well.'

The priest said, 'Yes, yes. Just take whoever can help you with it. Besides, my maid's been in many of these.'

His maid was thrilled and wanted to be the angel at the tomb because she knew the lines by heart. Eulenspiegel also looked for a couple of farmers, and found them. Well, he wanted the three of them to play the three Marys, so Eulenspiegel taught one farmer his lines in Latin. The priest was to be Our Lord God, Who was to rise from His tomb. Well, Eulenspiegel approached the tomb with his farmers dressed as the three Marys. At that point, the maid, as the angel at the tomb, spoke her lines in Latin, 'Quem queritis?' — 'Whom seek ye here?'

The farmer who was the first Mary answered as Eulenspiegel had taught him: 'We're looking for a priest's old one-eyed whore.'

When she heard this — that she was being mocked for her one eye — she became utterly furious with Eulenspiegel, sprang out of the tomb, and tried to attack him in the face with her fists. But she struck carelessly here, hitting one of the farmers, so one of his eyes swelled up. When the other farmer saw this, he also lunged out, hitting the maid on the head as well, so her wings fell off. When the priest saw that, he dropped his wings, rushed to help his maid, grabbed the hair of one of the farmers, and they dragged one another in front of the tomb. When the other farmers saw what was going on, they ran forward and there ensued a terrific uproar. Well, the priest lay at the bottom with his maid, and the two farmers (the two Marys) also lay underneath — so the farmers had to pull them apart from one another.

But Eulenspiegel had taken note of these events and promptly got out of there. He ran out of the church, walked out of the village, and did not come back.

God knows where they found another sacristan.

14. *How Eulenspiegel announced that he planned to fly off the roof at Magdeburg, and dismissed his audience with scathing language.*

Soon after Eulenspiegel's experience as a sacristan he arrived in Magdeburg and did lots of clever things. Well, his name became widely known there for the first time, so people knew Eulenspiegel as a name to talk about.

He was now challenged by the best citizens of the city to provide some sort of entertainment. He said he was eager to do so — and that he planned to mount the town hall and fly off the roof. There at once arose such a clamor in the city that young and old gathered at the market place, hoping to see him do it.

Well, Eulenspiegel took up his position on the roof of the town hall, flapping his arms, and acting as if he really meant to take off. The people stood there, with their eyes and mouths open, thinking he was really going to do some soaring. Eulenspiegel then laughed and said, 'I believed there was no greater fool or buffoon in the world than I. But I now see clearly enough that this whole city's utterly full of fools. If you'd all told me that you planned to do some flying, I wouldn't have believed it — and you think I'm a fool. How am I supposed to fly? I'm after all neither goose nor bird. After all, I've got no feathers, and without feathers or plumes nobody can fly. So you can see very well it's all been a lie.'

Whereupon he turned, ran off the roof, and left the crowd, one part cursing, the other part snickering and saying, 'There goes a charlatan. Still, he spoke the truth.'

15. *How Eulenspiegel pretended to be a doctor, and doctored the doctor of the Bishop of Magdeburg, who was deceived by him.*

At Magdeburg lived a Bishop called Bruno, a Count of Querfurt, who heard about Eulenspiegel's pranks and had him summoned to Greuenstein. Well, the Bishop enjoyed Eulenspiegel's tricks and gave him clothes and money. His servants liked him very much and had a lot of fun with him.

Now, the Bishop had a doctor of philosophy staying with him who thought himself quite learned and wise, with the result that the Bishop's royal household heartily disliked him. Well, this professor's attitude was that he disliked having fools around. The professor told the Bishop and his advisors, 'One should keep wise people around the Lords of courts, and not retain these clowns, for all sorts of reasons.'

The knights and the royal household agreed on this much, that this was not a fair opinion of the doctor's. If somebody disliked clowning, he could easily leave. Nobody had to join in.

The doctor-professor argued against this. 'Fools for fools, and wise men for wise men. If Princes had wise people around them, wisdom would stretch before them, but because they have fools about, they learn nonsense.'

Some immediately said, 'Who are the wise? Those who claim they are wise? One easily finds people like that who have been duped by fools. It's appropriate for Lords and

Princes to keep all types of people at their courts. For with fools they drive away lots of brooding thoughts, and where Lords are, there fools like to be.' So the people of the court approached Eulenspiegel, arranged certain schemes with him, and asked him to dream up an idea (they wanted to help him with it, and the Bishop did too) so the doctor might be repaid for his 'wisdom', for the Bishop had listened to it as well.

Eulenspiegel said, 'Of course, you Lords and Princes. If you'd like to help me, this doctor shall be taught a lesson.'

They agreed on it. Well, Eulenspiegel travelled off over open country for four weeks, giving some thought to how he might handle the professor. Once he had planned the thing through, he returned to Greuenstein and disguised himself, pretending he was a doctor himself, because the Bishop's doctor-professor was often physically ill and took a lot of medicine for what he had. The knights at once informed the professor that a medical doctor had arrived.

The professor did not recognize Eulenspiegel, went to visit him at his inn, and after a bit of conversation, took Eulenspiegel along with him to the palace. Well, they came to an understanding, and the doctor-professor told his physician that if he could help him with his sickness, he would reward him decently. Eulenspiegel answered with the sorts of words that doctors used in those days, and lured the man into spending a night at his house so he might better diagnose his condition. 'I would very much like to give you something before you go to sleep, to make you sweat.' Through the sweat he was supposed to discover what the man's infirmity might be.

The doctor of philosophy let all this be said to him, believed it all, and climbed into bed with Eulenspiegel. For he believed only that what Eulenspiegel told him must be true. Well, Eulenspiegel gave the doctor a powerful laxative. The doctor thought he was supposed to sweat from this, not realizing it was a powerful laxative.

Eulenspiegel found a hollowed-out stone, deposited a pile of his shit in it, and set the hollowed-out stone, with his excrement, on the bed between the wall and the philosopher. The philosopher lay closest to the wall, with Eulenspiegel lying on the outer side of the bed. Well, the philosopher simply lay here, and turned toward the wall. At that point the excrement in the hollowed-out stone stank right under his eyes, so he had to turn toward Eulenspiegel. Eulenspiegel now released a silent fart, so that he stank horribly. The philosopher turned back again, but at once the filth in the hollowed-out stone attacked the man again, stinkingly. Eulenspiegel kept this up with the philosopher for almost half the night.

Well, at that instant the laxative began to do its work, acting sharply, quickly and forcefully—causing the philosopher to make himself quite filthy and to stink most awesomely. Eulenspiegel now said to him, 'What's this, worthy Doctor? Your sweat's been stinking horribly for a long time. What's the matter with you that you sweat such a sweat? It stinks quite foully.'

The philosopher lay there thinking, 'I smell it all right.' Indeed he was so full of the smell that he could scarcely speak.

Eulenspiegel said, 'Just lie quietly. I want to get a light, so I can see how bad your condition may be.' As Eulenspiegel was pulling himself up, he let another weighty shit fall, and said, 'Ah, such pain! I, too, am getting weak. I must have picked this up from your sickness.'

The doctor simply lay there, so ill that he could barely raise his head, but he thanked God his physician had left him, so he might get a bit of air. For whenever the doctor had tried to get up during the night, Eulenspiegel had told him he must not move, saying he might first sweat enough.

Eulenspiegel now really got up, left the room, and took off. Meanwhile daylight arrived. The doctor spotted the hollowed-out stone, full of excrement, standing beside the wall, and became so ill that his face was soiled with stink.

Well, the knights and people of the court looked in on the philosopher and wished him a good morning. The philosopher spoke feebly, could not answer well, lying in his room on a bench, on a pillow. So the court people got the Bishop over to the room, and he asked him how things had gone with his physician.

The philosopher said, 'I've been hounded by a con man! I assumed he was a doctor of medicine, but he's really a doctor of knavery!' And he told them exactly what had happened to him.

The Bishop and all the people of the court began to laugh, saying, 'This happened precisely as you said it would. You said, "One had better not fool around with fools, because any wise man turns foolish among fools." But you'll see that one man at least will be made wise through fools. Your physician was Eulenspiegel. You didn't recognize him, and you trusted him. You were tricked by him. But we, who tolerated his foolishness, knew him well. Despite that, we didn't want to warn you—since and because you wanted to seem so wise. Ah, nobody's wise enough to recognize fools too. And if there were no fools, how would the wise be known?'

At that, the doctor fell silent and stopped his griping.

16. *How Eulenspiegel made a sick child shit at Peine and was highly praised.*

One sometimes shies away from true, proven doctors because they want a small sum of money, but one must often give just as much to tramps.

That's how it went once in the Bishopric of Hildesheim. On that occasion Eulenspiegel traveled there too, and arrived at an inn when the innkeeper was away from home. Now, Eulenspiegel was fabulously famous around there. Well, the innkeeper's wife had a sick child, so Eulenspiegel asked the wife what was wrong with her child and what sort of illness it had.

The innkeeper's wife said, 'The child can't make his stool. If only he could make his stool, things would go better for him.'

Eulenspiegel said, 'There's a solid remedy for that.'

The woman said that if he helped her child, she would give him whatever he wanted.

Eulenspiegel said he would take nothing for it. For him this was a craft simple to practise. 'Wait a little. It'll soon come on.'

Well, the woman had something to do back in the court-yard, and went there. Meanwhile Eulenspiegel shitted a huge pile beside the wall, quickly placed the child's toilet stool over it, and set the child on the stool.

When the woman came back from the courtyard and saw the child sitting on his little stool, she said, 'Oh, who managed that?'

Eulenspiegel said, 'I managed it. You said your child couldn't get his stool, so I put him on it.'

Then she noticed what lay under the little stool. She said, 'Look at this! This must have been hurting my child in his little body. I'll forever be grateful that you've helped my child like this!'

Eulenspiegel said, 'This sort of medicine I can practise often, with God's help.'

The woman asked him whether he would kindly teach her his skill as well. She would give him whatever he wished. Eulenspiegel said he was about ready to leave, but that when he returned, he would teach it to her. So he saddled his horse, rode toward Rosenthal, turned around, and rode back to

Peine, intending to ride through it toward Celle. The naked bastard page-boys were standing there, in front of the castle, and asked Eulenspiegel which road he had come by. Eulenspiegel said, 'I'm coming from Coldville,' because he saw they did not have much on.

They said, 'Listen a minute, if you're coming from Coldville. What does winter have to say to us?'

Eulenspiegel said, 'He's got no messages. He'll make his announcements to you in person.' And he rode off, leaving the naked boys standing there.

17. *How Eulenspiegel got all the patients at a hospital healthy in one day, without medicine.*

Once Eulenspeigel arrived at Nuremberg. He posted announcements on the church doors and at the town hall, describing himself as a solid doctor for all sorts of diseases.

Well, there were quite a few sick people at the new hospital there, where is preserved the most reverend holy lance of Christ, together with other remarkable objects.

Now, the director of the hospital would have been delighted to get rid of these sick people and would scarcely have begrudged them their health. So he went over to Eulenspiegel, the doctor, and asked him whether, according to the announcements he had posted, he could really help the sick: doing so would pay well. Eulenspiegel said he would certainly make his patients a lot better, if he would set aside two hundred guilders and promise them to him. The director of the hospital promised him the money, providing he helped his patients. So Eulenspiegel swore that if he could not make these sick people healthy, he need not give him a single penny. This pleased the director so well that he immediately gave him twenty guilders.

Well, Eulenspiegel went straight into the hospital, taking two assistants along with him, and asked the patients, each one separately, what was wrong with them. Finally, as he was leaving each patient, he made him swear an oath, and said, 'What I now reveal to you, you must keep secret and reveal to no one.' The patients, with a solemn oath, assured Eulenspiegel of this. He then told each one in private, 'If I'm to help you regain your health and get you on your feet, that won't be possible unless I burn one of you into a powder and give it to the others to drink down. That I must do. Therefore, whoever is sickest among you all and cannot walk, I'll burn him into the powder, so I can help the others with him. To get you all up, I'll take the director of the hospital, stand at the hospital door, and shout in a loud voice, "Whoever isn't sick in there—let him get out here." Don't be asleep when I do!'

He told this to each one individually—that the last one out would have to pay the reckoning. Everybody listened attentively to these little speeches, and on the appointed day they rushed forward, on their sick and lame legs, as no one wanted to be last. When Eulenspiegel summoned them, according to his promise, they began charging out of the place, including some who had not been out of their beds in ten years. Then, since the hospital was quickly empty, he demanded his payment from the director, telling him he had to hurry off to another town. The director paid him his money, thanking him profusely, and he rode away.

But in three days the sick people came back, groaning with their illnesses. The hospital director asked them, 'What's going on here? I got you the greatest master physician, who helped all of you enough to walk out of here by yourselves.'

They at once told the director that Eulenspiegel had warned them that whoever was last through the door when he called 'time' he planned to burn into a powder. Well, the director of the hospital realized he had been tricked by Eulenspiegel, but he was gone and the director could do nothing about him. So the patients stayed on at the hospital, and the money was lost.

18. *How Eulenspiegel purchased bread according to the proverb 'One gives bread to him who has it.'*

Honesty invents bread.

After Eulenspiegel tricked the doctor, he went on to 'Half-City'[1] and strolled through the market place. Seeing it was hard winter, he thought, 'The winter is hard and the wind blows bitterly as well. You've often heard that "One gives bread to him who has it."' So he purchased bread for two shillings, took a table, and went to stand in front of the Cathedral of Saint Stephan, offering his bread for sale. He sustained this foolish illusion till a dog came along, swiped a loaf from his table, and ran into the courtyard with it. Eulenspiegel ran after the dog.

Meanwhile, a sow with ten young piglets arrived, knocking over the table. Well, each of them took a loaf in its mouth and raced off with it. Eulenspiegel started laughing and said, 'Now I see well enough the falsity of the proverb "One gives bread to him who has it." For it's been swiped from me.' He went on, 'Oh, Half-City, Half-City, how well you've been named! Your beer and food taste good enough, but your penny-purses are plain pigskin.'

And he went back toward Brunswick.

19. How Eulenspiegel apprenticed himself as a baker's boy to a baker — and how he baked owls and long-tailed monkeys.

When Eulenspiegel returned to Brunswick, to the baker's establishment, there was a baker living nearby who beckoned him into his house and asked him what sort of journeyman he was. He said, 'I'm a baker's boy.'

The baker said, 'I've got no boy at present. Would you like to work for me?'

Eulenspiegel said, 'Yes.'

When he had been with him two days, the baker told him to bake during the evenings because he could not help him till morning. Eulenspeigel said, 'Yes, but what'll I bake?'

[1] Halberstadt.

The baker was a playful man, but he suddenly became irritated. Jesting, he said, 'You're a baker's boy and you ask what you're supposed to bake? What does one usually bake? — Owls and long-tailed monkeys!' And with that he went off to bed.

So Eulenspiegel went into the bakery and turned the dough into nothing but owls and long-tailed monkeys, till the bakery was full of them. He baked them.

His boss got up the next morning, planning to help him. But when he came into the baking room, he found, instead of either breakfast bread or wheat bread, only owls and long-tailed monkeys. The fellow at once got extremely angry and said, 'Ah! What've you been baking here?'

Eulenspiegel said, 'What you told me to bake — owls and long-tailed monkeys.'

The baker said, 'What'll I do with this foolish stuff? This bread is useless to me. I certainly can't turn it into money.'

And he grabbed him by the neck and said, 'Pay me for my dough.'

Eulenspiegel said, 'All right. If I pay you for the dough, then the goods that were baked from it ought to be mine.'

The baker said, 'What do I care about these goods? Owls and long-tailed monkeys can't do my business any good.'

So Eulenspiegel paid him for his dough, put the baked owls and long-tailed monkeys into a basket, and trundled them out of the house to the inn 'At The Wild Man'. Eulenspiegel now reflected, 'You've often heard that one can't bring anything so peculiar to Brunswick that one can't make money out of it.' Well, it was just the day before Saint Nicholas Eve. So Eulenspiegel took up a position in front of the church with his little business, sold all the owls and long-tailed monkeys, and made a lot more money out of them than he had been forced to give the baker for the dough.

The baker found out about this. It annoyed him, and he ran to Saint Nicholas Church, planning to charge Eulenspiegel for the fire-wood and the costs of baking the things. But Eulenspiegel was already gone, and the baker's trouble went for nothing.

20. *How Eulenspiegel sifted flour by moonlight into the courtyard.*

Eulenspiegel wandered around the country and came to Uelzen, to the village, where he again became a baker's boy. At home with his boss, the man arranged everything for baking. Eulenspiegel was supposed to sift the flour during the night, to have it ready by morning.

Eulenspiegel said, 'Chief, you ought to give me a light, so I can see to do the sifting.'

The baker told him, 'I'm not giving you any light. To this day I've never given my baker's boys any light. They've had to sift by moonlight. Well, you'll have to do so too.'

Eulenspiegel said, 'If they've sifted that way, I'll do so too.'

The baker went to bed, planning to sleep for several hours. Meanwhile, Eulenspiegel took the sifter, held it out of the window, and sifted the flour into the courtyard, where the moon shone, according to its light. When the baker got up, planning to begin his baking, Eulenspiegel was still standing there sifting. The baker noticed that Eulenspiegel was sifting the flour into the courtyard, which was utterly white with flour. His boss said, 'What the devil! What are you doing? Isn't that flour expensive enough, that you're sifting it into that filth?'

Eulenspiegel said, 'Come now, Chief, take it easy! It's been done both in and by moonlight — and there isn't much lost, just a handful. I'll quickly scoop that up again. This doesn't hurt the flour one little bit.'

The baker said, 'While you're busy scooping up the flour — during that time — no dough's being made. It'll take too long to bake.'

Eulenspiegel said, 'My dear boss, I've got a good idea. We want, after all, to bake as quickly as our neighbour. His dough is lying in his hutch. If you want it, I'll quickly get it — and stick our flour in its place.'

His boss looked rather riled and said, 'You ought to get yourself to the devil! Oh, get over to the gallows and drag a thief here.'

'Yes,' he said. So he left for the gallows. The skeleton of a thief was lying there, having fallen down. He lifted it onto his neck, brought it home, and said, 'What do you want this for? I've no idea what it's good for.'

The baker said, 'Didn't you bring anything else?'

Eulenspiegel said, 'There was nothing else there.'

The baker now became really furious, saying with some heat, 'You've insulted my lords' judiciary and robbed their gallows. I'll make a complaint about this to the mayor — you should see how I will.'

So the baker left his house for the market place. Eulenspiegel followed him. But the baker was in such a hurry that he did not look back, and so did not notice that Eulenspiegel was following. The bailiff or mayor was standing in the market place. The baker went right up to him and began to deliver his complaint.

But as soon as his boss began his complaining, Eulenspiegel quite nimbly took a place just beside him, opening wide both his eyes. When the baker caught sight of Eulenspiegel, he became so enraged that he forgot what he wanted to complain about, saying furiously to Eulenspiegel, 'What do you want?'

Eulenspiegel said, 'I don't want anything. But you said I should see how you were going to complain about me to the mayor. If I'm supposed to see it, I've got to open my eyes wide — so I can see it.'

The baker told him, 'Just get out of my sight! You're a scoundrel.'

Eulenspiegel said, 'That's what I'm often called. And if I'm sitting in your "sight", then I'll have to crawl out of your nostrils when you close your eyes.'

The mayor walked away from him, seeing well enough that this was foolishness, leaving them both standing. When Eulenspiegel saw him go, he pushed up against the baker, saying, 'When are we going to bake? The sun isn't shining anymore.' Then he ran off, and left the baker standing there.

21. *How Eulenspiegel always rode on a reddish-gray horse, and was miserable around children.*

Eulenspiegel was always cheerful in company. But for as long as he lived, there were three sorts of things he avoided. First, he never rode a gray horse, but always a reddish-gray horse, for the sake of a clownish appearance. Second, he never enjoyed staying wherever there might be children, because people worried more about their needs than his. Third, he disliked staying where there was an old, generous innkeeper. For an old, generous innkeeper did not take proper care of his possessions and was usually a fool; besides, his sort of company could not be found there: in his sort of company there would certainly be money around to be made, and the like.

He also crossed himself every day against healthy food, great good luck, and strong drink. For healthy food was merely weeds, no matter how healthy it might also be. He also crossed himself against nourishing things from the pharmacist's shop: no matter how healthy they are, they are also a sign of illness. It was the just same with great good luck. For if a stone falls from a roof, or a beam from a house, one might easily say, 'Had I been standing there, that stone or beam would have killed me. That was my great good luck.' Such good luck he could do without. And the strong drink was water. For while water may drive huge mill wheels with its power, many people of the best company will also drink their deaths from it.

22. *How Eulenspiegel hired himself out as a tower bugler to the Count of Anhalt; and how when enemies showed up, he failed to sound his horn; and how, when there were no enemies, he sounded it.*

Not long afterwards, Eulenspiegel, approached the Count of Anhalt, to whom he hired himself out as a tower bugler. Now, the Count had a lot of enemies, so during this time, both in the town and at his castle, he retained many knights and people of his court, and these had to be fed all day. The result was that Eulenspiegel, waiting in the tower, was forgotten and no food was sent up to him.

Well, that very day it happened that the Count's enemies rushed up to the town and, in front of his castle, stole his cows and drove them off. Now, Eulenspiegel was lying in the tower, looking through the window, but he sounded no alarm, either by bugling or shouting. But the noise reached the Count, and he rushed after them with his men.

Some of them looked up to the tower and saw Eulenspiegel lying in the window and laughing. The Count called up to him, 'How can you lounge about in the window that way, so completely unaffected?'

Eulenspiegel called down to him, 'Before eating, I neither shout nor like shouting.'

The Count called up to him, 'Aren't you going to sound the alarm for the enemy?'

Eulenspiegel called back, 'I don't need to sound the alarm for any enemy. The field's already full, and some have gone off with your cows. If I sound the alarm for more enemies, they'll beat you to death. Get moving, now! Everything's fine.'

The Count rushed after his enemies and busied himself with them, but Eulenspiegel and his food were forgotten again.

Well, for a while the Count was content. This was because he also took a quantity of bacon from his enemies, and cut it up for boiling and baking. Up in the tower, Eulenspiegel thought about how he too would like to get hold of some of this loot, and paid careful attention to the hour when it was time to eat. Then he began to shout and sound his horn. 'Enemy, ho! Enemy, ho!' The Count ran hastily from the table (on which the food was lying) with his men, laid on harness, took weapons in hand, rushed smartly out through the gate into the field, and searched for the enemy.

In the meantime, Eulenspiegel ran coolly and rapidly down from the tower and headed for the Count's table. He grabbed boiled and baked things from the table — and whatever he pleased — then quickly returned to the tower.

Well, when the knights and footsoldiers got outside, they spotted no enemies. They all agreed, 'The tower watchman has done this as a prank.' So they returned to the castle gate, and the Count shouted up at Eulenspiegel, 'Have you gone foolish and crazy?'

Eulenspiegel said, 'Utterly without evil design.'

The Count said, 'Why did you sound "Enemy, ho!" that way, when there was nobody there?'

Eulenspiegel said, 'Since enemies were lacking, I had to invent some.'

The count at once remarked, 'You're scratching yourself with your rogue's nails. When the enemy's around, you don't like sounding the alarm, and when no enemy's there, you sound the alarm for the enemy. This might well be called treason.' He dismissed him on the spot, engaged another tower bugler in his place, and Eulenspiegel had to follow them on foot as a footsoldier.

This was pretty irritating to him, and he would have been glad to get out of there altogether, but he certainly could not get out through fair play. So whenever they moved out against the enemy, he delayed in all sorts of ways and was always last through the gate. But when they had finished their business and turned toward home, he was always first inside the gate.

The Count finally asked him how he was supposed to understand him: whenever he went out with the Count against the enemy, he was always last, and on going home he was first.

Eulenspiegel said, 'You shouldn't be angry about that. While you and your royal household were all eating, I was sitting up in the tower and getting thin. As a result, I've become fairly feeble. If I'm now supposed to be first out against the enemy, I'll have to make up for that time and rush up here, so I'm both the first at the table and last to leave it. Once I get strong again, I'll be the first and last against the enemy.'

'So you're now telling me,' said the Count, 'that you plan to go on with this for the whole length of time you spent sitting up in the tower?'

Eulenspiegel said, 'Everybody's right about something, depending on how you take him.'

The Count said, 'You won't be mine for long,' and let him go. Eulenspiegel was happy about this, since he had little enthusiasm for fighting with enemies all day.

23. *How Eulenspiegel had his horse shod with gold shoes, for which the King of Denmark had to pay.*

So fine an entertainer was Eulenspiegel that his cleverness attracted the attention of a number of princes and lords, and he was widely talked about. He greatly pleased these princes and lords and they offered him clothes, horses, money, and food. Well, he visited the King of Denmark, who liked him a lot and told him that if he could manage some sort of trick, he would have his horse shod for him with the very best horseshoes.

Eulenspiegel asked the King whether he should take him at his word. The King said, 'Yes,' for he kept his word.

Eulenspiegel rode his horse over to the goldsmith and had

his horse shod with gold shoes and silver nails. Then he returned to the King and announced that he would like him to pay for the shoeing. The King said, 'Yes,' and instructed his accountant to pay for the shoeing. The accountant thought this must be an ordinary horseshoeing, until Eulenspiegel took him to the goldsmith and the goldsmith asked for one hundred Danish marks. The accountant had no intention of paying it, left, and reported the matter to the King. The King had Eulenspiegel summoned and told him, 'Eulenspiegel, what an expensive horseshoeing you've gotten! If I had to have all my horses shod like this, I'd soon have to sell both country and people. It wasn't my intention to have the horse shod with gold shoes.'

Eulenspiegel remarked, 'Gracious Sire, you said they were to be the best horseshoes, and that I ought to take you at your word.'

The King said, 'You're the most valuable of all the people at my court: you do what I tell you!' And he started laughing — and paid the hundred marks.

Eulenspiegel at once went to have the gold shoes removed and settled with the smith. He had iron shoes put on his horse, and remained with that King to the end of his days.

24. *How Eulenspiegel, with a superior trick, humiliated the King of Poland's jester.*

In those days His Highness Casimir was King of Poland. Staying with him was an adventurer of unusual humour and clowning who could also play the fiddle well. Eulenspiegel, who was also in Poland, visited the King. The King had heard a great deal about Eulenspiegel, who was very welcome as a guest at his palace. For the King had seen him, heard of his adventures before this, and quite enjoyed him as an entertainer.

Well, Eulenspiegel and the King's fool met, and soon things fell out as they often say: two fools in one house seldom go well together. The King's jester disliked Eulenspiegel, but at the same time did not wish to be thrown out himself. The

King noticed this, so he summoned them both to his chamber. He said, 'Whichever of you makes the wildest performance — one that the other cannot repeat after him — I'll give that fellow new clothes and twenty guilders. And let's get started right now.'

So the two set about their clowning, performing a lot of absurd tricks, with funny faces and peculiar speeches. Whatever the one could think up for the other, and whatever Eulenspiegel did, this same fool repeated as well. The King laughed, along with his knights, and they saw all sorts of bizarre acts.

Eulenspiegel then reflected, 'Twenty guilders and a new wardrobe — that would be rather nice. I shall thus do something I would otherwise find unpleasant.' For he saw clearly what the King's attitude was — that it was all the same to him who won the prize, and by whatever means.

So Eulenspiegel walked into the middle of the room, lifted his behind, shitted a pile right in the center, took a spoon and split the excrement in half, down the middle. Then he called the other fool over and said, 'Fool, get over here and do some lapping up after me now, as I plan to do it before you.' And he took up the spoon, scooped half the excrement into it, and ate it. Then he presented the spoon to the clown and said, 'Look here, you eat the other half, and after that you produce a pile too, divide it up also, and I'll eat after you.'

The King's fool at once said, 'No, not a chance! Put your spoon away. Do you want me to be embarrassed for the rest of my life? I certainly won't eat from you, or you from me, like this.'

So Eulenspiegel won the championship of clowning, and the King gave him the new clothes and the twenty guilders. Eulenspiegel rode off, taking the King's prize with him.

25. *How Eulenspiegel was banished from the Duchy of Lüneburg, and how he cut open his horse and stood in it.*

Eulenspiegel practised his extraordinary buffoonery in the province of Lüneburg at Celle. As a result, the Duke of Lüneburg banished him from the province. If he were found anywhere there, he was to be seized and hanged. But Eulenspiegel did not avoid the province on that account. If his path took him that way, he rode or walked through the district anyhow.

A time soon came when he wanted to ride through Lüneburg. The Duke suddenly appeared, heading toward him, and when Eulenspiegel realized it was the Duke, he thought, 'It's the Duke, and if you're careless, they'll catch up with you with their nags and yank you off your horse. Next thing, the angry Duke hangs me from a tree.' He rapidly came up with a good idea. He got off his horse, quickly slit open its stomach, shook out its bowels, and took a standing position in its trunk. When the Duke and his knights got closer, they saw Eulenspiegel standing in his horse's stomach.

The Prince came abreast of him and said, 'Is that you? What're you doing in this carcass here? Don't you realize that I've banished you from my territory — and that if I find you in it, I'm going to have you hanged from a tree?'

Eulenspiegel simply said, 'Gracious Lord and Prince, I haven't done anything so awful that it's worth a hanging.'

The Duke said to him, 'Get over here to me and explain your innocence. — And what do you mean by this, that you're standing in a horse's carcass?'

Eulenspiegel walked over to him, replying, 'Gracious and high-born Prince, I worried about your displeasure and feared terribly for myself, but all my life I've heard that a man is entitled to be left in peace — in his four-poster.'

Well, the Duke began to laugh, and said, 'Will you stay out of my territory from now on?'

Eulenspiegel said, 'Gracious Lord, as your princely Grace wishes.'

The Duke rode off, calling back, 'Stay as you are.'

But Eulenspiegel quickly jumped out of the horse — and to his dead horse he said, 'Thanks, my dear horse, that you've helped me out of this and saved my life. And that, in addition, you've made me a respectable man again. Stay where you are.

It's better that ravens eat you than that they might have eaten me.' And he continued on foot.

26. *How Eulenspiegel bought some land from a farmer in the province of Lüneburg, and sat in it, in a tumbrel.*

Somewhat later, Eulenspiegel traveled that way again. He went into a village near Celle, and waited for the moment when the Duke might again be riding toward Celle. A farmer was going into a field there. Now, Eulenspiegel had gotten himself another horse and a tumbrel, and drove up to the farmer and asked him whose field it was.

The farmer said, 'It's mine, and I've inherited it.'

Eulenspiegel next asked how much he would have to pay him for a cartful of earth from his field.

The farmer said, 'I'll take a shilling for it.'

Eulenspiegel paid him a shilling coin, filled the cart full of earth from the field, crawled into it, and drove up to the castle at Celle on the Aller. When the Duke came riding by, he noticed that Eulenspiegel was sitting in the cart — and sitting in earth up to his shoulders.

The Duke said, 'Eulenspiegel, didn't I banish you, from my land? — If I found you in it, I intended to have you hanged?'

Eulenspiegel said, 'Gracious Lord, I'm not in your land. I'm sitting in my land, which I bought for a shilling. What's more, I bought it from a farmer who told me it was his inheritance.'

The Duke said, 'Get yourself and your earthy empire out of my earthy empire, and don't come back — or I'll have you hanged, along with horse and cart.'

Eulenspiegel quickly leaped out of the cart and jumped onto his horse. He rode out of the district, leaving his cart standing before the castle. And that is why Eulenspiegel's earthy empire is still standing there, in front of the bridge.

27. *How Eulenspiegel painted for the Landgrave of Hesse, doing it in white, so whoever was illegitimate could not see it.*

Eulenspiegel set amazing things going in the country of Hesse. When he had roamed the country of Saxony through and through, and was almost too well known — so he was no longer quite able to get away with his mischief-making — he moved into the country of Hesse, and arrived near Marburg, at the court of the Landgrave. This Lord asked what he could do. He replied by announcing, 'Gracious Lord, I am an artist.' This pleased the Landgrave, because he thought Eulenspiegel was a performer and could do alchemy. The Landgrave occupied himself quite a lot with alchemy. The Landgrave asked whether he was an alchemist.

Eulenspiegel said, 'No, gracious Lord. I am a painter — one whose equal will not be found in many countries. For my work far exceeds the work of others.'

The Landgrave said, 'Let's see something.'

Eulenspiegel said, 'Yes, gracious Lord.' Now, he had with

him various paintings on canvas and *objets d'art*, which he
had bought in Flanders. He pulled these out of his sack and
showed them to the Landgrave. The Lord certainly liked
them, and said to him, 'Dear master-painter, what would you
ask for painting over our chamber here—showing the arrival
of my wife, the Landgrave of Hesse, how she initiated my
friendship with the King of Hungary, and other Princes and
Lords, and how long all this has lasted? And we would want
to have this thing done as sumptuously as possible.'

Eulenspiegel replied, 'Gracious Lord, if Your Grace were
to let me do it, it would probably cost four hundred guilders.'

The Landgrave said, 'Master, just let it be well done for us.
We plan to pay you well for it.'

So Eulenspiegel took the job on, and of course the Landgrave had to give him one hundred guilders right away, so he
could buy paints and hire assistants. But when Eulenspiegel,
with three assistants, was ready to start, he instructed the
Landgrave to allow no one other than his helpers into the

room while he was working. That way he would not be
disturbed in practising his art. The Landgrave allowed him
this. Eulenspiegel next came to an agreement with his assistants. He ordered them to keep silent and let him do everything. They were not to work. They would receive their pay
anyway. Their greatest labour would consist of playing back-
gammon. His assistants were delighted that they were to earn
the same money for doing nothing.

All this went on for about four weeks — till the Landgrave
decided to see what master and company might be painting,
and whether it would really be as good as the samples.
Whereupon he said to Eulenspiegel, 'Ah, dear master, we very
much wish to examine your work. We request that we be
allowed to go into the room with you to view your painting.'

Eulenspiegel said, 'Yes, gracious Lord. But I've got to tell
Your Grace one thing. Whoever enters with Your Grace and
views the painting — if he is not of proper and legitimate birth,
he won't be able to see my painting.'

The Landgrave said, 'Master, it must be something
fantastic.'

As they spoke, they were walking into the room. Eulenspiegel had spread a long linen cloth across the wall where he was
supposed to have been painting. Eulenspiegel now drew this
back a little, pointed at the wall with a small white stick, and
began to speak. 'Look, gracious Lord. This man — he was the
first Landgrave of Hesse and a pillar of Rome, who afterwards
became Kaiser and had as his Princess and Lady mild
Justinian's daughter, a Duchess of Bavaria. Look here, gracious Lord. Adolphus was born of him. Adolphus sired
William the Black. William sired Ludwig the Pious — and so
on, to Your Princely Grace. And indeed I know this much:
no one can censure my work, so artistic is it and managed
with such beautiful colours.'

The Landgrave saw nothing other than the white wall before
him and thought to himself, 'Maybe I'm supposed to be the
son of a whore, but I don't see anything here but a white
wall.' Nonetheless, he said (wishing to be fair), 'Dear master,
we are well satisfied — but we aren't sophisticated enough to
judge.' With that, he left the room.

When the Landgrave approached his Princess, she asked him, 'Ah, gracious Lord, what is your master painter painting? You've seen it. How do you like his work? I myself have but little faith in it. He looks like a charlatan.'

The Prince said, 'Dear Lady, I like his work enormously. You do him an injustice.'

'Gracious Lord,' she said, 'may we not also view it?'

'Yes, with the master's permission.'

She had Eulenspiegel brought to her and requested that she might see the painting too. Eulenspeigel told her what he had told the Prince: whoever was illegitimate would not be able to see his work. Then she, along with eight ladies-in-waiting and a female court jester, went into the room. Eulenspiegel now drew back the cloth, as before, and told the Princess too about the arrival of the Landgrave's wife, one section after the other. But the Princess and the ladies-in-waiting remained silent; no one praised or condemned the painting. Everyone was afraid she might be illegitimate, either on her father's or mother's side. But finally the court jester roused herself and said, 'Dear master, maybe I'm to remain a whore's daughter for the rest of my life, but I don't see any painting there.'

Eulenspiegel thought quickly. 'This isn't good at all. If fools start telling the truth, then I, in truth, must do some travelling.' But he tried to laugh it off.

In the meantime the Princess returned to her Lord, and he asked her whether she liked the painting. She answered him, 'Gracious Sir, I like as much as Your Grace. But our jester doesn't like it. She says she doesn't see any painting at all. Our ladies-in-waiting say the same—and I am afraid there may be knavery in this business.'

The Prince looked into his heart, realizing he had been tricked. Nonetheless, he had Eulenspiegel informed that if he were to pay for this stuff, everyone at court would have to see his work. The Prince said he wished to find out who among his noblemen might be legitimate or illegitimate.

Well, Eulenspiegel went to his assistants and dismissed them. Then he charged the steward another hundred guilders, and got them. Then he left at once. The next day the Prince inquired after his painter—he was gone. Whereupon the

Prince, with all the people of his court, went into the room to discover whether anyone could see the painting. But no one could say he saw anything. As they all remained silent, the Landgrave said, 'We acknowledge that we have been tricked. Oh, I never wanted to be troubled with Eulenspiegel. He visited us anyhow. We can forget easily enough about the two hundred guilders, though. You can't stop him from being the scoundrel that he is. For that reason he had better stay out of our realm.'

But Eulenspiegel was gone from Marburg and had no wish to engage in any more painting.

28. *How Eulenspiegel debated with the students at the University of Prague, in Bohemia, emerging victorious.*

Eulenspiegel travelled through Bohemia to Prague when he left Marburg. Now, at that time good Christians were still living there—before the days when Wycliffe brought his heresy from England to Bohemia and it was spread further by John Huss. Well, Eulenspiegel advertised himself as a great scholar there in the answering of great questions—to which any other scholar would be able to offer neither explanation nor reply. He had this written into announcements, and posted them on the church doors and at the lecture halls.

This irritated the rector. The students, professors, and other scholars were annoyed about it, as was the whole university. So they met to find a way by which they could offer Eulenspiegel problems he would be unable to solve. If he did badly, they would be justified in seizing and humiliating him. And it was arranged and agreed among them (and they also concluded and ordained it) that the rector ought to present these questions. So they had Eulenspiegel notified through their porter that he should show up the next day to answer these problems and questions, which would be presented to him in writing before the whole university, if he wished to be tested and desired to have his abilities accepted as genuine. Otherwise he would not be accepted at all.

Eulenspiegel, by way of reply, told their porter, 'Inform your superiors that I shall do this thing, and that I still hope to come through it a clever fellow—as I have till now.'

The next day all the professors and learned men assembled. Eulenspiegel also arrived, bringing with him his innkeeper, several other townspeople, and various good acquaintances, in case of any sudden attack that might come his way from the students. When he entered their meeting, they told him to mount a podium and to answer the questions which would be presented to him.

Well, the first question the rector put to him was that he should state, and prove with true facts, how many currents of water there were in the sea. If he could not solve and answer this question, they would condemn and punish him as an uneducated corruptor of scholarship.

He made a quick answer to this question. 'Worthy Lord Rector, tell the rest of the water, which runs from all ends of the sea, to stand still, and I shall measure, prove and report the truth about this matter. For that will be easy to do.'

It was impossible for the rector to stop the water from flowing — so he dropped this subject and excused Eulenspiegel from measuring it. But the rector stood there, now looking rather embarrassed, and put his next question. 'Tell me, how many days have passed from Adam's time till today?'

Eulenspiegel answered briefly. 'Only seven days. And when they've passed, then seven more days commence. This process continues till the end of the world.'

The rector presented him with his third question. 'Tell me now, how or where is the centre of the world located?'

Eulenspiegel answered, 'It's right here. I'm standing in exactly the centre of the world. And to see whether that's true, have it measured with a string. If I'm off by even a straw's length, I'll admit I'm wrong.'

Rather than measuring it, the rector chose to let this question go to Eulenspiegel. Then, with real fury, he offered Eulenspiegel his fourth question. He said, 'Tell me, how far is it from the Earth to Heaven?'

Eulenspiegel replied, 'It's quite nearby. If one speaks or calls from Heaven, one easily hears it down here. Just climb up there. I'll call softly from down here. You'll certainly hear it in Heaven. Of course, if you don't hear me, I'll admit I'm wrong.'

The rector had to accept this, and asked his fifth question. 'How big is Heaven?'

Eulenspiegel answered immediately. 'It's a thousand fathoms wide and a thousand ells[1] high. I can't be wrong about that. If you don't want to believe it, take the sun, moon and all the stars of Heaven, and measure them together. You'll find I'm right, even though the idea doesn't appeal to you.'

What could they say? Eulenspiegel was never at a loss for an answer, and they had to admit he was right about everything. But he did not wait long after he had defeated these learned men with quackery. He was afraid they might offer him something to drink to trip him up. So he took off his long academic robe, left, and headed for Erfurt.

---

[1] Probably about 250 feet, though the ell, as a unit of measure, varied considerably from place to place.

29. *How Eulenspiegel, at Erfurt, taught an ass to read from an old psalter.*

After playing that game in Prague, Eulenspiegel felt a great longing for Erfurt. He was worried that they might still be coming after him. When he got to Erfurt, at which there is a remarkably large and famous university, Eulenspiegel posted his announcements there too. Now, the students of the university had heard a great deal about his jests, and wondered what they ought to set him as a problem, so things would not go for them as they had gone for those who came up against him at Prague, and they would not be humiliated.

Well, they decided to offer Eulenspiegel an ass to teach — since there are many asses at Erfurt, both old and young. They sent for Eulenspiegel and told him, 'Professor, you've stuck up announcements that you can teach any creature to write and read pretty quickly. Well, the Lords of the University are here and plan to send you a young ass to teach. Are you up to taking it on too?'

Eulenspiegel said, 'Certainly,' but added that he would need some time for this particular case, since an ass was a speechless and unintelligent creature. They agreed on twenty years. Eulenspiegel thought, 'There are three of us. If the rector of the university dies, I'm free. If I die, who can hold me accountable? If my pupil dies, I'm free anyway.' So he took the problem on, and agreed on five hundred old groschen to do it. Of this they paid him some gold in advance.

Well, Eulenspiegel led the ass away with him, and moved into the inn 'At The Tower', where at that time there happened to be a uniquely tolerant innkeeper. He engaged a stall for his pupil alone, and acquired an old psalter. This he placed before the ass, in the manger, inserting oats between each of the pages. The ass was alerted to these, and tossed the pages over with its mouth to get at the oats, but on finding no more oats, it screamed, 'Eee — aa, eee — aa!'

Eulenspiegel took stock of this, went to the rector, and said, 'My dear Lord Rector, when would you like to see a bit of what my pupil's managing to do?'

The rector said, 'Dear Professor, can he, too, accept instruction?'

Eulenspiegel said, 'He's awfully clumsy with his skills, and it's very hard for me to teach him. Nonetheless, with a lot of effort and work, I've accomplished enough so he recognizes some letters and vowels, and can name them. Would you like to go with me to hear and see this?'

Now, his good pupil had been kept fasting all that time, till three in the afternoon. When Eulenspiegel got there, with the rector and several professors, Eulenspiegel stuck a new book in front of his pupil. As soon as the ass discovered it in the manger, he flipped the pages back and forth, looking for the oats. When the ass did not find any, he began to scream, in a loud voice, 'Eee — aa — eee — aa!'

Eulenspiegel at once said, 'Observe, dear gentlemen, the two vowels "e" and "a". These he can do so far. I am hoping he may yet do nicely.'

Well, the rector died pretty soon afterwards. Eulenspiegel thereupon set his pupil free, letting him go where his nature might take him. Then Eulenspiegel got out of there with the

money he had kept. He thought, 'If you had to make all the
asses in Erfurt wise, you'd need quite a few lifetimes.' He had,
moreover, no desire to do so, and let the place stay as it was.

30. *How Eulenspiegel, at Sangerhausen, in the province
of Thüringen, washed pelts for the ladies.*

Eulenspiegel arrived in the province of Thüringen, near Nien-
stetten, at the village there, and asked about accommodations.
The innkeeper, a woman, gazed at him and asked him what
sort of fellow he was.

Eulenspiegel said, 'I'm not a journeyman. Instead I practise
telling the truth.'

The woman said, 'I enjoy accommodating the truth, and
I'm especially well disposed to those who tell the truth.'

Now, as Eulenspiegel was looking around, he noticed that
the lady was squinting, and so he said, 'Squint-eyed lady,

squint-eyed lady, where shall I sit and where shall I put my staff and sack?'

The innkeeper said, 'Ah! May nothing good ever come your way! In all my life nobody's ever mentioned to me that I'm squint-eyed.'

Eulenspiegel said, 'Dear innkeeper, if I'm always to tell the truth, I can't keep silent about it.'

The woman was pleased with this and laughed over it.

As Eulenspiegel was staying there overnight, he struck up a conversation with the innkeeper, and they happened to discuss the fact that he knew how to wash furs. Now, this very much delighted the woman, so she asked him whether he would like to wash pelts. She would tell her neighbours about it, and they would bring all their pelts for him to wash. Eulenspiegel said, 'Absolutely.' The woman invited all her neighbours, and the women brought all their pelts.

Eulenspiegel said 'You'll need some milk for this.'

The women were overjoyed, since they had a yen for clean furs, and brought all the milk they had in their houses. Eulenspiegel then stuck three kettles on the fire, poured milk into them, stuck the pelts in as well, and let them boil and cook. When everything looked ready to him, he told the women, 'You'll have to go to the woods and bring me white linden wood from young trees. And strip it, because when you come back I'm going to hoist the pelts out. They'll be soaked enough by then, and I want to wash them through — and for that I'll need the wood.'

The women set off for the woods enthusiastically, and their children ran along with them. They took their children by the hands and jumped and sang, 'Oh-ho, good new pelts! Oh-ho, good new pelts!'

But Eulenspiegel just hung back, laughing, and said, 'Ah, wait, your pelts aren't ready yet.'

As soon as they were off in the woods, Eulenspiegel dipped their pelts under once more, left the kettles standing with the pelts, got out of the village, and took off. He had no intention of coming back to wash the pelts. Well, the women returned with the linden wood, failed to find Eulenspiegel, and guessed he might be gone. They then tried, each before the rext, to get their pelts out of the kettles. But these had been so ruined by the washing that they fell apart. So they left the pelts standing, hoping he might still come back to wash them out.

But he simply thanked God that he had gotten out of there unhurt.

31. *How Eulenspiegel wandered around with a death's-head, amazing people with it, and made quite a profit from doing so.*

Eulenspiegel made himself notorious in every single country with his malicious tricks. Where he had once been he was no longer welcome. It thus happened that he disguised himself so as not to be recognized. Nonetheless, it finally became clear to him that he could no longer simply trust himself to make a living by idleness—despite his having been a cheery fellow from his youth up and having made money enough through all sorts of clever games. Now that his fame for roguery was spreading through country after country, and his profits were declining, he reflected on what he might undertake—to support himself in idleness anyhow—and got the idea of doing himself up a wandering monk and riding, with relics, through the surrounding districts. So, with a student, he dressed himself to look like a priest, got hold of the skull of a dead man, had it mounted in silver, and went into the country of Pomerania, where priests care more about drinking than praying.

From then on, wherever there might be a dedication of a church in a village, or a wedding, or some other gathering of country people, Eulenspiegel presented himself to the priest as somebody who could pray and preach religion to the farmers, and this so well that they would find themselves utterly entranced. He agreed to give the priest half of whatever he might get in offerings. The uneducated priests agreed to everything—as long as they got some money.

Well, when all the people arrived in church, Eulenspiegel mounted the pulpit, said something from the Old Testament, tossed in the New as well, with Noah's Ark and the Golden Bucket, in which the bread of Heaven lay—and said, moreover, that all this stuff was the greatest holiness. Then at the same time he began to speak of the head of Saint Brendan, who had been a holy man. He had Brendan's head right there—and it had been commanded of him that he use it to collect for the building of a new church, and to do so with purest goodness, never (on pain of death) accepting any offerings from any woman who might be an adulteress.

'And whoever here may be such women, let them stand back. For if they offer me something—those who are guilty of adultery—I won't take it, and they will be revealed in shame unto me! So—know yourselves!'

Then he offered the people the head to be kissed, a smith's head, maybe, that he had stolen from a church graveyard, and gave the farmers and their wives the blessing. After this, both guilty and innocent wives approached the altar with their offerings, rushing so much that they gasped for breath. And he took the offerings, from guilty and innocent alike, refusing none. Well, so firmly did these foolish wives believe in this sly, roguish business that they considered any woman impious who might still be holding back. And those women who had no money offered a gold or silver ring—and each one eyed the next to see if she gave too; and those who had given thought they had confirmed their honour and destroyed their evil reputations. There were also those who offered two or three times, so that everyone could see them do so and leave them out of their malicious gossip. Well, he received the most splendid donations, the likes of which had never been heard of before. And when he had taken up the donations, he commanded, on pain of excommunication, that all those who had given him something never act with deceit, for they were free of it—since if there had been any such deceitful wives there, he could not have accepted any offerings from them. Well, those wives were thoroughly pleased.

As a result, wherever Eulenspiegel went, he preached, and he became rich through doing so. And the people took him for a pious preacher, so well was he able to conceal his knavery.

32. How Eulenspiegel led the city patrol of Nuremberg into following him over a narrow bridge and falling into the water.

Eulenspiegel was inventive in his roguishness. After he had travelled about widely with the head, thoroughly deceiving people, he came to Nuremberg, planning to spend the money he had made with his relic. But when he had spent a bit of time there, and had seen all parts of the city, he was unable to repress his true nature. He needed to pull off a clever stunt there as well.

Now, he saw that the city patrol slept, with armour on, in a large chamber under the city hall. Eulenspiegel had gotten to know very well the roads and narrow bridges of Nuremberg—and had especially examined the narrow bridge between the hog market and the 'Little House', which is dangerous to cross during the night, as many innocent girls out to get wine have been assaulted there. Well, Eulenspiegel delayed his little prank till everyone had gone to sleep and all was quiet. Then he broke three planks from this very bridge and heaved them into the river (called the Pegnitz). He walked up to the city hall, started cursing, and beat on the plaster with an old knife, till the sparks flew.

When the watchmen heard this, they were soon up and running. As Eulenspiegel heard them coming after him, he raced ahead of the watchmen, took flight toward the hog market, and once there, had them still behind him. He arrived, barely ahead of them, at the place where he had thrown away the three planks, and managed, as best he could, to get across the bridge. But once he made it across, he yelled, 'Hey! Hey! What're you waiting for, you weak-hearted scoundrels?' When the watchmen heard this, they raced after him, quite without thinking, as each wanted to be first. As a result, they fell, one after the other, into the Pegnitz. And the passageway across the bridge was so narrow that they started quarrelling with each other all along it. So Eulenspiegel called out, 'Hey!

Hey! Aren't you moving yet? Tomorrow you might run after me some more. You'd have arrived at this bath early enough — tomorrow morning. Even if you hadn't wanted to go hunting half as much, you'd still have got here on time.' Well, one man broke his leg, the next his arm, the third received a gash on his head — with the result that none of them got out of there unhurt.

When he had pulled off this bit of mischief, he did not stay at Nuremberg too long and went travelling again. He had, after all, no real wish that he be recognized as the jester in this case. He might be flogged. The people of Nuremberg would probably not take it as a joke.

33. *How Eulenspiegel ate for money at Bamberg.*

Through cunning, Eulenspiegel once earned money at Bamberg, after he left Nuremberg and felt pretty hungry. He arrived there at the house of a lady innkeeper, whose name was Mrs Königen. She was a cheerful innkeeper and told him he was welcome there, since she could see by his clothes that he was a rare guest.

When he wanted his morning meal, the woman asked him how he would like to have it, whether he preferred to sit at the table for complete meals, or whether he would like to eat *à la carte*. Eulenspiegel answered that he was a poor fellow. He asked her whether, for the sake of God, she would give him something to eat.

The woman said, 'Friend, at the butcher's or the baker's I get nothing for free. I've got to pay for it. So I've also got to get money for the food.'

Eulenspiegel then said, 'Ah, woman, I too like to eat for money. For what—or how much—ought I to eat and drink here?'

The woman said, 'At the Gentlemen's Table for twenty-four pennies, at the next table there for eighteen[1] pennies, and with my servants for twelve pennies.'

Eulenspiegel replied, 'Woman, the most money would serve me best.' So he sat down at the Gentlemen's Table and soon ate his fill. When he felt good, and had eaten and drunk well, he told the innkeeper that she ought to wind up their business, as he had to be on his way so he would not have too much of a bill.

'My dear guest,' said the woman, 'give me the meal's price of twenty-four pennies, and go wherever you like. May God speed you.'

'No,' said Eulenspiegel. 'You've got to give me twenty-four pennies, as you said. For you said, at this table one eats a meal for twenty-four pennies. Well, I took that to mean that I should earn money for it—for things have been getting pretty rough for me. I've been eating till the sweat's broken out all over me, and if life and limb depended on it, I couldn't eat any more. So just give me my hard-earned reward.'

'Friend,' said the woman, 'it's true you've eaten enough for three men. But that I'm also supposed to pay you for eating—these two things don't rhyme together at all. All right, this

---

[1] An error? Grüninger has twenty-eight here.

meal is finished and you may as well go. However, I won't give you any money for it. That's lost. And I'll ask no money of you. Just don't come back here again. If I had to feed my guests this way all year round, and raise no more money than from you, I'd soon have to give up house and home.'

So Eulenspiegel said goodbye to that place, without earning much in the way of thanks.

34. *How Eulenspiegel travelled to Rome and visited the pope, who took him for a heretic.*

Eulenspiegel was dedicated to cunning roguishness.[1] After he had tried all sorts of tricks, he thought of the old saying, 'Go to Rome, pious man: come back worthless.' So he went off to

---

[1] The edition of 1519 has 'With thoroughgoing cunning Eulenspiegel equipped himself lavishly,' a reference to his apparently elegant appearance in this tale.

Rome, to give his mischief a chance there too, and took lodgings with a widow. She could see that Eulenspiegel was a rare fellow, and asked him where he was from. Eulenspiegel said he was from the district of Saxony, was an Easterner, and that he had come to Rome to speak with the pope.

The woman at once said, 'Friend you can easily see the pope, but to speak to him, that I doubt. I was born and brought up here, and am of the best sort of family, but have never yet been able to exchange one word with him. How could you manage it so fast? I'd easily give a hundred ducats to speak with him.'

Eulenspiegel said, 'My dear innkeeper, if I get the chance to place you before the pope, so you can speak with him, will you give me the hundred ducats?'

The woman was quick to promise him the hundred ducats, on her honour, if he could arrange it. But she thought it would be impossible for him to manage anything like it, as it would cost him a great deal of trouble and work.

Eulenspiegel said, 'My dear innkeeper, if this happens somehow, I'll ask for the hundred ducats.'

She said, 'Yes.' But she thought, 'You're still nowhere near the pope.'

Eulenspiegel waited. Every four weeks the pope had to read a mass in the chapel called Jerusalem, at Saint John in Lateran. Well, after the pope had finished his mass, Eulenspiegel pushed himself forward in the chapel, as close to the pope as he could. Then as the pope said low mass, Eulenspiegel turned his back on the sacrament. The cardinals noticed this. And when the pope said the blessing over the communion cup, Eulenspiegel turned his back again. When the mass was over, they told the pope that a peculiar person, a rather distinguished-looking man, had been at mass and had turned his back on the altar during low mass.

The pope said, 'It's important to investigate this, as it concerns the Holy Church. For if disbelief were not punished, it would be a sin against God. If the man has in fact done this, it may well be feared that he has fallen into disbelief and is not a good Christian.' The pope ordered that Eulenspiegel be brought to him.

The cardinals immediately approached Eulenspiegel and directed him to appear before the pope, and at the appointed hour Eulenspiegel went to an audience with him. The pope now asked him what sort of man he was. Eulenspiegel said he was a good, Christian man. The pope asked what sort of beliefs he held. Eulenspiegel said he held the same beliefs as his lady-innkeeper, and named her, for she was a woman who was well known there. At that point, the pope summoned the woman. The pope asked the woman about the nature of her beliefs. The woman said she believed in the Christian religion and in what the Holy Christian Church allowed her and forbade her. She held no other beliefs.

Eulenspiegel was standing nearby, and he at once began to bow elaborately, and said, 'Most Gracious Father, Thou Servant Among All Servants, I hold the same beliefs as well. I am a good, Christian man.'

The pope said, 'Why do you turn your back on the altar during the low mass?'

Eulenspiegel said, 'Most Holy Father, I am a poor, great sinner and was so glaring in my sins that I wasn't worthy — till I had confessed my sins.'

The pope seemed pleased with this, released Eulenspiegel, and went off to his palace. But Eulenspiegel returned to his inn and asked his innkeeper for the hundred ducats. She had to give them to him. Well, Eulenspiegel stayed the same person then as he had been before, and was not much improved by his trip to Rome.

35. How Eulenspiegel cheated the Jews at Frankfurt-on-the-Main out of a thousand guilders, by selling them his excrement as prophet's berries.

No one should mind if the cunning Jew has his eye closed.[1]

When Eulenspiegel got back from Rome, he travelled to Frankfurt-on-the-Main, where it was just fair-time. Eulenspiegel walked here and there and observed the sorts of

---

[1] i.e., does not see and gets cheated.

merchandise everybody had for sale. Then he spotted a young, clever fellow wearing fine clothes, who had a very small shop, with musk from Alexandria, which he sold at a cost far beyond its possible value.

Eulenspiegel thought, 'I'm also a lazy, clever scoundrel who doesn't like to work. If I could support myself as easily as this fellow, it would please me very much.' So he lay without sleeping all that night, thinking and speculating on business. In the meantime, a flea bit him in the behind. He quickly fumbled about for it, and found several small knots on his behind. He reflected, 'These must be the little rough sources (which one calls "Lexander"[1]) from which the musk comes.'

When he got up the next day, he bought gray and red taffeta, wrapped the little knots in it, found a seller's bench, bought some spices for it, and took up a position in front of the town hall with his stall. Many people approached him,

---

[1] There is evidently a pun involved here: on 'Alexandria', the source of musk, and the Low German expression for 'it licks itself', 'leckts selbander'.

inspected his curious shop, and asked him the nature of the odd things he had on sale there. For it was an unusual item. It was wrapped, like musk, into a little bundle, and smelled most strangely. But Eulenspiegel gave no one accurate information about his merchandise — until three rich Jews came up to him to inquire about his wares. He told them they were prophet's berries, and that whoever put one of them into his mouth, and then stuck one in his nose, would speak the truth forever after. The Jews withdrew to consult for a while. Finally one old Jew said, 'With this we'll be able to prophesy when our Messiah is to come — something that would be of no small comfort to us Jews.'

So they decided they would buy up all these wares, no matter what they might have to pay for them. They at once returned to Eulenspiegel and said, 'Merchant, what, in a word, would one of these prophet's berries cost?'

Eulenspiegel thought quickly and said, 'Indeed, whenever I've got merchandise, Our Lord bestows buyers on me. These delicacies please Jews especially.' And he added, 'I'll give you one for a hundred guilders — and if you don't wish to pay them, you dogs, take off and leave the junk where it is.'

As they did not wish to anger Eulenspiegel, and as they wanted to obtain what he had for sale, they immediately paid him the money, took one of the berries, and quickly went home. Then they had all the Jews, old and young, rung[1] into *schule*. When they met, the oldest Rabbi (named Alpha) stood up and told how, by the grace of God, they had acquired a prophet's berry, which one of them was to put in his mouth to be able to prophesy the coming of the Messiah. In order that salvation and comfort might come to them from it, they ought to prepare themselves with fasting and praying. Then after three days, one Isaac would consume it with great reverence.

And so it happened.

When the man had it in his mouth, Moses asked him, 'Well, dear Isaac, how does it taste?'

---

[1] Actually, 'klopfen', or 'knocked', it being the custom then to dispatch someone to Jewish homes to knock on the doors to summon the people to the synagogue.

'Servant of God! We've been cheated by that Goi! This is nothing other than human excrement.'

So they all tasted the prophet's berry — until they saw the 'tree' on which the berry had grown.

But Eulenspiegel was gone, and he enjoyed himself enormously for as long as the Jews' money lasted.

36. *How Eulenspiegel bought chickens at Quedlinburg, and left the farmer's wife one of her own chickens as a pledge for the money.*

People were not always as sophisticated as they are now, especially country people.

Eulenspiegel once arrived at Quedlinburg. It was just market-time, and Eulenspiegel had few provisions. For just as he acquired his money, so it left him again, and he wondered how he might acquire provisions. Well, a countrywoman was sitting in the market place, and she had a basketful of good chickens for sale. Eulenspiegel asked what a pair of them would cost.

She answered, 'By the pair, two Stevens-shillings.'

Eulenspiegel said, 'Won't you sell them for less?'

The woman said, 'No.'

So Eulenspiegel picked up the chickens, with the basket, and walked off toward the castle gate.

The woman ran after him, saying, 'Sir — buyer — how am I to understand this? Don't you intend paying me for my chickens?'

Eulenspiegel said, 'Yes, with pleasure. I'm the Abbess' scribe.'

'I'm not asking about that,' said the woman. 'If you want to keep the chickens, pay for them. I hope never to have to do with your Abbot or Abbess. My father taught me that I should not buy from or, still less, sell or give credit to those before whom one must bow or raise one's cap. So pay me for the chickens, do you hear?'

Eulenspiegel said, 'Woman, you're of little faith. It wouldn't be good if all merchants were as you are. Good comrades would have to go about poorly dressed. But just so you can be sure of your money, take this one chicken as a pledge till I bring you the basket and the money.'

The good woman fancied herself well taken care of, and took one of her chickens as a pledge. But she was deceived. For Eulenspiegel — and the chickens and the promised money — did not appear. It went with her as it does with those who are most meticulous in their supervision of what is theirs: they are the first to be cheated.

So Eulenspiegel left that place, and left the woman furious over the single chicken she had taken for her chickens.

37. *How the priest of Hoheneggelsen ate one of Eulenspiegel's sausages — something which subsequently did not make him happy.*

Eulenspiegel was at Hildesheim, and he bought a good red sausage at the butcher's stall and went on to Hoheneggelsen.

He was well known to the priest there, and it was a Sunday morning. When he got there, the priest was saying the early mass, as he wanted to eat pretty soon. Eulenspiegel went into the parsonage, and asked the girl doing the cooking to roast the red sausage for him.

The girl said, 'All right.'

Eulenspiegel then went into the church. There, early mass was just finished, and another priest was taking over the high mass, which Eulenspiegel heard to its end.

In the meantime, the priest went home and asked his servant girl, 'Isn't anything cooked, so I can eat a little?'

The girl said, 'Nothing's ready, except a red sausage that Eulenspiegel brought. That's cooked. He'd planned to eat it after he got back from church.'

The priest said, 'Let me have the sausage. I wouldn't mind eating a bit of it.'

The girl handed him the sausage.

The priest enjoyed the taste of the sausage so much that he ate it all. And he said to himself, 'God bless me, that tasted good. The sausage was good.' He said to the girl, 'G ve Eulenspiegel bacon and cabbage, as he's used to eating. Th it's much better for him.'

Now, when the service was over, Eulenspiegel went back to the parsonage, planning to eat his sausage. The priest greeted him, thanked him for his sausage, told him how good it had tasted, and offered him bacon and cabbage. Eulenspiegel kept quiet, ate what had been cooked there, and left on Monday.

The priest called after Eulenspiegel, 'Listen, when you come back, bring two sausages with you—one for you and one for me. I'll pay you back whatever you have to spend for them. Then we'll really enjoy ourselves—till our mouths simply foam.'

Eulenspiegel said, 'Yes, Father, that's what'll happen. I'll certainly be thinking of you when I get the sausages.' He went back to Hildesheim.

Now, it happened, as he hoped it would, that the commercial pig-slaughterers were carrying a sow to their slaughters' burial place. Eulenspiegel asked a slaughterer whether, for money, he would make two red sausages out of his sow, and paid him some silver pennies for them right there. The slaughterer did so, making him two fine red sausages. Eulenspiegel took them, boiled them half through, as was customary with such sausages, and went back to Hoheneggelsen the following Sunday. It happened that the priest was holding early mass. Eulenspiegel went over to the parsonage, brought his sausages to the cook, and told her to roast them for breakfast. The priest was to have one, and he the other. Then he went into the church.

Well, the girl placed the sausages on the fire and roasted them. When the mass was over, the priest noticed Eulenspiegel and immediately left the church for the parsonage, where he said, 'Eulenspiegel is here. Did he bring the sausages too?'

She said, 'Yes, two sausages, finer than almost any I've ever seen, and they're both just about roasted.' She went over and took one out of the hot fire. Now, she was as greedy for the sausages as the priest, so they both sat down to eat together. But as they were eating the sausages so lustily, their mouths began to foam with decayed fat. Another man saw and heard the priest saying to his servant girl, 'Oh, my dear girl! How your mouth is foaming!'

But the girl replied, 'Oh, dear sir! Your mouth is just the same!'

Just at that moment, Eulenspiegel came in from church. The priest said to him, 'Look here, what kind of sausages did you bring? Look how messy my mouth and my servant girl's mouth are!'

Eulenspiegel laughed. 'God bless you,' he said. 'What's happening to you is exactly according to your wishes when you asked me to bring two sausages from which you planned to eat till your mouth simply foamed. But I paid no attention to the kind of foam—as long as vomit didn't follow it. I understand, though. That'll soon come. For these two sausages were made out of a dead sow. As a result, I had to boil them clean with soap. The mess comes from that.'

The girl began to gag, and vomited all over the table. The priest did the same. He said, 'Get out of my house, you rogue.' He grabbed a club to beat him with.

Eulenspiegel said, 'This doesn't become a pious man. You told me to bring these two sausages. Well, you've eaten both of them, and now you plan to beat me. First pay me for the sausages. I'll forget about the third one.'

The priest became furious and almost crazy with rage and said Eulenspiegel himself ought to have eaten his mouldy sausages made from the corpse of a sow, and not have brought this sort of stuff into his house.

Eulenspiegel said, 'I certainly haven't made you sick against your wishes. Besides, I wouldn't want these sausages. I might have liked the first one, though. That one you ate against my wishes. Since you've gobbled up the first, good sausage—eat the bad ones too.' And he said, 'Adieu! Good night!'

38. *How Eulenspiegel, with a false confession, talked the priest of Kissenbrück out of his horse.*

Eulenspiegel could not keep out of terrible mischief at Kissenbrück, a village in the Asseburg jurisdiction. A priest was living there too, who had a very pretty girl as his maid and a little, pretty, smart horse, both of which the priest liked, the horse as much as the girl.

The Duke of Brunswick was at Kissenbrück just then, and had asked the priest, through other people, to let him have the horse: he would give the priest whatever would satisfy him for it. The priest continually refused the prince, as he had no desire to give up his horse. And the prince was also not entitled simply to have the horse taken away, since the law there was under his own administration of Brunswick. Well, Eulenspiegel heard about this problem, thought it over, and told the prince, 'Gracious Lord, what will you give me if I get that horse away from the priest of Kissenbrück?'

'If you can manage it,' said the Duke, 'I'll give you the coat I'm wearing.' Well, it was a red camlet coat, woven with pearls.

Eulenspiegel accepted this challenge, and rode out of Wolfenbüttel to take lodgings with the priest in the village. Now,

Eulenspiegel was well known at the priest's house, for he had often stayed with him before and was welcome there. When he had been at the priest's house for about three days, Eulenspiegel pretended to be ill, complained loudly of pain, and lay down. The priest and his cook, the girl, were unhappy about this, but had no idea what they ought to do about it. Finally Eulenspiegel became so sick that the priest spoke to him, exhorting him to confess and receive God's mercy. Eulenspiegel was quite inclined to do so — as long as the priest would confess him and question him as closely as possible. So the priest told him to consider well the state of his soul, for he had done a lot of crafty things during his lifetime. He had better prove himself true, so God would forgive him his sins.

Eulenspiegel spoke rather pitifully, telling the priest he knew of nothing he had done — aside from one sin, one he dared not confess to him. He would rather he got another priest: he would confess it to him. For Eulenspiegel feared that were he to confess it to the priest, he would become extremely angry. When the priest heard this, he reflected that there must be some secret here, and since he wanted to find out what it was, he told Eulenspiegel, 'Eulenspiegel, the road is long. I can't find another priest all that quickly, and if you should die in the meantime, you and I shall bear the blame before Our Lord God, if you now miss your chance. Tell me what it is. Your sin cannot be so awful. I want to absolve you of it. Besides, what good would it do me to get angry? I cannot betray a confession.'

Eulenspiegel said, 'All right. I'll confess it.' It would not be so awful either, but he was sorry that the priest would probably get angry, for the sin concerned him. The priest now ached even more to know what it was, and told him that whether he had stolen something or done him some harm — no matter what it might be — Eulenspiegel should confess it to him. The priest would forgive him and never despise him.

'Ah, dear Father,' said Eulenspiegel, 'I know that you'll be very angry about it. But I know and fear that soon I must take my leave of this place. So I'll tell it to you, letting God decide whether you become calm or angry. And, dear Father, it's this: I've slept with your servant girl.'

The priest asked how often this had happened.

Eulenspiegel said, 'Just five times.'

The priest thought, 'She ought to get five lashes for this.' Then he quickly absolved Eulenspiegel, went to his room, and called the girl. He at once asked her whether she had slept with Eulenspiegel.

The girl, his cook, said, no, it was a lie.

But the priest said Eulenspiegel had confessed it to him— and he believed it.

She said, 'No.'

He said, 'Yes.'

And he took up a stick and beat her black and blue. Eulenspiegel lay laughing in bed, and thought, 'This game ought to turn out well now and have a decent result.' And he lay there all day.

During the night he became pretty healthy again. The next day he got up, saying he was getting better, and had to leave for another district, so the priest should figure out how much he had eaten there. The priest did the figuring with him, but was so confused he had no idea what he was doing—so he took money but it was no money, for he was happy enough that Eulenspiegel was leaving. The girl felt the same, since it was because of him that she had been beaten.

When Eulenspiegel was ready to go, he said, 'Sir, you should be warned that you have revealed my confession. I plan to go to the Bishop of Halberstadt and expose you.'

The priest forgot his sin of malice when he heard that Eulenspiegel intended to bring him difficulties and begged him earnestly to keep silent. It had happened because of rashness. He would give Eulenspiegel twenty guilders as long as he did not sue him.

Eulenspiegel said, 'No. I wouldn't take a hundred guilders to keep silent about this. I shall go, and prefer charges, as is proper.'

With tearful eyes, the priest called his servant girl, and said she should ask Eulenspiegel to tell her what he should give him: she could give it to him. Finally Eulenspiegel said: if the priest would give him his horse, he would keep silent and the betrayal would remain unknown. Eulenspiegel would, moreover, take nothing but the horse. The priest liked his horse enormously and would rather have given Eulenspiegel all his ready cash than lose his horse. But he gave it up against his will, as necessity forced him to. The priest gave his horse to Eulenspiegel and let him ride off with it.

Eulenspiegel immediately rode to Wolfenbüttel with the priest's horse. Well, he arrived at the moat. The Duke was standing there, on the drawbridge, and saw Eulenspiegel trotting up on the horse. At once the prince took off the coat he had promised Eulenspiegel, went straight over to him, and said, 'Look here, my dear Eulenspiegel. Here is the coat I promised you.'

Eulenspiegel dismounted, saying, 'Gracious Lord, here's your horse.' Well, he thanked the Duke profusely, and had to tell him how he had gotten the horse away from the priest. This made the prince laugh, and he was glad about it — and he gave Eulenspiegel another horse in addition to the coat.

But the priest mourned his horse, and beat the girl quite cruelly because of it — so much so that she left him. Thus he lost both.

39. *How Eulenspiegel hired himself out to a blacksmith, and how he carried the blacksmith's bellows into his courtyard for him.*

Eulenspiegel went over to Rostock, in the district of Mecklenburg, and hired himself out as a blacksmith's assistant. Now, this blacksmith had a favourite saying. Whenever his assistant was supposed to pump hard on the bellows, he said, 'Hey! Hey! Follow with the bellows!' Well, Eulenspiegel was standing at the bellows and pumping. And the smith, in a harsh voice, said to Eulenspiegel, 'Hey! Hey! Follow with the bellows!' With these words, he went into the courtyard, planning to drain off his water.

Eulenspiegel immediately placed one of the bellows on his shoulder, and followed his boss, saying, 'Chief, I'm bringing one bellows here. Where should I stick it? I'll go and get the other one too.'

His boss looked around and said, 'Dear apprentice, I didn't mean it like that. Go put the bellows back.'

Eulenspiegel did so, returning it to its proper place. Now, his boss wondered how he might get even with him for this, and decided to get up at midnight every night for five days, wake up his assistant, and make him work. In fact he woke up both his assistants, and let them do some forging.

Eulenspiegel's fellow assistant questioned him. 'What can the boss mean by waking us up so early? He doesn't usually do so.'

So Eulenspiegel said, 'If you like, I'll ask him.'

The boy said, 'All right.'

Eulenspiegel said, 'My dear boss, why're you waking us up so early? It's just midnight.'

His boss said, 'It's my custom that at the beginning—and for eight days—my boys don't sleep longer than half the night.'

Eulenspiegel kept quiet, and his companion dared not

speak, till the next night. Then his boss woke them up and Eulenspiegel's companion went to work. But Eulenspiegel took his bed and tied it onto his back. Then, when the iron was hot, he came running down from the garret to the anvil, crashing the bed against the anvil, so the sparks spewed into the bed.

The blacksmith said to him, 'Look here! What're you doing? Have you gone crazy? Can't the bed stay where it's supposed to be?'

Eulenspiegel said, 'Chief, don't be angry. This is my custom — that during the first weeks I lie on the bed for half the night, and for the second half of the night the bed lies on me.'

His boss became furious, ordering him to bring back the bed he had taken. Then he rashly went on, 'Now, you maddening fool, get up and out of my house!'

Eulenspiegel said, 'Yes.' So he climbed up into the garret, putting back the bed he had taken, found a ladder, stuck it against the coping, broke the roof open, went out onto the roof with the ladder, pulled the ladder up after him, set it into the street from the roof, climbed down, and so got away.

The blacksmith heard him making loud noises, and followed him into the garret with his other assistant. There he saw that Eulenspiegel had broken the roof open and climbed out. He now got even more furious and hunted for a skewer, throwing it after him out of the house. But his assistant calmed the blacksmith, saying, 'Chief, take it easy! Admit he hasn't done anything other than what you told him to. When you told him to get up and out of the house, he did so, as you now see.' The smith let himself be pacified.

What else could he do? Eulenspiegel was gone and his boss had to have the roof mended, and had to be satisfied with that.

His assistant said, 'Not much to be gained from a fellow-worker like that one. Whoever doesn't know Eulenspiegel — just let him deal with him, and he'll get to know him.'

40. *How Eulenspiegel forged a blacksmith's hammer, tongs, and other tools together.*

When Eulenspiegel left the blacksmith, it was nearly winter. Well, the winter was cold and froze cruelly. Eulenspiegel fell on hard times because of it, as many workers were going without work. Well, Eulenspiegel had no money to waste, so he wandered on and came to a village where there was another blacksmith, who took him in as an assistant. Eulenspiegel certainly had no great desire to stay on there as a smith's boy, though his hunger and the need of winter forced him to do it, so he thought, 'Bear what you can bear, and do what the smith wants till you can stick your finger into the spongy earth of spring again.'

The smith had no intention of hiring him just because times were hard. So Eulenspiegel told the smith that if he would give him any sort of work, he would do whatever he wanted—

and eat whatever nobody else wanted. Well, the smith was a wicked man, and he thought, 'Take him on for eight days' trial. He won't eat me into poverty that soon.'

The next morning they began forging, and the smith drove Eulenspiegel mercilessly, at hammer and bellows, till mealtime, when it was getting on toward noon. Well, the smith had an outhouse in the courtyard. As they were preparing to go to table, he took Eulenspiegel into the courtyard, led him to the outhouse, and said to him, 'Look, you say you're willing to eat whatever I want as long as I give you work. Now, nobody'd enjoy what's in here—so you eat it all.' He went into the house, ate something, and left Eulenspiegel standing at the outhouse.

Eulenspiegel kept quiet, but he thought, 'You've run the wrong way here, and done such things yourself to many people—to the extent that it's now being measured out to you. How do you plan to pay him back for this? For it's got to be paid back, though the winter were twice as harsh.'

Eulenspiegel worked for the man until evening. Then the smith gave Eulenspiegel something to eat, for he had gone hungry all day, and besides it stuck in the smith's head that he had shown him to the outhouse. As Eulenspiegel was getting ready to go to bed, the smith said to him, 'Get up tomorrow morning. The girl will work the bellows, and you forge whatever you've got, one thing after the other. And cut horseshoe nails till I get up.'

Eulenspiegel went to sleep. But when he got up, he thought he would now pay the blacksmith back, even if he had to run through snow up to his knees. He built a fierce fire, took the tongs, melted them in the sand-ladle, and forged them together, doing the same to two hammers, the firing spit, and the poker. Then he took the box in which the horseshoe nails lay, poured the nails out of it, and cut the heads off them, sticking the heads together and the stumps as well. Then, as he heard the smith getting up, he grabbed his leather apron and got out of there.

The smith came into his workshop and saw that the nails and heads had been cut apart and that his hammer, tongs, and other tools had been forged together. He got pretty angry and screamed at the girl to tell him where his assistant had gone. The girl said he had gone out.

The smith said, 'He's gone — like a rogue. If I knew where he was, I'd ride after him and give a fine slapping.'

The girl said, 'He was writing something over the door as he left. It's a face that looks like an owl's.'

Now, Eulenspiegel had this custom whenever he did some mischief where he was unknown: he took chalk or coal and drew an owl and a mirror over the door, and underneath wrote, in Latin, *Hic fuit*. And this Eulenspiegel had drawn on the smith's door too.

When the smith came out of his house that morning, he found it, as the girl had told him. But because the smith could not read the language, he went over to the priest and asked him to come read the writing over his door. The priest went with the smith to his door, and saw the writing and the picture.

He told the smith, 'It simply means "Eulenspiegel was here."' In fact the priest had heard a great deal about Eulenspiegel — about the sort of fellow he was — and scolded the smith because he had not let him know, for he would greatly have liked to have seen Eulenspiegel.

The smith instantly got angry with the priest and said, 'How could I let you know about it, when I didn't know myself? But I know now that he was definitely at my house. That you can see well enough by my working tools. But that he never comes back, there isn't much against it.' He took the coal-brush, whisked off what was above his door, and said, 'I don't want any fool's coat of arms over my door.'

The priest walked off, leaving the smith standing there. But Eulenspiegel did not appear, and did not return.

41. *How Eulenspiegel told something true to a blacksmith, his wife, his assistant, and his servant girl in front of his house.*

After he left the smith, Eulenspiegel went to Wismar, on a holy day. He saw a proper wife and her maid standing in front of the smithy there. It was the blacksmith's wife. Well, he took lodgings opposite the smithy, and during the night broke all four horseshoes off his horse, marching up in front of the smithy the next day. That way he was recognized.

When he came up to the smithy, and they realized it was Eulenspiegel, the wife and maid stood at an entrance of the house, as they wanted to hear and see Eulenspiegel's business. Eulenspiegel asked the smith whether he would shoe his horse.

The smith said, 'All right.' Now, it pleased the smith to be able to converse with Eulenspiegel. After much talk, the smith happened to say to Eulenspiegel that if he could tell him one true thing—something that was really true—he would give his horse one horseshoe.

Eulenspiegel said, 'All right:
If you've got irons and coals
And wind for your bellows' holes—
You can forge well.'

The smith said that, by his soul, that was true, and gave him a horseshoe.

His assistant was putting the irons on the horse and felt compelled to say to Eulenspiegel that if he could also tell him something true concerning him, he would give his horse a horseshoe too.

Eulenspiegel said, 'All right:

If they want to set about something,
A blacksmith and his boy
Must stand to hard employ.'

The boy said, 'That's true too,' and gave him a horseshoe as well.

The wife and maid saw this, and pressed closer, to be able to speak with Eulenspiegel too, and they told him that if he could say something true to them too, they would give him one horseshoe each.

Eulenspiegel said, 'Very well.' He said to the wife:

'The wife who stands before her doors
With lots of white in her eye,
If she had the time and were free of chores—
There wouldn't be fish to fry.'

The wife said, 'By my soul, that's true.' And she gave him a horseshoe as well.

Then he told the maid, 'When you eat, guard against beef. You won't have to pick your teeth, and your stomach won't bother you.'

The maid said, 'God protect us, how true that is!' And she gave him an iron horseshoe also.

So Eulenspiegel rode off, with his horse well shod.

42. *How Eulenspiegel worked for a shoemaker, and how Eulenspiegel asked him what shapes he should cut. His boss said, 'Large and small, like those the swineherd runs past the gate.' So Eulenspiegel cut out oxen, cattle, calves, rams, and the like, and ruined the leather.*

There was once a shoemaker who much preferred strolling around the market place to working, and he hired Eulenspiegel for cutting. Eulenspiegel asked what sort of shapes he would like, and the shoemaker said, 'Cut both large and small — like those the swineherd runs out of town.'

Eulenspiegel said, 'Sure.'

The shoemaker went out, and Eulenspiegel to cutting — and he made pigs, oxen, calves, sheep, goats, rams, and all sorts of beasts out of the leather. In the evening his boss returned, planning to see what his assistant had cut, and he found these animals cut out of his leather. He got angry, saying to Eulenspiegel, 'What've you made out of it? How could you cut up my leather so uselessly for me?'

Eulenspiegel said, 'My dear boss, I've done it as you wanted it.'

His boss said, 'You're lying. I didn't mean that you should destroy it. I didn't ask you to do that.'

Eulenspiegel said, 'Chief, what's the reason for this anger? You told me I should cut large and small out of the leather — like the swineherd runs past the gate. I did so. That's obvious.'

His boss said, 'I didn't mean it that way. I meant this: they should be large and small shoes, and you should stitch them, one after the other.'

Eulenspiegel said, 'If you'd asked me to do that, I'd gladly have done so. And I'd still be glad to do so.'

Well, Eulenspiegel and his boss were reconciled, and the shoemaker forgave him that cutting. Even more than that, Eulenspiegel promised him he would do it for him as he told him he wanted it done. So the shoemaker cut out leather for soles, placed it in front of Eulenspiegel, and said, 'Now look, stitch the small with the large, one after the other.'

Eulenspiegel said, 'Sure,' and began stitching.

His boss put off going out, as he wanted to watch Eulenspiegel to see how he planned to do it, since he had realized that Eulenspiegel would do exactly what he had told him to do.

Well, Eulenspiegel acted according to his boss's instructions. He took one small shoe and one large, stuck the small into the large, and stitched them together. Well, as his boss was going strolling, he became nervous about what he might be doing. It was then that he saw that Eulenspiegel was stitching one shoe inside the other.

His boss said, 'You're my proper assistant. You do everything I tell you to.'

Eulenspiegel said, 'He who does what he's told doesn't get punished. On the contrary.'

His boss said, 'Yes, my dear assistant, that's true. My words ran this way—but my meaning certainly didn't. I meant you should make a pair of small shoes, and afterwards a large pair. Or the large first, the small next. You're acting according to the words, not the meaning.' He got quite angry, snatched up some leather, and said, 'Pay attention a little! Look, here's more leather. Cut the shoes out over a last.' Then he thought no more about it, as he had to go out.

His boss was tending to his affairs, and had been out almost an hour, when he realized that he had told his assistant to cut the shoes over a last. He dropped everything and rushed home. Well, during this time Eulenspiegel had been sitting there, and had taken the leather and cut all of it over a single last.

His boss at once said, 'Why're you doing the large shoes with the small?'

Eulenspiegel said, 'Well, you wanted it that way. I still plan to do everything well. So now, afterwards, I'll cut the large ones.'

His boss said, 'You can more easily cut small shoes out of large than large out of small. You're using one last, and the other is sitting around unused.'

Eulenspiegel said, 'True enough, Chief. You told me to cut the shoes out over a last.'

His boss said, 'I might go on telling you — till I have to run you to the gallows.' And he went on to say that Eulenspiegel should pay for the leather he had ruined, since he would now need to buy more leather.

Eulenspiegel said, 'The tanner can fix your leather again.' Then he stood up, went to the door, turned round in the house, and said, 'If I don't come back to this house — at least I've been here.' And he left.

43. *How Eulenspiegel sprinkled a soup for a farmer, putting filthy-smelling fish oil on it instead of bread and drippings, and thought that was good enough for the farmer.*

Eulenspiegel did a great deal of mischief to shoemakers, not just in one place but in many. When he had done this last bit of nonsense, he arrived in Stade. There too he hired himself out to a shoemaker.

On the first day, when he started working, his boss went off to the market and bought a cartload of wood. Well, he agreed to give the farmer a soup as well as money, and brought the farmer, along with the wood, to his house. There he found no one at home (his wife and maid had gone out) but Eulenspiegel, who was alone in the house, stitching shoes. As his boss had to return to the market, he told Eulenspiegel to take whatever he found and make the farmer a soup: he had left him something in the cupboard.

Eulenspiegel said, 'All right.'

Well, the farmer threw down his wood and came into the house. Eulenspiegel cut pieces of bread into a bowl for him, but found no melted-down fat in the cupboard. So he went to the tank in which the shoemaker's awful-smelling fish oil was kept, and sprinkled the farmer's soup with that. The farmer began eating, and tasted how awful it was, but he was hungry and ate all the soup.

In the meantime, the shoemaker came in and asked the farmer how the soup had tasted. The farmer said, 'It tasted very good—and just a little like new shoes.' And with that the farmer left the house.

The shoemaker began to laugh and asked Eulenspiegel what he had used to sprinkle the farmer's soup with.

Eulenspiegel said, 'You told me to take what I had. Well, I had no fat other than fish fat—as I looked into the cupboard in the kitchen and didn't find any fat. So I took what I had.'

The shoemaker said, 'Well, that's all right. It's good enough for the farmer.'

44. *How a bootmaker in Brunswick larded Eulenspiegel's boots, and how Eulenspiegel knocked the windows out of his room.*

'Christopher' was the name of a bootmaker at the coal market in Brunswick. Eulenspiegel went over to him, planning to have his boots oiled. When he got to the bootmaker's, he said, 'Dear master-bootmaker, would you lard[1] these boots for me, so I can have them back by Monday?'

The bootmaker said, 'Very well.'

Eulenspiegel left the house and thought no more about it. When he was gone, the apprentice told his boss, 'That's Eulenspiegel, who's too mischievous with everybody.' — And that if he were to tell him to do 'What he told you to do,' he would do it and not fail to.

His boss said, 'Well, what did he tell me to do?'

---

[1] 'Lard' was evidently a bit of bootmaker's jargon for 'oil'.

The apprentice said, 'He really told you to "lard" his boots — and he meant to "oil" them. Now, I wouldn't oil them. I'd lard them, as one bastes a roast.'

His boss said, 'That we'll do — just as he told us.' So he took bacon, cut it up, and larded the boots with a larding-needle — like a roast.

Well, on Monday Eulenspiegel came back, and asked whether they had his boots ready for him. The bootmaker had hung them on the wall, and pointed them out to him, saying, 'There they hang.'

Eulenspiegel saw that his boots had in fact been larded — and began to laugh, saying, 'What a straightforward master-bootmaker you are! You've done it as I told you to. What do you want for this?'

The bootmaker said, 'One old shilling.'

Eulenspiegel presented the old shilling, took his larded boots, and left the house. Well, the bootmaker and his apprentice watched him go, laughing after him, and they said to one another, 'How could that happen to him? Now he's been made a fool of.'

In the meantime Eulenspiegel rammed his head and shoulders through the window from the street — for the room was on the ground floor and gave onto the street — and said to the bootmaker, 'Dear master-bootmaker, what sort of fat did you use for my boots? Is it sow's fat or boar's fat?'

The bootmaker and his apprentice were puzzled. Finally they realized that Eulenspiegel was lying in the window and knocking the window panes fully half out — with the result that they were falling toward the bootmaker into the room. The bootmaker at once got furious and said, 'You tricky liar! If you don't stop, I'll beat you over the head with this stick!'

Eulenspiegel said, 'Dear master-bootmaker, don't lose your temper. I'd like to know what sort of fat it was that you larded my boots with. Is it sow's fat or boar's fat?'

The bookmaker went mad with rage, saying he had better leave his windows unbroken.

'If you don't want to tell me what kind of fat it is, I'll have to ask somebody else.' And Eulenspiegel jumped back out of the windows.

Well, the bootmaker now got simply furious with his apprentice too, telling him, 'You advised me to do this! Now give me advice on how to have my windows fixed!'

The apprentice was silent. His boss became indignant, saying, 'Who's made a fool of whom? I've always heard that whoever's bothered by tricksters should cut the traces and let them go. If I'd done so, my windows would still be in one piece.'

The apprentice was fired because of this. His boss wanted his windows paid for—since the apprentice had given him the idea to lard the boots.

45. *How Eulenspiegel sold a shoemaker of Wismar frozen filth for tallow.*

Eulenspiegel once did a lot of damage in leather-cutting to a shoemaker of Wismar, destroying much of his leather and

making the good man quite unhappy. Eulenspiegel took stock
of this, returned to Wismar, and told the shoemaker to whom
he had done the damage that he planned to obtain a huge load
of leather and tallow that ought to yield the shoemaker quite
a profit, so he might recover his loss.

The shoemaker said, 'Well, you're acting fairly, since you've
made me a poor man. When you get the goods, let me know.'

Then they parted. Well, it was wintertime, and the harnessmakers were cleaning the outhouses. Eulenspiegel went to
them and promised them ready money if they would fill
twelve barrels for him with the material they were otherwise
planning to dispose of in the water. The harnessmakers did
so, packing the barrels quite full, so they were four fingers
from the top, and left them standing till they had frozen stiff.
Eulenspiegel then hauled them away. Well, he caked six
barrels over thickly with tallow, beating them tightly shut;
smeared six barrels over with cooking fat, beating these all
tightly shut; had them brought to his inn, 'At the Golden
Star', for a Dutch guilder; and sent a messenger to the
shoemaker. When the shoemaker arrived, they opened the
goods on top, and the shoemaker was quite pleased with
them. They settled their purchase, with the shoemaker giving
Eulenspiegel twenty-four guilders for the load. He was to give
Eulenspiegel twelve guilders at once, the rest in a year.
Eulenspiegel took the money and left, as he was worried
about what would happen.

The shoemaker received his goods and was as happy as one
who has overcome hopeless injury or debt. He summoned
help to be able to oil his leather the next day. The shoemaker's
boys showed up in strength, thinking they might at least get a
good meal, and set about the work, singing loudly, as they
usually do. But when they had placed the barrels on the fire
and they began to get warm, they regained their natural smell.
Everybody said to everybody else, 'I think you've been
shitting in your pants.'

The shoemaker said, 'If somebody's stepped in some filth,
wash your shoes. It stinks terribly everywhere.'

They looked around and found nothing, and began to pour
the tallow into a kettle and begin oiling. But the deeper they

dug with their oiling the more foully it stank. Finally they realized what it was and left the work standing.

The shoemaker and his helpers ran to look for Eulenspiegel to hold him for the damages, but he had left with the money. He was even supposed to return for the other twelve guilders. So the shoemaker had to take his barrels of tallow to the slaughterers' graveyard, and sustain double his loss.

46. *How Eulenspiegel became a brewer's assistant at Einbeck, and how he boiled a dog called Hops, instead of hops.*

Once again Eulenspiegel made himself useful in his work.

After people at Einbeck had forgotten about his shitting on the plums,[1] he came back to Einbeck and offered his services

---

[1] Possibly a reference to the eighty-seventh story.

to a brewer of beer. It happened that the brewer wanted to go to a wedding, so he told Eulenspiegel to brew beer with his servant girl as best he could. The brewer would return to help him in the evening. Now, above all, Eulenspiegel should work hard and boil the hops well, so the beer would taste strong afterwards and the brewer could sell it. Eulenspiegel said, yes, he would do his best. With that, the brewer and his wife left the house.

Eulenspiegel began his boiling enthusiastically. The servant girl instructed him, as she knew more about it than he did. Well, when the time came for boiling the hops, the girl said, 'The boiling of the hops, dear, that you can do very well on your own. Let me go watch the dance for an hour.'

Eulenspiegel said, 'Sure.' But he thought, 'If the girl leaves too, you've got a chance for some fun. What sort of joke would you like to play on this brewer?'

Well, the brewer had a large dog called Hops. When the water was very hot, Eulenspiegel took it, threw it into the water, and let it boil through till its skin and hair came off and all the flesh fell off its legs. Well, when the servant girl thought it was time to go home — for the hops must have boiled enough by now — she came back, planning to help Eulenspiegel. She said, 'My dear brother, that's enough now. Drain it off.'

But when they moved the straining basket and started to dig into it, one shovelful after the other, the girl said, 'Did you put hops in here too? I don't notice any yet on my shovel.'

Eulenspiegel said, 'You'll find it at the bottom.'

The girl fished around and lifted the skeleton on her shovel. She began to scream horribly. 'God help me, what did you put in here! The devil drink this beer!'

Eulenspiegel said, 'I only put into it what our brewer told me to put into it. Why, it's nothing other than Hops, our dog.'

At that moment the brewer came home, quite drunk, and said, 'What're you doing, my dear children? Are you being good little things?'

The girl said, 'I don't know what the devil we're doing. I

went to watch the dance for half an hour, and told our new assistant to boil the hops well in the meantime. He boiled our dog. You can see its spine here.'

Eulenspiegel said, 'Yes, sir. You both told me to do so. Isn't it terrible? I do everything that people tell me to — and never seem to earn much thanks at all. There may be some brewers somewhere who'll be satisfied if their servants do only half what they're told to do.'

So Eulenspiegel quit, and left the place — without earning much in the way of appreciation.

47. *How Eulenspiegel hired himself out to a tailor and sewed under a tub.*

When Eulenspiegel went to Berlin, he hired himself out as a tailor's boy. When he was sitting in the workshop, his boss said, 'Boy, when you want to sew, sew well and sew so nobody sees it.'

Eulenspiegel said, 'Yes,' and took the needle, and material with it, crawled under a tub, folded a seam over one knee, and began to sew it there.

The tailor stood watching this, and said to him, 'What're you doing? This is strange needlework.'

Eulenspiegel said, 'Boss, you said I should sew so nobody sees it. Well, nobody sees it.'

The tailor said, 'No, my dear assistant. Stop and don't sew that way any more. Start sewing so it can be seen.'

This went on for maybe three days. Then it happened that they worked till nightfall. The tailor was tired and wanted to go to bed. A gray farmer's coat was lying there, half unsewn, which he tossed to Eulenspiegel, saying 'Look, finish the wolf[1] and go to bed too.'

Eulenspiegel said, 'Yes. You just go ahead. I'll do it properly.'

His boss went to bed and thought no more about it. Eulenspiegel took the gray coat and cut it up, making a head like a wolf's out of it, with body and legs, and stretching it over separated sticks, so it quite resembled a wolf. Then he went to bed too.

The next morning his boss got up, woke Eulenspiegel as well, and found the wolf standing in his workroom. His boss was outraged, but he understood well enough what had happened. Eulenspiegel came in just then, and the tailor said, 'What the devil did you make out of it?'

He said, 'A wolf—as you told me.'

The tailor said, 'I didn't mean that sort of wolf. I simply called the gray farmer's coat a wolf.'

Eulenspiegel said, 'My dear boss, that I didn't realize. If I'd known your thoughts ran that way, I'd have preferred making the coat to making the wolf.'

Well, the tailor accepted that, since it had happened just once. But after about four days it chanced that his boss felt

[1] A slang term for such coats. See Notes on the Tales. The same word play recurs in Tale 53.

tired one evening and decided to go to sleep early. It seemed to him, however, that it was still too early for his assistant to go to bed. Now, a coat was lying there that had been finished up to its arms. So Eulenspiegel's boss took the coat and its loose arms, tossed them over to Eulenspiegel, and said, 'Cast these arms on the coat, and then go to bed.'

Eulenspiegel said, 'Yes.'

His boss went to bed — and Eulenspiegel hung the coat on a hook and lit two lamps, one on either side of the coat. He took one arm and threw it at the coat, and went to the other side and threw the other at it too; and when the two lamps burned out, he lit two more, casting the arms on the coat straight through the night till morning. His boss now got up and came into the room. Eulenspiegel ignored his boss, and kept casting the arms at the coat.

The tailor stood there, looking at this, and said, 'What sort of devilish fraud are you engaged in?'

Eulenspiegel said, quite seriously, 'This isn't any devilish fraud for me. I've been standing here all night — throwing these crazy arms at this coat, and they won't stay there. It would have been better if you'd told me to go to bed than telling me to "cast on". And you knew perfectly well that this was pointless work.'

The tailor said, 'Is it my fault? Could I know that you would interpret me that way? I didn't mean it that way. I meant that you should sew the arms on the coat.'

Eulenspiegel at once said, 'The devil reward you for it. If you've a fancy to say something other than what you mean, how is one to rhyme the things together? If I'd known your intentions clearly, I'd have sewed the arms on all right — and gotten a few hours of sleep. Well, you sit and sew all day, and I'll lie down and sleep.'

His boss said, 'Oh, no, not a chance! I'm not going to keep you on here as a loafer.'

Well, they began to quarrel with each other — and so much so that during their quarreling the tailor addressed Eulenspiegel about the lamps: he ought to pay him for those he had used during this business. At that point Eulenspiegel took up his things and walked away.

48. *How Eulenspiegel made three tailor's boys fall off a bench — and told people the wind had blown them off it.*

Eulenspiegel stayed at an inn near the market place in Bernburg for about fourteen days. Now, hard by the inn lived a tailor who had three boys sitting on a bench and sewing. Whenever Eulenspiegel passed by, they mocked him or threw their remnants at him. Eulenspiegel kept quiet, biding his time. But one day when the market place was full of people, Eulenspiegel had sawn off the supporting posts of the bench the night before, leaving them standing on their foundations.

That morning the apprentices placed the bench on its posts, sat down, and sewed. But when the swineherd began his yelling — that everybody ought to let his pigs be driven out — the tailor's pigs came out of his house, rushed under his window, and began to rub themselves against the benchposts. The result of the rubbing was that the posts were punched out from under the window, and the three boys sitting under the window tumbled into the lane. Eulenspiegel caught sight of them, and as they fell, began calling in a loud voice, 'Look, look, the wind's tossing three boys out of this window!' — calling it so stridently that he could be heard all over the market place. Well, the people ran over and laughed and jeered, but the boys were embarrassed, and had no idea how they had fallen from under the window. Finally they noticed that the benchposts had been sawed through — and realized also that Eulenspiegel had done it. They pounded new posts into place, and did not dare make fun of him again.

49. *How Eulenspiegel called all the tailors of Saxony together to teach them a skill that would help them and their children.*

Eulenspiegel announced a convocation and assembly of the tailors of the Wendish towns and of the district of Saxony —

also of those in the districts of Holstein, Pomerania, Stettin, and Mecklenburg; also of Lübeck, Hamburg, Sunt, and Wismar. In his letter he assured them of a grand opportunity — namely, that if they would meet with him (he was in the city of Rostock) he would teach them a tailoring method that would help them and their children forever, for as long as the world lasted.

The tailors in the cities, country towns, and villages wrote one another their views of this idea. They all wrote that they were ready to come to the city at an appointed time and would all assemble there. Each longed more than the next to learn what it might be that Eulenspiegel planned to say, or what sort of method he would teach them, since he had written to them so urgently. Well, they arrived in Rostock at the appointed time — all according to their pledges — with the result that many people wondered what all these tailors were doing there.

When Eulenspiegel heard that the tailors had actually responded to his invitation, he had them draw together in a tight little group. The tailors at once told Eulenspiegel that they had come there and answered him because of his announcement, in which he had alluded to the fact that he could teach them a method that would help them and their children. They asked that he enlighten them, make his method public, and inform them about it. They would reward him well.

Eulenspiegel said, 'All right. Let's all meet in a meadow, so each of you can hear me.'

They all met on a broad plain. Eulenspiegel climbed up inside a house, peered out of a window, and said, 'Honourable men of the craft of tailoring! You should note and understand: if you have a pair of scissors, tape-measure, thread, and a thimble, along with a needle, you've got the right equipment for your profession. Getting hold of this stuff is hardly a difficult proposition for you. In fact, it follows of itself, if you wish to engage in your profession. But here's a method you'll receive from me, and you'll thank me for it. When you've threaded your needle, don't forget to make a knot at the other end, or you'll sew a lot of stitches uselessly, as the thread will have no reason not to slip out of the needle.'

Each tailor looked at the next, and they said to one another, 'We all knew this skill well enough before—along with everything else he's told us.' And they asked him whether he had anything more to say, since they had not planned on travelling ten or twelve miles, and sending messengers to each other, for this nonsense. Tailors had known this method for a long time, for more than a thousand years.

Eulenspiegel responded to this by saying, 'There isn't anybody who remembers what happened a thousand years ago.' He also said that if his advice did not meet with pleasure and thanks, they might as well take it in displeasure and no thanks—and that the crowd could just go back to where it had come from. The tailors, who had come from so far away, and who really wanted to be instructed by him, at once became pretty angry, but they could not manage to get at him. So the tailors simply dispersed. Some were furious, cursed, and were thoroughly annoyed that they had gone such a great distance for nothing. But those who lived in nearby houses laughed and jeered at the others because they had made such fools of themselves, and said it was their own fault if they believed country rogues and knaves—for they ought to have realized long ago what sort of bird Eulenspiegel was.

50. *How Eulenspiegel beat wool on a holy day, because the clothier had forbidden his having Monday off.*

When Eulenspiegel arrived in Stendal, he made out that he was a wool-weaver. On Sunday his wool-weaver boss told him, 'Dear apprentice, you fellows take your days off on Mondays—but whoever's used to doing that I don't want in my business. A boy's got to work right through the week.'

Eulenspiegel said, 'Yes, Chief, I like it that way too.'

So the next morning Eulenspiegel got up and beat wool, doing the same on Tuesday, and this quite pleased the wool-weaver. Now, Wednesday was an Apostle's day, which they had to celebrate, but Eulenspiegel acted as though he knew nothing about the holy day. He got up that morning, and started to clean and beat wool—doing it so it could be heard through the whole street. The wool-weaver at once shot out of his bed, saying, 'Stop! Stop! This is a holiday.'

Eulenspiegel said, 'My dear boss, you informed me about no holiday on Sunday. On the contrary, you told me to work the whole week through.'

The wool-weaver said, 'Dear assistant, I didn't mean it that way. Just stop and don't beat any more. I'll gladly give you whatever you might have earned today.'

Eulenspiegel was happy about that, took the day off, and that evening had a conference with his boss. The wool-weaver now told him that he was succeeding quite well with his beating of the wool—only he ought to beat it a little higher.

Eulenspiegel said, 'Sure.'

He got up early the next morning, stretched the bow over the lath, and placed a ladder against it. Then he climbed up, arranging it so the beater could follow him from the basket, took the wool from the basket (which was standing on the ground) up to the oast and beat the wool so it scattered all over the house. The wool-weaver was lying in bed. He could hear by the beating that Eulenspiegel was not doing it properly. He got up to watch him.

Eulenspiegel said, 'Chief, what do you think? Is this high enough?'

His boss said, 'Ha! Terrific fellow! If you stood on the roof, you'd be even higher. If you want to beat the wool that way, you could just as well do it sitting down on the roof instead of standing up here on this ladder.' With that he left the house for church.

Eulenspiegel took his advice. He took the beater, climbed onto the roof, and beat the wool on the roof. His boss, outside in the lane, caught sight of it. He ran right back, shouting, 'What the devil are you doing! Stop! Is beating wool on the roof how it's usually done?'

Eulenspiegel said, 'What're you saying now? You just said it would be better on the roof than on the ladder, because that's higher than the rungs of the ladder.'

The wool-weaver said, 'If you want to beat wool, beat it. If you want to fool around, fool around. Climb off the roof and shit in the wool-basket.' With that the wool-weaver went into his house and out into his courtyard. Eulenspiegel at once climbed off the roof, went into the sitting room of the house, and deposited a huge pile of filth in the wool-basket. The wool-weaver came back from the courtyard, saw him shitting in the parlour, and said, 'Oh, may you never have any happiness! You're behaving like a scoundrel!'

Eulenspiegel said, 'Chief, I'm doing nothing but what you told me to. You told me to climb off the roof and shit in the wool-basket. Why are you so angry about it? I'm doing what you told me.'

The wool-weaver said, 'You'd shit on my head—without being told. Take that excrement and stick it where no one will have it.'

Eulenspiegel said, 'Yes,' and putting the excrement on a piece of wood carried it into the dining room.

The wool-weaver said, 'Leave that outside! I don't want that in here!'

Eulenspiegel said, 'I know perfectly well you don't want it in here. Nobody would want it in here. But I'm doing what you told me.'

The wool-weaver got really angry, and ran to the stable, planning to beat Eulenspiegel over the head with a log. But Eulenspiegel left the house, saying, 'Can't I earn any gratitude anywhere?'

The wool-weaver then tried to grab the piece of wood on which Eulenspiegel had stuck his shit, but he was in too much of a hurry and made his fingers dirty. He let the filthy thing drop and ran to the well to wash his hands.

In the meantime, Eulenspiegel left.

51. *How Eulenspiegel hired himself out to a furrier and shitted in his workroom for him, because one stink is supposed to drive out another.*

Eulenspiegel once arrived in Aschersleben. Now, it was deep winter and a bitter time, and he thought, 'What'll you take up now, to bring you through the winter?' There was no one who needed an assistant, but a furrier was living there who wanted to hire an apprentice, if one showed up who worked his trade. Eulenspiegel thought, 'What'll you do? It's winter, and hard because of it. You've got to bear what you can bear and bear the winter out.' So he hired himself out as an apprentice to the furrier.

When he went into the workshop to sew pelts, he was unused to their stink, and said, 'Fie, fie! You may be white as chalk, but you stink like filthy garbage.'

The furrier said, 'You don't like the smell — and still you're sitting here? That it smells is only natural. It's from the wool the sheep has on the outside.'

Eulenspiegel kept quiet and thought, 'One evil is supposed to drive off another.' And he released such a sour fart that both his boss and his wife had to hold their noses.

The furrier said, 'What're you doing? If you like making filthy farts, get out of the room into the courtyard and fart as much as you like.'

Eulenspiegel said, 'For the health of a human being this is much more natural than the stink of sheepskins.'

The furrier said, 'Whether it's healthy or not, if you want to fart, go into the courtyard.'

Eulenspiegel said, 'Chief, there it'll be lost. No fart enjoys being out in the cold. They're always where it's warm. To prove it, release a fart. It'll immediately run back to your nose, to the warmth from which it came.'

The furrier kept quiet. He knew perfectly well that he was being made the butt of a joke and was certain he would not keep Eulenspiegel for long. Eulenspiegel remained sitting there, and sewed, farted, and breathed out, coughing the hairs out of his mouth. The furrier sat and watched him, keeping quiet till evening, after they had eaten.

Then his boss said to him, 'Dear assistant, it seems clear to me that you aren't happy with this trade. I'm convinced you aren't a true furrier's apprentice. That I can see by your attitude. Or you can't have been at it for long, if you aren't used to the work. If you'd merely slept with it for four days, you wouldn't be turning up your nose that way and complaining about it. It wouldn't be offensive to you. Therefore, my dear assistant, if you haven't any wish to stay on here, tomorrow please go wherever your horse takes you.'

Eulenspiegel said, 'Chief, you're telling the truth when you say I haven't been at this for long. If you'll just let me sleep near the work for four nights, till I'm used to it, then you'll see what I can do.'

The furrier was happy with that, since he needed Eulenspiegel and he could sew well.

52. How Eulenspiegel slept among pelts for a furrier — dry and damp, as the furrier told him to.

The furrier and his wife went happily to bed. Eulenspiegel took the prepared hides that were hanging on the frames, the dry hides that had been tanned, and the wet ones too. He piled them together on the floor, crawled between them, and slept till morning.

His boss now got up and saw that his hides were gone from their frames. He quickly ran over to his workshop to ask Eulenspiegel whether he knew anything about the hides. But he did not find Eulenspiegel, and saw that his pelts, both dry and damp, were lying in a pile on the floor — all mixed up with one another. He got pretty anxious, and in a tearful voice called his maid and wife.

Well, his shouting roused Eulenspiegel, who peered out of the pelts and said, 'My dear boss, what on earth is wrong, that you're shouting so much?'

The furrier was amazed, not realizing that he was in the pile of hides and pelts, and said, 'Where are you?'

Eulenspiegel said, 'Here I am, in here.'

His boss said, 'Ah! May nothing good ever come your way! You've taken my pelts off the frames, the dry hides, and the wet ones out of the limewater — and piled them up together here. You're destroying the one with the other for me. What sort of nonsense is this?'

Eulenspiegel said, 'Chief, if you're angry about it, and I haven't slept in here more than one night, you'd be much angrier if I slept in here for four nights — as you told me to yesterday evening because I wasn't used to the work.'

The furrier said, 'You're lying like a knave! I didn't tell you to drag the finished hides across the floor, and the damp ones, and sleep in them.' And he looked for a stick to beat him with.

In the meantime, Eulenspiegel hurried downstairs, meaning to run out through the door. The wife and maid were standing at the bottom of the stairs. They tried to stop him. So he screamed wildly, 'Let me go for a doctor! The boss has broken his leg!'

They let him go and ran upstairs. But the furrier was coming downstairs, running fiercely after Eulenspiegel, and he stumbled, falling on his wife and maid, and all three piled onto each other.

Well, Eulenspiegel ran out through the door, leaving them in the house together.

53. *How Eulenspiegel, in Berlin, made wolves for a furrier, instead of 'wolf-pelts.'*

Swabians are extremely sly people. If they try one sort of thing to make a living, and cannot get by, another must be worse. In reality, they are more fond of the beer mug and of drinking than of working, and for this reason their workshops often stand empty.

A furrier who was a Swabian once lived in Berlin. Now, he was quite skilful in his profession and also careful with his expenditures. As a result, he was also rich and ran a fine workshop. He had among his clientele the prince of the district, the nobility, and many good people and citizens. Well, it happened that the prince decided to hold a great court that winter, with races and tournaments. He wrote announcements of it to his noblemen and other lords. Since no one wished to be left out, many 'wolf-pelts'[1] (or coats) were ordered from the aforementioned furrier just then. Eulenspiegel found out about this, and went to this master-furrier to ask for work.

The furrier, who needed helpers at that time, was happy that he had come, and asked him whether he also knew how to make 'wolves'. Eulenspiegel said, sure: in the district of Saxony he was by no means the least known for this sort of thing.

The furrier said, 'Dear boy, you've come to me at just the right moment. Come on. We'll arrive at a good understanding between ourselves about your wages.'

Eulenspiegel said, 'Yes, boss. I see that you're honest enough to know very well yourself what they should be, once you see my work. But I don't work with the other workers. I wish to be alone, so I can perform my job according to my wishes and without interference.'

So the furrier gave him a little room, offering him many wolf skins that had been scraped and were prepared as pelts, giving him a mass of various pelts, both large and small. Well, Eulenspiegel began to apply himself to the wolf hides, and cut them up, making wolves out of all of them and stuffing them with hay and shaping legs for them with sticks, to make them lifelike. When he had cut up all the hides and made wolves out of them, he said, 'Chief, the wolves are all ready. Is there anything else?'

His boss said, 'Yes, my dear boy. Sew up as many of them as you can.' With that he went up to the room where the wolves, both large and small, were lying on the floor. His boss looked at them and said, 'What's this supposed to be? May the plague shake you! What a disaster you've brought on me! I'll have you imprisoned and punished!'

Eulenspiegel said, 'Chief, are these supposed to be my

---

[1] See Tale 47, in which this term also appears.

wages, then? And I've acted in precise accordance with your own words. You told me to make wolves. If you'd said, "Make me wolf-coats," I'd have done that too. And if I'd known I wasn't to earn any more gratitude, I wouldn't have used up so much energy.'

So Eulenspiegel took his leave of Berlin, leaving nowhere a good reputation behind him, and went on to Leipzig.

54. *How Eulenspiegel, in Leipzig, sold the furriers a live cat sewn into a rabbit skin, in a sack, for a live rabbit.*

How quickly Eulenspiegel could invent a fine jest—as he proved to the furriers of Leipzig on Shrove-Tuesday Eve, when they held their feast, or drinking bout, together. Now, it happened that they wanted to eat wild game. Eulenspiegel heard about this and thought, 'The furrier in Berlin gave you nothing for your work. These furriers ought to pay for it.'

So he went to his inn, where his innkeeper had a fine, plump cat—which Eulenspiegel stuck under his coat. Then he asked the cook for a rabbit skin: he planned to arrange a smart little jest with it. The cook gave him a skin, into which he sewed the cat. Then he dressed in farmer's clothes and took up a position in front of the town hall, keeping his wild game concealed in his jacket until one of the furriers came by. Eulenspiegel asked him whether he would not like to buy a good hare, and let him look under his jacket. They soon agreed on his giving Eulenspiegel four silver guilders for the hare and six pennies for the old sack in which the hare was kept. The furrier took it off to their guildmaster's house, where they all gathered, with great boisterousness and merriment, and announced that he had bought the finest hare he had seen in a year. One after another, they handled it all over. Then, since they planned to have it on Shrove-Tuesday, they let it run live in an enclosed grass-garden—and got some young dogs, because they wanted to hold a rabbit-hunt.

Well, when the furriers got together, they let the hare loose, with the dogs after it. Since the hare could not run well, it jumped into a tree and cried 'Mieow!'—and that it would rather go home again. When the furriers saw this, they shouted fiercely, 'You good comrades, come on! Come on! Whoever's made fools of us with this cat—we'll beat him to death!'

This might well have happened. But Eulenspiegel had taken off his clothes and so altered his appearance that they did not recognize him.

55. *How Eulenspiegel boiled leather—along with chairs and benches—for a tanner in Brunswick on the Damme.*

Shortly after Eulenspiegel left Leipzig, he went on to Brunswick, to a tanner who tanned leather for shoemakers. Well, it was wintertime, so he thought, 'You'd better put up with this tanner for the winter.' He hired himself out to the tanner.

When he had been with the tanner for eight days, it happened that the tanner was invited out to dinner. That day Eulenspiegel was to tan the leather—completely—by himself.

The tanner told Eulenspiegel, 'Boil a full load of leather in the tub.'

Eulenspiegel said, 'All right. What should I use as wood for this?'

The tanner said, 'What sort of question is that? If I haven't got any wood in the woodshed, I've still got lots of chairs and benches with which you can quite finish the leather.'

Eulenspiegel said, 'Sure.' It would be fine.

The tanner went out to his friends'.

Eulenspiegel hung up a kettle, stuck the leather inside it, one hide after the other, and boiled the leather through till it could be pulled apart with one's fingers. Then, when Eulenspiegel had boiled the leather through, he broke up chairs and benches — all of them that were in the house — stuck them under the kettle, and boiled the leather even longer. When this was done, he took the leather out of the kettle, laid it out in a heap, left both house and city, and went on his way.

The tanner sensed nothing wrong, drank all day, and went

pleasantly to bed that evening. The next morning the tanner wanted to see how his assistant had done his leather, so he got up and went into the tanning house. Well, he found the leather utterly boiled through, found neither bench nor chair in either house or courtyard, became quite miserable, and went to his room, to his wife, and said, 'Woman, something awful has happened. I have a feeling that our new assistant was Eulenspiegel because he seems to be in the habit of doing everything that he's told. He's gone—and he's chopped all our chairs and benches into the fire and boiled the leather far too much.'

His wife began to cry, and said, 'Get after him, wild and fast, and bring him back!'

The tanner said, 'No, I don't want him back. If only he stays away till I send for him.'

56. *How Eulenspiegel cheated the wine-tapster at Lübeck, by giving him a jug of water instead of a jug of wine.*

Eulenspiegel kept wisely on his guard when he arrived in Lübeck, and conducted himself properly, playing no tricks on anyone, for justice in Lübeck is harsh indeed.

At that time there was a wine-tapster at Lübeck, at the Ratskeller, who was a haughty, proud man. He had managed to convince himself that no one was as clever as he was. He said himself, and made sure it was said about him, that he longed to have a look at the man who could trick him and outsmart him. Well, because of this, a lot of citizens thoroughly disliked him.

When Eulenspiegel heard about this wine-tapster's presumptuousness, he found it impossible to suppress his mischievous nature any longer, and thought, 'You've got to find out what he can do.' He took two jugs that had been made exactly alike, putting water into the first jug and leaving the other empty. The jug of water he carried hidden under his coat, the empty jug out in the open. Then he went into the wine cellar with the jugs, had a measure of wine poured out for him, and put the jug with the wine under his coat, setting the water jug in its place. He put it on the little shelf, so the wine-tapster did not see it, and said, 'Bartender, what does a measure of wine cost?'

'Ten pennies,' he said.

Eulenspiegel said, 'That's too expensive. I've got just six pennies. May I have it for that much?'

The wine-tapster got angry and said, 'Are you trying to set the price of wine for these gentlemen here? This is a fixed price. If you don't like it, just leave your wine in the Gentlemen's Cellar.'

Eulenspiegel said, 'That's what I wanted to know. I've got these six pennies. If you don't want them, pour the wine back again.'

The wine-tapster grabbed the jug in anger, thinking it was wine when it was water, poured it back into the bung-hole, and said, 'What sort of fool are you—having wine measured out for you, and you can't pay for it?'

Eulenspiegel took his jug and walked off, saying, 'I see

rather that you're a fool. There's nobody too wise to be tricked by fools — even if he's a wine-tapster.'

With that he left, carrying the jug of wine under his coat, but the empty jug, in which the water had been, he carried out in the open.

57. *How people tried to hang Eulenspiegel at Lübeck; and how, with clever trickery, he got out of there.*

Lambrecht, the wine-tapster, listened to the words Eulenspiegel uttered as he left the cellar. Then he went to get a policeman, ran after Eulenspiegel, and caught up with him in the street. The policeman grabbed him, and they found the two jugs with him, the empty jug and the jug with the wine. They pronounced him a thief and led him to prison. Now, some offered it as their judgement that he deserved the gallows for this; and some said it was no more than a subtle jest and thought the wine-tapster should have been more cautious when he asserted that no one could outsmart him. Eulenspiegel had only done what he did because of the wine-tapster's presumptuousness. But those who disliked Eulenspiegel said it was theft: he must hang for it. Well, sentence was passed on him—death on the gallows.

Now, when the day of judgement arrived, on which Eulenspiegel was to be led out and hanged, there was an uproar through the whole city, with everyone up and out on horse or foot. The Council of Lübeck feared that he might have worked the people up or fixed it so he would not be hanged. Some wanted to see how he would take his end, after his having been so wild a fellow. Others declared he knew the black arts and could escape by them. Most would have rejoiced at his escape.

Now, Eulenspiegel kept still on being led out, saying not a word, with the result that everyone was amazed and thought he was in despair. This continued till they reached the gallows. Then he spoke, calling the whole Council before him, and asking, with great humility, that they grant him one request. He would ask them for neither life nor limb, nor for either money or property, but for something small to be done afterwards—neither eternal mass, nor eternal alms-giving, nor everlasting remembrance—but a different thing that would cause no damage in its accomplishment and that it would be easy for the honourable Council of Lübeck to do—without its costing a penny.

The members of the Council gathered and moved to one side to consult; and they were satisfied that they could grant him his request, since he had already stipulated what he would not ask for. Besides, a number of them very much wanted to know what he intended to request. They told him that whatever he asked for would be done, as long as he did not ask for any of the things he had mentioned earlier. If he agreed, they would grant him his wish.

Eulenspiegel at once said, 'I won't ask you for any of the things I mentioned before. But if you plan to keep your word with me with respect to what I ask of you, give me your hands on it.'

This they did, all together, swearing by hands and oaths.

Whereupon Eulenspiegel said, 'You honourable gentlemen of Lübeck, as you've pledged on your honour, I'll make my request of you. And this is it, that after I've been hanged, the wine-tapster come here every morning for three days — the bartender first and the skinner, who'll dig my grave, second — and that before they eat, they kiss me with their mouths on my arse.'

Well, they vomited and said this was hardly a civilized request.

Eulenspiegel said, 'I consider the esteemed Council of Lübeck honest enough to keep its word with me — that it has pledged me by their hands and sworn oaths.'

They all went off to consult about this — with the result that, by permission and for other appropriate reasons, it was decided that they would let him go. Well, Eulenspiegel went on from there to Helmstädt, and was never again seen in Lübeck.

58. *How Eulenspiegel had a giant purse made at Helmstädt.*

Eulenspiegel arranged still another jest, with a purse. A pursemaker was living at Helmstädt. Eulenspiegel visited him, asking whether the pursemaker would like to make him a large, pretty purse.

The pursemaker said, 'Of course. How big should it be?'

Eulenspiegel said that he would like to have it made big enough, for those were times in which one carried large purses that were big and roomy. The pursemaker made Eulenspiegel a big purse. When he came for it and saw the purse, he said, 'This purse isn't big enough. It's a mere purselet. If you'll make me one that's big enough, I'll pay you nicely.'

The pursemaker made him a purse out of an entire cowhide, making it so big that one might easily have put a yearling calf into it — a purse that one had to drag along.

When Eulenspiegel came for it this time, he was still not happy with the purse and said the purse was still not big enough. If the pursemaker really wanted to make him a purse, he should make one big enough for him: he would give him two guilders for it. The pursemaker took the two guilders and made him a purse for which he used three oxhides. Three men would have had trouble carrying it on a bier. You could have poured a bushel of corn into it.

When Eulenspiegel came back, he said, 'Chief, this purse is big enough, but the big purse I had in mind isn't this purse. So I don't want it either—it's still too small. If you can make me a purse big enough so I can take one penny out of it and two more are still left inside it—so I'd never be without money and never have to grovel for a living—I'd buy it from you and pay up. These purses you've made me are empty. They're useless to me. I've got to have full purses. Otherwise I can't go out among people.'

And he left, leaving his purses with the pursemaker, and said, 'You keep them in case of a good sale.' Eulenspiegel also left him the two guilders, although the pursemaker had easily cut him ten guilders' worth of leather.

59. *How Eulenspiegel cheated a butcher of Erfurt out of a roast.*

Eulenspiegel could not suppress his clownish nature when he arrived at Erfurt, where he soon became well known among both citizens and students.[1] Once he went to the butchers' stalls because meat was on sale. A butcher immediately told him that he ought to get something to take home with him.

Eulenspiegel said, 'What should I take with me?'

The butcher said, 'A roast.'

Eulenspiegel said, 'All right.' He grabbed a roast by one end and left with it.

The butcher ran after him, saying, 'Not like this! You've got to pay for the roast.'

Eulenspiegel said, 'You said nothing to me about paying. You spoke instead about whether I wouldn't like to take something with me.' The man had pointed out the roast so he

---

[1] For Eulenspiegel's experience with the students of Erfurt, see Tale 29.

might take it home with him. This Eulenspiegel could prove with his neighbours, who were standing nearby.

The other butchers came over and—out of malice—said yes, that was true. The other butchers disliked him, for whenever customers approached them and tried to buy something, this butcher called them over to him and lured them away. So they declared absolutely that Eulenspiegel should keep the roast. While this butcher argued with them, Eulenspiegel stuck the roast under his coat and went off with it— leaving them to settle things among themselves as best they could.

60. *How Eulenspiegel cheated a butcher of Erfurt out of another roast.*

Eight days later, Eulenspiegel returned to the butchers' stalls. The same butcher now solicited Eulenspiegel again, with flattering words, 'Come on over and get a roast.'

Eulenspiegel said, 'Yes,' and tried to touch the roast, but the butcher was quick and grabbed it tightly.

Eulenspiegel said, 'Just leave the roast lying there. I fully intend to pay for it.'

The butcher laid the roast on his counter.

Eulenspiegel went on, 'If I tell you a word that will be in your interest, will the roast be mine?'

The butcher said, 'Well, you may tell me such words as will be useless to me ... but you may also tell me words that could indeed be in my interest, and then you might take the roast.'

Eulenspiegel said, 'I don't plan to touch your roast unless my words please you.' And he went on, 'I'll say this: "Come on, Mr Moneybags, and pay the people!" How do you like that? Don't you like it?'

The butcher said, 'These words quite please me—and certainly are to my liking.'

Eulenspiegel said to those who were standing around them, 'Dear friends, you've heard him. Well, the roast is mine.'

Eulenspiegel took the roast and walked off with it, saying sarcastically to the butcher, 'Well, I've got another roast—as you promised me.'

The butcher stood there, not knowing what he could possibly say to this. Twice he had been tricked, and made to feel the shame of his fellow butchers' ridicule as they stood around him and laughed at him.

61. *How Eulenspiegel became a carpenter's boy in Dresden, and failed to win much praise.*

Eulenspiegel soon cleared out of the district of Hessen for Dresden, near the Bohemian Forest on the Elbe. There he took on the role of carpenter's boy. A cabinet-maker hired him. The cabinet-maker needed an apprentice, as his own apprentice had given up the trade and gone travelling.

Now, a wedding was being held in the city, to which the cabinet-maker was invited. He told Eulenspiegel, 'Dear boy, I've got to go to the wedding and won't be back during the

day. Do well and work hard and install the four planks on
that table, in the glue, as tightly as possible.'

Eulenspiegel said, 'Yes. Which planks belong together?'

The carpenter placed them on top of one another for him—
those that belonged together—and went off to the wedding
with his wife. Eulenspiegel, the trusty helper who always
aimed at doing his work more absurdly than properly, started
off and bored through the finely milled table planks or counter
planks, which his boss had stacked there for him, in three or
four places. Then he piled them into plank blocks, wedged
them together, boiled glue in a large kettle, stuck the planks
in, carried them up inside the house, and shoved them out of
the window, so the glue could dry in the sun. Then he took
time off.

That evening his boss came home, having had a lot to drink,
and asked Eulenspiegel how he had worked that day.

Eulenspiegel said, 'Chief, I've stuck the four table planks

together as tightly possible in the glue — and had a decent time off as well.'

This quite pleased his boss, and he said to his wife, 'This is a fine assistant. Treat him well. I'd like to keep him a long time.' They went off to bed.

But the next morning his boss told Eulenspiegel to bring him the table he had finished. Eulenspiegel came along, dragging his work in from the work-floor. When his boss saw that the rogue had ruined his planks, he said, 'Look here, my apprentice, have you ever been taught carpentry?'

Eulenspiegel answered: why was he asking this?

'I'm asking it because you've ruined these fine planks for me.'

Eulenspiegel said, 'My dear boss, I've done it as you told me to. If it's ruined, that's your fault.'

The carpenter got angry, saying, 'You damned fool! I'll throw you out of my workshop for this! I've no use for your sort of work!'

Eulenspiegel took his leave of that place and did not earn much thanks — despite his having done all he was told to do.

62. *How Eulenspiegel became an optician, and found no demand for his services in any country.*

The electors were angry and contentious among themselves, with the result that there was no Roman Kaiser or King. Well, it came about that the Count of Supplenburg was chosen as Roman King by the mass of electors, but there were a number among them who fancied themselves able to take over the empire by force. So this newly elected King had to camp near Frankfurt for six months to see whether anybody might try to overthrow him. Since he had assembled a very large crowd, on horse and foot, Eulenspiegel speculated on what it might be possible for him to do there: 'Lots of foreign Lords are arriving, who won't think of me as lacking in talent. If I can manage to join their retinue, I'll do well.' He set out for the place.

The Lords of all countries were going there. Thus it

happened that the Bishop of Trier and his company found Eulenspiegel in the Wetterau near Friedburg, on the road to Frankfurt. As he was oddly dressed, the Bishop asked him what sort of fellow he was.

Eulenspiegel replied, 'Gracious One, I am an optician and come from Brabant. There is nothing to do there, so I'm wandering in search of work. But there seems to be absolutely no demand for our skills.'

The Bishop said, 'I should think your craft would be thriving, better with each day — the reason being that each day the people become more sickly and lose their vision. As a result, a lot of eyeglasses are certainly needed.'

Eulenspiegel answered the Bishop, 'Yes, gracious Lord, Your Grace speaks the truth. But there's one thing that's ruining our craft.'

The Bishop said, 'What is it?'

Eulenspiegel said, 'If only I might tell Your Grace without your getting angry!'

'No,' said the Bishop. 'I'm used to such things from you and your kind. Just speak freely.'

'Gracious Lord, it is ruinous to the craft of spectacle-making—so much so that one may well fear that it may vanish—that you and other great Lords, Popes, Cardinals, Bishops, Kaisers, Kings, Princes, Councilors, Governors, Justices of cities and countries (God save us!) presently just wink at what is right—and this, presently, because of gifts of money. But in ancient times, one finds it written, Lords and Princes, as many as there were of them then, were in the habit of reading and studying after justice, so that injustice might be decently avoided. To do so, they needed lots of eyeglasses, so in those days our craft did well. Moreover, popes studied a lot more then than now, so eyeglasses are disappearing. Of course, they are now so well educated from the books they buy that they know their pages by heart—so they don't open their books more than once in four weeks. For this reason our craft lies in ruins, and I'm running from one country to the next and finding work nowhere. This evil condition has spread so widely that farmers in the country are concerned and are keeping an eye on it.'

The Bishop understood this text without any further explanation, and told Eulenspiegel, 'Follow us to Frankfurt. We shall offer you our festive regalia and clothes.'

This Eulenspiegel did. He remained with the Lords till the Count was confirmed as Kaiser. Then he travelled with the Kaiser back to Saxony.

63. *How Eulenspiegel hired himself out as a cook and houseboy to a merchant in Hildesheim, and behaved quite mischievously.*

On the right, in the street that one takes out of the hay-market in Hildesheim, there lived a rich merchant. Once he went walking in front of his house, intending to go into his garden. On the way, in a green field, he came across Eulenspiegel, who was lying down. The merchant greeted Eulenspiegel, asked him what sort of fellow he was, and what his trade might be. Eulenspiegel answered him with concealed roguishness and cunning: he was a cook's apprentice and was out of work.

The merchant quickly said, 'If you can be trusted, I'll take you on myself — and give you new clothes and a nice piece of change. I've got a wife who complains all day long about cooking, and I'd very much like to earn her gratitude.'

Eulenspiegel promised him enormous loyalty and honesty. So the merchant hired him, asking him his name.

'Sir, my name is Barto-lo-me-us.'

The merchant said, 'That's a long name. It can't easily be said. You'll be called "Crazy".'

Eulenspiegel said, 'Of course, my dear Squire. It's all the same to me what I'm called.'

'Well, well,' said the merchant, 'you're the boy for me. Come on, come on. Come into my garden with me. We're going to take some herbs home with us, and young chickens as well. I've invited guests for next Sunday, whom I'd like to treat nicely.'

Eulenspiegel went into the garden with him and cut rosemary, with which he was to stuff the chickens in Swiss style — and others with onions, eggs, and other herbs. Then they went home together. When his wife saw her guest's odd clothes, she asked the master of the house what sort of fellow this was and what her husband planned to do with him — or whether her husband was just worried that their bread might be moulding.

The merchant said, 'Woman, be content. He's to be your very own servant. He's a cook.'

His wife said, 'Yes, dear husband, he looks as if he ought to be able to cook fine things.'

'Just be happy,' said her husband. 'Tomorrow you'll see very well what he can do.' And he called Eulenspiegel: 'Crazy!'

Eulenspiegel answered: 'Squire!'

'Get a sack and follow me to the butcher's. I want to get meat and a roast.'

Eulenspiegel followed him. His Squire bought meat and a roast there, and said to him, 'Crazy, put the roast to one side tomorrow to let it cool and brown slowly, so it doesn't burn. Put the other meat beside it, so it'll be hot for eating.'

Eulenspiegel said yes, got up early, and put the food on the fire. But he put the roast on a spit and placed it between two barrels of Einbeck beer in the cellar, so it would stay cool and not burn. As the merchant had invited the City Secretary and other guests for dinner, he came to find out whether his guests had arrived and whether the food was ready — and asked his new servant.

Eulenspiegel answered, 'Everything's ready but the roast.'

'Where's the roast?' said the merchant.

'It's lying in the cellar, between two barrels. I knew of no cooler place in the house where I could put it, according to your instructions.'

'But is it ready?' said the merchant.

'No,' said Eulenspiegel. 'I didn't know when you wanted to have it.'

While this was going on, the guests arrived. The merchant

told them about his new servant and how he put the roast in the cellar. Well, they laughed and made a good joke of it. But the wife was unhappy for her guests' sake, and told the merchant he ought to let the boy go: she could no longer bear him in the house; she could see he was a rogue.

The merchant said, 'Dear wife, just keep calm. I'd like to use him for a trip to the City of Goslar. When I get back, I'll have him take off.' He could barely persuade his wife to be satisfied with this.

When they had eaten and drunk and there had been good cheer all evening, the merchant said, 'Crazy, get the carriage ready, and grease it. Tomorrow we're going to Goslar. There's a priest living there, called Father Heinrich Hamenstede. The man is here and will travel back with us.'

Eulenspiegel said yes, and asked what sort of grease he ought to use. The merchant threw him a shilling and said, 'Go buy wagon grease and have my wife mix old fat under it.'

Eulenspiegel did precisely that, and when everyone was asleep, he greased the carriage inside and out, and especially where one was supposed to sit. The merchant got up early the next morning, with the priest, and told Eulenspiegel to hitch up the horses. He did so. They seated themselves and drove off. At once the priest began to heave about, and said, 'What, by the gallows, is so fatty here? I'd like to stop, so this carriage stops throwing me around and making my hands so filthy everywhere.'

They ordered Eulenspiegel to stop and told him they were both being smeared with grease, front and back. They also began to get angry with him. In the meantime a farmer came by, driving to market with a load of straw. They bought several bundles from him, wiped off the carriage, and seated themselves inside once more.

The merchant now said angrily to Eulenspiegel, 'You damned fool! May nothing good ever come your way! Drive to beat the gallows!'

Eulenspiegel did so. When he arrived under the gallows, he stopped short and unhitched the horses.

The merchant said, 'What're you trying to do — or what do you mean by this — you fool!'

Eulenspiegel said, 'You told me to drive under the gallows. Here we are. I thought we wanted to rest here.'

At this, the merchant saw by looking out of the carriage that they were stopped under the gallows. What could they do? They began to laugh at the joke, and the merchant said, 'Hitch up, you fool, and drive straight on and don't look to either side!'

Eulenspiegel now unhitched the coupling pins from the travelling carriage. When he had driven an acre's length further, the carriage separated, and the rear portion of it, with the roof, remained standing still. But Eulenspiegel went on by himself. They shouted after him, and had to run till their tongues hung out of their mouths before they caught up with him. The merchant tried to beat him to death. The priest helped, as best he could.

Well, they completed their journey and returned home. His wife asked how it had gone.

'Strangely enough,' said the merchant, 'but at least we're back.' With that he called Eulenspiegel and said, 'Fellow, stay here tonight. Eat and drink what you like. But tomorrow clear out of my house. I won't have you here anymore. You're a tricky fool—wherever you come from.'

Eulenspiegel said, 'Dear God, I do everything I'm told—and still earn no gratitude. But if you're not pleased with my service, I'll clear out of your house, and leave tomorrow, according to your words.'

'Yes, do that,' said the merchant.

The next day the merchant got up and told Eulenspiegel, 'Eat and drink yourself full and get yourself out of here. I'm going to church. Don't let yourself be found here again.'

Eulenspiegel kept quiet. As soon as the merchant was out of the house, he began clearing out—chairs, tables, benches. Whatever he could carry and haul he dragged into the lane—copper and pewter pots and candles. The neighbours started wondering what was going on there, with all these things being lugged into the street.

The merchant found out about it. He came puffing up to Eulenspiegel and said, 'You trusty servant—what're you doing here! Do I still find you here?'

'Of course, Squire. I wanted first to obey your words—since you told me to clear out the house, and then leave.' He went on, 'Grab here with your hands. This load is too heavy for me. I can't manage it alone.'

'Leave it lying!' said the merchant. 'And go to the devil! These things cost too much to be thrown into filth like this!'

'Dear Lord God,' said Eulenspiegel, 'isn't it a great wonder? I do everything I'm told—and still earn gratitude nowhere! I'm not deceived—I was born in an unlucky hour.'

Well, Eulenspiegel took his leave of that place, letting the merchant take back what he had cleared out. The merchant's neighbours laughed at him, to his face and behind his back.

64. *How Eulenspiegel became a horse-dealer in Paris, and removed the tail from a Frenchman's horse.*

Eulenspiegel played an amusing trick on a horse-dealer at the lake at Wismar. A horse-dealer always stopped by there who refused to buy any horse unless, during the bargaining, he pulled the horse by its tail. He did this even to horses that he did not buy, as he thought he could find out, by pulling, his own sign whether the horse would live long. His sign was this. If a horse had a long tail, he pulled it by the tail: if the long hair on its tail was curly, he did not buy it, since he believed that it did not have long to live. If the hair on the tail was straight, he bought it, and was convinced that it would live long and had a hardy constitution. Well, this had become so common an idea at Wismar that everyone swore by it.[1]

Eulenspiegel found out about this, and at once thought, 'You ought to play some trick on him, be it what it may, to set these people free of this superstition.' Well, Eulenspiegel was able to help himself with black magic. He got hold of a horse, practised black magic on it according to his purposes, and rode to the market with it. There he asked such a high price for the horse that everybody refused to buy it from him,

---

[1] As this tale has to do neither with Paris nor with a Frenchman, it may be assumed that some sort of editorial error has taken place here.

until the very merchant arrived who pulled horses by their tails. Eulenspiegel asked a good price of this fellow for his horse.

The merchant could see very well that the horse was a fine one, and fine for its money. He went over to it, planning to pull hard on its tail. Now, Eulenspiegel had so arranged things that as soon as he pulled on the horse's tail it came off in his hand, while the horse appeared to have lost its tail.

The merchant stood there, getting more and more worried. But Eulenspiegel started shouting, 'Curses on this villain! Look, dear fellow citizens, how he's insulted and ruined my horse!'

The citizens rushed right over and saw that the merchant had the horse's tail in his hand and that the horse no longer had a tail. Well, the merchant was terrified. But the citizens intervened and arranged that the merchant paid Eulenspiegel ten guilders, and that Eulenspiegel kept his horse. So Eulenspiegel rode off on his horse, and replaced its tail.

But after that experience, the merchant never again pulled a horse by the tail.

65. *How Eulenspiegel played a huge joke on a pipemaker at Lüneburg.*

At Lüneburg lived a pipemaker who had been a country tramp and had been run out of the country with other lazy logs. He was sitting at his beer. Well, Eulenspiegel arrived at these festivities and found much company there. So the pipemaker invited Eulenspiegel to dinner—but with this purpose, to make a fool of him—and told him, 'Come by tomorrow at noon and eat with me, if you can.'

Eulenspiegel said yes, not understanding his words right away, and went along the next day, planning to go to dinner at the pipemaker's. When he came up to his door, the door was bolted above and below and all the windows were closed. Eulenspiegel walked back and forth before the house two or three times, till it was after midday, but the house remained shut. He realized that he had been tricked. He left the place and kept quiet till the next day.

Eulenspiegel now came up to the pipemaker in the market place and said to him, 'See here, my worthy fellow, are you in the habit of doing things like this — of inviting people for dinner, then going out yourself and shutting the doors above and below?'

The pipemaker said, 'Didn't you hear how I invited you? I said, "Come by tomorrow at noon and eat something with me — if you can." Well, you found the doors locked, so you couldn't come by.'

Eulenspiegel said, 'Thanks very much. I didn't realize that. I'm learning something new every day.'

The pipemaker laughed and said, 'I don't want to annoy you. Go there now. My door's open. You'll find cooked and baked things on the fire. Go on ahead. I'll come after you. You may eat by yourself. I don't want any guests but you.'

Eulenspiegel thought, 'That'll be fine.' So he went at once to the pipemaker's house, and found everything as the pipemaker had said. The maid was turning the roast, and his wife was moving about arranging things. So Eulenspiegel went into the house and told the wife that she and her maid were to leave immediately. The master of the house had just been presented with a large fish, a sturgeon, which they were to help him carry home. Eulenspiegel would turn the roast in the meantime.

The woman said, 'Of course, dear Eulenspiegel. I'll go with the girl and be back in a flash.'

Eulenspiegel said, 'Go, quickly!'

The woman and her maid hurried off toward the market. But the pipemaker met them on the way and asked them why they were in such a rush. She said Eulenspiegel had come to the house and told them that he had been presented with a huge sturgeon which they were to help him carry home.

The pipemaker got angry, saying to his wife, 'Couldn't you have stayed at home? He hasn't done this for no reason. There's some trick here.'

Now, in the meantime Eulenspiegel had bolted the door,

above and below, so when the pipemaker, together with his wife and maid, arrived at the house, they found the door locked.

He said to his wife, 'Now you see the sort of sturgeon you were supposed to get.'

They knocked on the door.

Eulenspiegel came to the door and said, 'Stop this knocking. I'm not letting anyone in. The master of the house ordered and definitely said I was to be in here alone. He wants no guests but me. Go away and come back after dinner.'

The pipemaker said, 'That's true. I said that. But I didn't mean it. Well, let him eat. I'll play another trick on him for this.' And he went, with wife and maid, to a neighbour's house to wait till Eulenspiegel was finished.

Well, Eulenspiegel prepared the food thoroughly, sat down at the table, stuffed himself, and put what was left back on the fire, taking his good time about it. Then he opened the door and left it open.

The pipemaker now came in and said, 'Fine people don't do the sorts of things you've done, Eulenspiegel.'

But Eulenspiegel said, 'Should I have done with another what I was supposed to do by myself? If I'm invited to dinner, and the master of the house wants nobody but me—and I let in more guests—the fellow certainly won't be happy.' With these words he left the house.

The pipemaker gazed at him: 'I'll pay you back for this, rogue that you are.'

Eulenspiegel said, 'Whoever can do so best is master.'

Well, the pipemaker went that very hour to the horse-slaughterer and told him, 'There's a good man at the inn, Eulenspiegel by name, whose horse has died.' The slaughterer ought to pick it up. The pipemaker showed him the house. The horse-slaughterer recognized the pipemaker at once, and said, yes, he would do it. So he drove his slaughterer's cart up to the inn the pipemaker had shown him and asked for Eulenspiegel. Eulenspiegel came to the door and asked what he wanted. The horse-slaughterer said the pipemaker had come to him and told him that Eulenspiegel's horse had died, that he ought to pick it up: but was he indeed Eulenspiegel and was this true? Eulenspiegel turned around, pulled down his pants, and stuck up his arse. 'Look here, and tell this to the pipemaker: if Eulenspiegel hasn't been sitting in this alleyway, then I don't know what street he's sitting in.'

The slaughterer was furious, drove his slaughterer's cart to the pipemaker's house, left the cart standing there, and complained to the pipemaker so strongly that the pipemaker had to give the horse-slaughterer ten guilders.

Eulenspiegel saddled his horse and rode out of town.

66. *How Eulenspiegel was tricked by an old farmer's wife and lost his purse.*

A long time ago, at Gerdau in the district of Lüneburg, there lived an old couple who had been married to each other for about fifty years, and who had grown children whom they had well provided for and established. Now, there was an extremely greedy priest living in the parish at that time, a man who particularly liked being wherever people might be feasting or carousing. This priest arranged things among his parishioners as follows—that every farmer had to invite him to dinner at least once a year and take care of him and his maid for one or two days, and feed them very well indeed. But for many years the two old people had had no wake, baptism or banquet that the priest might have turned into a wild party. This annoyed him, so he thought of a scheme to force the farmer to offer him a feast. He sent him a messenger to ask him how long he and his wife had been established in the state of matrimony.

The farmer answered, 'Dear Father, it's been so long that I've forgotten.'

The priest responded, 'This could be a dangerous situation for your holy soul. If you've been together fifty years, the vows of matrimony expire, like a monk's in a cloister. So talk to your wife, come back to me, and let me know the facts, so I may recommend help for your blessed soul, as I am required to do for you and all my parish children.'

The farmer did so and discussed it with his wife, but was unable to give the priest an accurate reckoning of the years of his marriage. Full of worry, they returned to the priest, so he might offer them sound counsel in the matter of their unworthiness.

The priest said, 'Because you do not know the exact number of years, and out of concern for your souls, I shall, next Sunday, unite you anew—so in case you are not in a state of matrimony you shall arrive in it. Slaughter a fine ox for the event, and sheep and pigs. Invite your children and good friends to your banquet. And enjoy yourselves, because I'll be there too.'

'Ah, dear Father, just be there. For us this won't be a matter of just a pile of chickens. That we have lived so long with one another—and now for the first time may be out of wedlock—that would not be good.' With that they went home to make their preparations.

The priest invited various prelates and priests with whom he was acquainted to the affair. Among these was the Prior of Ebsdorf, who always had a decent horse or two and also greatly enjoyed eating. Eulenspiegel had been staying with him for some time. The Prior said to him. 'Take my young stallion and come along. You'll be welcome.'

Eulenspiegel did so. When they arrived there—and were eating and drinking and growing merry—the old woman, who was supposed to be the bride, was sitting on the table, as brides are supposed to do. But as she was tired and felt weak, she was allowed to go outside. She went behind the house, to the River Gerdau, and dangled her feet in the water. At the same time, the Prior and Eulenspiegel came by, riding home to Ebsdorf. Well, Eulenspiegel honoured the bride with some fine jumping of the young stallion, but did so a bit too much, with the result that his belt-purse, which was carried on one's side in those days, fell off. When the good woman saw it fall, she got up, took the purse, and went back to the river, sitting down over the purse. When Eulenspiegel had ridden an acre's length further, he missed his purse for the first time, and raced back to the Gerdau to ask the good old farmer's wife whether she had not picked up or found an old, rough purse.

The old woman said. 'Yes, friend. For my wedding I picked up a rough purse indeed. I still have it and am sitting on it. Is that the one?'

'Ha,' said Eulenspiegel. 'If you've had it since your wedding it must be quite a rusty purse by now. I've no need of your old purse.'

Thus was Eulenspiegel—roguish and cunning as he was— nonetheless tricked by an old farmer's wife and forced into losing his purse. The women of Gerdau still have that same rough bride's-purse. I believe that the old widows there are even holding it for safekeeping. Whoever is interested ought to ask about it.

67. *How Eulenspiegel tricked a farmer at Ueltzen out of some green fabric from London by making him believe it was blue.*

Eulenspiegel always preferred eating cooked and baked things, so he was ever alert to where he might get them. Once he

went to the fair at Ueltzen, as a lot of Wends and other
country people were coming to it. He strolled here and there,
observing everywhere what there was to do. Among other
things, he saw that a country fellow was purchasing a green
fabric from London and planning to go home with it. Eulenspiegel thought, in the end, that he might enjoy tricking this
farmer out of that fabric. He asked about the village where
the farmer lived, picked up a Scottish priest and a tramp, and
went out of the city with them to the road by which the
farmer had to travel. He then laid his plans for how they
would handle him, so the farmer with the green fabric would
be persuaded it was blue. Each of them was to station himself
an acre's length away from the other on the road leading out
of the city.

When the farmer came out of the city with his fabric,
meaning to bring it home, Eulenspiegel asked him where he
had bought that fine, blue material. The farmer replied that it
was green, not blue. Eulenspiegel said it was blue. He would

bet twenty guilders on it — and the first person to come up to them, who knew green from blue, would tell them so well enough, so they could be clear about it. Eulenspiegel then gave a signal to the first fellow to come over.

The farmer said, 'Friend, we two have just bet twenty pennies on the colour of this fabric. Tell the truth, whether it's green or blue. As you say it, that's how we'll let it be.'

The first fellow lifted it and said, 'It's a fine blue fabric.'

The farmer said, 'No! You're both rogues — and probably set this up with each other to trick me.'

Eulenspiegel now said, 'Just a minute. To let you see I'm right, I'll let this first test pass, and let the matter be settled by this pious priest who's just coming over. What he says will either make or break me.' The farmer agreed.

When the priest came up to them, Eulenspiegel said, 'Father, just tell the truth — what's the colour of this fabric?'

The priest said, 'Friends, that you can see well enough yourselves.'

The farmer said, 'Yes, Father, that's true. But these two are trying to convince me of something I know must be a lie.'

The priest said, 'Why should I bother with this quarrel of yours? What do I care whether it's black or white?'

'Ah, dear Father,' said the farmer, 'settle it for us. I beg you to do so.'

'If you really want it that way,' said the priest. 'Well, I can't say anything other than — the fabric is blue.'

'Do you hear that?' said Eulenspiegel. 'The fabric is mine.'

The farmer said, 'Indeed, Father, if you weren't an ordained priest, I'd think you were lying and that all three of you were rogues. But as you're a priest, I have to believe it.'

So he gave Eulenspiegel and his companions the fabric, with which they clothed themselves against winter, while the farmer had to go about in his torn coat.

68. *How Eulenspiegel shitted in the baths at Hanover,
believing that the place was a House of Cleansing.*

The bathkeeper at the baths in Hanover, near the Lein Gate,
did not like having his place called a 'Bathhouse' but a 'House
of Cleansing'. Eulenspiegel found out about this, and when he
got to Hanover, went to these baths, undressed, and said, as
he stepped into the bathing room, 'God bless you, sir, and
your house servants, and everyone whom I find in this clean
house.'

The bathkeeper was pleased with this remark, told him he
was welcome, and said, 'Dear guest, you're speaking the truth.
This is a clean house and also a house of cleansing—and not a
bathhouse. For dust is in the sun, and is also in earth, ashes,
and sand.'[1]

---

[1] This sentence has no intelligible meaning. Something has perhaps been omitted;
see also Notes on the Tales.

Eulenspiegel said, 'That this is a house of cleansing is obvious, for we come into it unclean and come out of it clean.' With these words, Eulenspiegel deposited a great pile of shit in the water trough in the middle of the bathing room, creating a stink through the whole place.

The bathkeeper said, 'It seems clear to me that your words aren't quite appropriate to your deeds. Your words pleased me well enough, but your deeds don't please me in the least. Your words were fine, but your deeds stink horribly. Is this how one behaves in a house of cleansing?'

Eulenspiegel said, 'Isn't this a house of cleansing? I needed cleansing more inside than outside — otherwise I wouldn't have come in here.'

The bathkeeper said, 'One usually does your sort of cleansing in the lavatory. This is a house of cleansing-by-sweating — and you're turning it into a shithouse.'

Eulenspiegel said, 'Doesn't this filth come from the human body? If one wants to cleanse oneself, one must cleanse oneself inside as well as outside.'

The bathkeeper got pretty angry and said, 'One cleanses oneself of this sort of stuff in the shithouse, and the horse-slaughterer takes it out to the slaughterer's burial place. But I'm not in the habit of washing and scouring it.' With these words, the bathkeeper ordered Eulenspiegel out of the baths.

Eulenspiegel said, 'Mr Keeper, let me bathe for my money. You'd like having a lot of money, and I'd like a good bath.'

The bathkeeper said Eulenspiegel should simply get out of his place; he had no interest in Eulenspiegel's money. If Eulenspiegel refused to leave, he would show him the door at once.

Eulenspiegel reflected, 'This would be dirty fighting — naked with razors.' He started out through the door, and said, 'How nicely I've bathed for a bit of filth.' He then left and got dressed in a room in which the bathkeeper and his employees usually took their meals.

The bathkeeper tried to trap him in there and frighten him by pretending to hold him prisoner and threatening him. While this was going on, Eulenspiegel realized that he had not cleansed himself quite enough in the bathing room. He spotted a folding table, opened it, shitted a pile on it, and folded it up again. Well, the bathkeeper soon let him out, and they settled their quarrel.

Eulenspiegel at once told him 'Dear Keeper of the Baths, in this room I cleansed myself thoroughly for the first time. You'll be thinking about me a great deal before noon. I'm leaving this place.'

69. *How Eulenspiegel bought milk from the countrywomen in Bremen, and mixed it all together.*

Eulenspiegel did strange and amusing things in Bremen. Once he went to the market there and observed that the farmers' wives brought a lot of milk to sell. He waited for a market-day when a good deal of milk was being delivered, acquired a large vat, set it up in the market place, purchased all the milk that was brought for selling, and had it all poured into the vat. Now, for each woman he marked a ring around the vat—the first had this much, the next had that much, and so on. He told the women to wait till he had collected all their milk. Only then would he pay each woman separately.

The women sat in a circle in the market place, and Eulenspiegel kept buying milk till no more women were arriving with it, and the vat was nearly full.

Eulenspiegel now turned to them, making a joke of the thing, and said, 'I haven't any money just at present. Whoever doesn't want to wait fourteen days may take her milk out of the vat.' With that, he left.

The women created an uproar and riot. One had this much, the next that much, the third the same, and so on — till they began beating and smashing one another over the head with their pails, little casks and bottles, and pouring milk into their eyes and over their clothes and on the ground, and it looked as though it had rained milk.

The farmers, and everybody who stood there watching, laughed at the absurdity — that women would go to market like this — and Eulenspiegel was praised a good deal for his roguishness.

70. *How Eulenspiegel gave twelve blind men twelve guilders — how they took them, how they spent them, and how in the end they lived miserably because of them.*

Since Eulenspiegel was always wandering from one district to the next, the time came when he arrived in Hanover again and engaged in many curious exploits. Once he went riding an acre's length on the road by the gate and ran into twelve blind men.

When Eulenspiegel drew abreast of them, he said, 'You blind men — where are you coming from?'

The blind men stopped. They could hear very well that he was mounted on a horse. They thought he must be a high-ranking personage, doffed their hats and caps, and said, 'Dear Squire, we've been to the city. A rich man died there, for whom a funeral was held, and alms were given out. But it was horribly cold.'

Eulenspiegel told the blind men, 'It's cold indeed. I'm only afraid you may freeze to death. Look, here are twelve guilders for you. Go on back to the city, to the inn from which I've just come'—and he told them which house it was—'and spend these twelve guilders, for my sake, till winter is over and you can go on your way again before frost-time.'

The blind men stood there, bowing and thanking him profusely. The first blind man thought the second had the money, the second thought the third had the money, the third thought the fourth had the money, and so on, till the last thought the first had it. Well, they went back into the city to the inn that Eulenspiegel had told them about. When they got to the inn, the blind men all said that a good man had ridden up behind them, and given them, by the grace of God, twelve guilders which they were supposed to spend, for his sake, till winter was over. The innkeeper was eager for their money and took them in for the twelve guilders. He did not reflect that he ought to have asked them which blind man had the twelve guilders. He said, 'Yes, my dear brothers, I'll treat you nicely.' He slaughtered and chopped and cooked for the blind men, and let them eat, till it seemed to him that they had used up the twelve guilders. At that point he said, 'Dear brothers, if we do a reckoning, the twelve guilders are just about spent.'

The blind men agreed, and each asked the next which of them had the twelve guilders, so they might pay the innkeeper. The first did not have the guilders; the second did not have them either; the third likewise did not; the fourth the same; and the last had the twelve guilders no more than the first. The blind men said so, and scratched their heads. They had been tricked.

So had the innkeeper. He sat down to think. 'If you lose them now, your food won't be paid for. But if you keep them on, they'll stuff themselves and eat even more — and still leave you with nothing — till you've got twice your loss.' He led them out to his pigsty, locked them in, and offered them a bed of straw and hay.

Eulenspiegel started thinking that the blind men must have used up that money by now, so he disguised himself and rode into the city, to the very same inn. When he reached the courtyard, planning to tie up his horse in the stable, he saw the blind men lying in the pigsty. He went straight into the house and said to the innkeeper, 'Mr Innkeeper, what reason can you have for keeping poor blind men in your pigsty? Haven't you got any sympathy for them? They must be eating stuff there that's doing harm to life and limb.'

The innkeeper said, 'I wish they were where all rivers meet[1] — and I had my food paid for.' And he told Eulenspiegel everything about how he and the blind men had been tricked.

Eulenspiegel said, 'What, Mr Innkeeper, can't they offer any security?'

The innkeeper thought, 'Oh, if I just had some!' And he said, 'Friend, if I could get some definite security, I'd take it and let those unhappy blind men go.'

Eulenspiegel said, 'Fair enough. I'll ask around in the city, and see whether I can find you a pledge.'

---

[1] i.e., in the sea. See Lappenberg, p. 271.

Eulenspiegel next visited a priest and said, 'My dear Lord Priest, how would you like to perform a genuinely friendly deed? My innkeeper was possessed of the evil spirit last night. He desperately wants you to exorcise it for him.'

The priest said, 'Of course. But he'll have to wait patiently for one or two days. One can't be in too much of a hurry about these things.'

Eulenspiegel quickly said to him, 'I'll get his wife, so you can tell her that yourself.'

The priest said, 'Yes, just have her come.'

Eulenspiegel went back to the innkeeper and said, 'I've found you a pledge. The man's your priest, who will promise it to you and give you what you want. Just let your wife go along with me to him. He'll tell her all about it.'

The innkeeper was agreeable—in fact delighted—and sent his wife with him to the priest.

Eulenspiegel started right in. 'Dear Father, here's his wife. Just tell her yourself what you told me and what you promised me.'

The priest said, 'Certainly. My dear woman, just wait one or two days, and I'll help him with this.'

The woman said, 'All right.' She went home with Eulenspiegel and told her husband what she had heard. The innkeeper was thrilled, let the blind men go, and sent her off. Eulenspiegel now made his own travel arrangements and sneaked out of there.

On the third day the wife went back and asked the priest for the twelve guilders the blind men had spent.

The priest said, 'Dear woman, is that what your husband told you to do?'

The woman said, 'Yes.'

The priest said, 'I was told that your husband was possessed by the evil spirit. Bring him to me, so I can help free him of it, with God's help.'

The wife said, 'Charlatans, who are liars, act this way when they're supposed to pay up. You'll find out right away whether my husband has been captured by an evil spirit.' And she ran home and told her husband what the priest had said.

The innkeeper prepared himself—with pikes and halberds — and raced over to the priest's house. The priest saw him coming, and called on his neighbours for help. He crossed himself and said, 'Come help me, my dear neighbours! Just see! This man is possessed of the evil spirit!'

The innkeeper said, 'Priest! Think about your promise — and pay me!'

The priest simply stood there, crossing himself.

The innkeeper attempted to attack the priest. His neighbours got between them, but were able to separate them only with enormous efforts. Then, as long as that innkeeper and the priest lived, the innkeeper demanded payment for his expenses. The priest, however, said that he owed the innkeeper nothing — rather that the innkeeper was possessed of the evil spirit. The priest wished only to free him of it. This state of affairs dragged on for as long as they both lived.

71. *How Eulenspiegel, in Bremen, basted his roast from his behind, so nobody wanted to eat it.*

After Eulenspiegel played that joke[1] in Bremen, he became quite well known there. It went like this in the city of Bremen: all the citizens enjoyed having him around and wanted him to play all sorts of pranks. As a result Eulenspiegel spent a long time in that city.

An association existed there at that time. It included citizens and other inhabitants, such as merchants. They had an agreement among themselves that each of them in succession would prepare a feast, with a roast, cheese, and bread. Whoever failed to attend, without a good excuse, would have to pay the host for the whole meal, at prevailing Bremen-market prices. Eulenspiegel came to one of their meetings. They welcomed him as a fun-maker, and he was allowed to join their organization.

As the question of hosting the feast went around, it fell to Eulenspiegel as well. He invited his fellow members to his

---

[1] Cf. other Bremen stories, such as Tale 69. See also the commentary on the various orderings of the tales, in the Introduction.

inn, purchased a roast, and stuck it on the fire. As the hour of the feast approached, the invited members gathered in the market place and discussed among themselves whether they ought to go along to Eulenspiegel's to eat. Each asked the next whether anybody knew if he had cooked something. They did not want to go there for nothing. Well, they came to an agreement that they would go there together: better that everybody discover the trick than one person alone.

When they all arrived at Eulenspiegel's inn, he took a piece of butter, stuck it into the groove of his behind, turned his arse backwards to the fire, over the roast, and basted the roast like that, with the butter from his groove. As his guests arrived at the door, stopped, and tried to see whether he had cooked anything, they saw him standing there like that, near the fire, and basting the roast.

They said things like this: 'The devil be his guest! I certainly won't eat that roast.'

But Eulenspiegel demanded payment from them for the

food—which they all cheerfully offered as long as they did not have to eat it.

72. How Eulenspiegel sowed stones in a city in Saxony; and how, when he was asked about it, he said he was sowing rogues.

Soon after that, Eulenspiegel came to a city on the Weser. There he took careful note of the people's business, and what their commercial transactions were like, till he was familiar with all their ways and how affairs were handled there.

Since he had fourteen inns available to him, what he lacked in one place he found in the next, and soon came to hear and see nothing that he did not already know about. But the people tired of him, and he likewise tired of them. So he collected little stones near the river, walked back and forth through the lanes near the city hall, and sowed his 'seeds' to left and right.

Foreign merchants came up to him and asked him what he was sowing.

Eulenspiegel said, 'I'm sowing rogues.'

These merchants said, 'There's no need for you to sow them here. There are more than enough of them here already.'

Eulenspiegel said, 'That's true. But they're living in the houses. They ought to be run out of town.'

They said, 'Why don't you also sow honest people?'

Eulenspiegel said, 'Honest people? They wouldn't grow here.'

These words attracted the attention of the city council. Eulenspiegel was sent for and ordered to collect his 'seeds' and leave the city. He did so—and arrived, ten miles from there, in another city, planning to sow his seeds in Ditmarschen. But reports about him had preceded him to that particular city. If he wanted to enter it, he had to promise to travel through it, with his 'seeds', without eating or drinking. Since nothing else seemed possible, he rented a little boat, planning to have his 'seeds' and belongings lifted into it. As his sack was being lifted, it tore open in the middle and he left both 'seeds' and sack behind.

Well, Eulenspiegel ran off. He is still supposed to return.

73. *How Eulenspiegel hired himself out to a barber in Hamburg, and entered his shop through his windows.*

On one occasion Eulenspiegel went to Hamburg and went into the hops market. As he was standing there looking around, a beard-shearer came by who asked him where he was from.

Eulenspiegel said, 'I come from here and there.'

The barber asked him, 'What sort of craft are you apprenticed to?'

Eulenspiegel said, 'Well, in a word, I'm a barber.'

The barber hired him.

Now, this barber lived at the hops market, just across from where they were standing. His house had high windows that faced the street, where his shop was located. The barber told

Eulenspiegel, 'See that house over there? Where those high windows are? Go in there, and I'll be along after you in a minute.'

Eulenspiegel said yes, went straight through the high windows into the house, and said, 'God, Almighty God, bless this craft.'

The beard-shearer's wife was sitting in the shop and spinning. She got frightened and said, 'Good Heavens! Is the devil himself after you? How come you're climbing in through the windows? Isn't the door wide enough?'

Eulenspiegel said, 'Dear woman, don't be angry with me. Your husband told me to do this, and hired me as an apprentice.'

The woman said, 'It's a trusty servant indeed who does his boss real damage.'

Eulenspiegel said, 'Dear woman, shouldn't a servant do what his boss has told him to do?'

At this point his new boss came in and heard and saw the

argument Eulenspiegel had started. His boss said, 'Boy, why couldn't you have come in through the door and left my windows in one piece? Why on earth did you break into my house through the windows?'

Eulenspiegel said, 'My dear boss, you told me to go in where the high windows were. You were to come along after me in a minute. Well, I did what you told me—but you didn't really come along after me, although you told me to go first.'

His boss said nothing, as he needed him, and thought, 'If I want to recoup my loss here, I'd better accept what he's done—and deduct it from his wages.'

His boss let Eulenspiegel work for about three days. The barber then told Eulenspiegel to sharpen the shearing knives.

Eulenspiegel said, 'Yes, gladly.'

His boss added, 'Make them even on the back, like the blade.'

Eulenspiegel said yes, and started sharpening the shearing knives, making the reverse edges like the blades. His boss came over to see what he was doing, and saw that he was sharpening the knives, reverse edges and blades alike, and that he was also about to sharpen the knives he had lying on the grindstone.

The barber at once said, 'What're you doing! This is getting to be awful.'

Eulenspiegel said, 'How's it getting to be awful? I'm not hurting you, since I'm doing what you told me to.'

His boss got pretty angry and said, 'I'm telling you that you're an awful, damned fool! Stop! Just leave off all this sharpening! And go back where you came from!'

Eulenspiegel said yes, went into the shop, and jumped back out through the windows—where he had come from. The beard-shearer now got even angrier, and raced after him with the bailiff to catch him to make him pay for the windows he had broken.

But Eulenspiegel was quick. He boarded a ship and got out of the country.

74. *How a woman who had snot hanging out of her nose invited Eulenspiegel for a meal.*

It once chanced that a court was to be held, and Eulenspiegel wanted to ride to it. But his horse was lame, so he went on foot.

Now, it was quite hot and he began to get hungry, and there was a small village on the way. There was no inn at the small village, but it was high noon, so he went on into the village anyway, as he was well known there. He came into a house where a woman was sitting and making cheese. She had a lump of whey in her hands. Since she was bending over the whey, neither of her hands was free—and a huge piece of snot was hanging out of her nose. Eulenspiegel wished her good day, and saw the snot. She noticed it, but could not wipe her nose with her arms. Neither could she suck the snot back in.

She told him, 'Dear Eulenspiegel, go sit down and wait. I'm going to give you good, fresh butter.'

But Eulenspiegel turned and started back out through the door.

The woman called after him, 'Wait and eat something first.'

Eulenspiegel said, 'Dear woman, after that falls off.' He went across to another house, thinking, 'You wouldn't like that butter. Whoever's got a little dough doesn't need to throw eggs into it. It'll get fatty enough from her snot.'

75. *How Eulenspiegel got to eat a white jam by himself, by letting a lump fall into it, out of his nose.*

Eulenspiegel played quite a trick on a farmer's wife, so he could eat her white jam all by himself. He came into a house and was hungry. Well, he found the wife alone, sitting by the fire and cooling a white jam. It looked so tasty and good to him that he ached to eat it, so he asked the woman whether she would simply give him her white jam.

The woman said, 'Yes, my dear Eulenspiegel, gladly. If I could do without it myself, I'd give it to you to eat all by yourself.'

Eulenspiegel said, 'My dear woman, that may indeed occur, precisely according to your words.'

The woman set all the white jam down before him, putting the bowl of white jam on the table, with bread as well. Eulenspiegel was hungry, and began to eat, but the woman came over, planning to eat with him, as farmers usually do.

Eulenspiegel reflected, 'If she joins in too, there won't be anything here before long.' So he coughed up a big ball of phlegm and threw it into the bowl of white jam.

The woman got angry and said, 'Shame on you! Now, you rogue, you'll have to eat that white jam by yourself!'

Eulenspiegel said, 'My dear woman, your first words were thus: you would like to do without it yourself, and I could then eat the white jam by myself. Just now, though, you were coming over to eat with me—and you'd have eaten this bowlful of white jam in three gulps.'

The woman said, 'May nothing good ever come your way! If you won't allow me to have my own food, how would you ever allow me to have yours?'

Eulenspiegel said, 'Woman, I'm simply acting according to your words.'

So he ate up all the white jam, washed out his mouth, and left.

76. *How Eulenspiegel shitted inside a house and blew the stink through a wall to a host who disliked him.*

Eulenspiegel travelled fast and arrived at Nuremberg and stayed there for fourteen days. A pious man lived next door to the inn where Eulenspiegel was staying—a man who was rich and liked going to church and had little use for musicians. If musicians were about, or showed up wherever he was, he left. This man also had a custom, that once a year he invited his neighbours to dinner, and treated them handsomely, with food, wine, and the best sorts of drinks. If the neighbours

whom he usually invited had a stranger staying with them—
business people, two or three—he always invited them too
and welcomed them. Well, the time came around when
everybody was offering invitations. Eulenspiegel was staying
at the inn next door to the man's house. Well, the man offered
an invitation to his neighbours, as was his custom, and to the
guests they had, who were strangers, but he did not invite
Eulenspiegel, who looked like a clown and musician, like the
sorts of people whom he was not in the habit of inviting.

Now, when the neighbours went to dinner at the house of
this pious man, along with the respectable strangers whom he
had also invited and who were staying with them, Eulenspiegel's innkeeper (with whom he was staying) went along too,
taking his own guests who had also been invited to dinner.
His innkeeper told Eulenspiegel that the rich man had taken
him for a clown and so had not invited him.

Eulenspiegel had to accept that, but he thought, 'If I'm a
clown, I ought to show him some clowning.' Of course, it
annoyed him that the man had treated him with contempt.

Well, it was just after Saint Martin's day, when parties like this usually took place. The host sat in a well appointed room with his guests, where he served them their meal. Now, the room was hard by the wall of Eulenspiegel's inn. When they were seated and truly enjoying themselves, Eulenspiegel bored a hole through the wall into the room in which the guests were sitting, took a bellows, produced quite a pile of his excrement, and blew on it with the bellows, into the hole he had bored into the room. Now, this created a stink so awful that nobody had any desire to remain in that room. Everybody looked at the person next to him. The first thought the second must be making the stink, the second thought the third was doing so. Well, Eulenspiegel did not stop working his bellows till the guests had to get up and could no longer remain there amid the stink. They searched under the benches. They looked in every corner, to no avail. Nobody knew where it was coming from, and everybody went home.

Eulenspiegel's innkeeper now came by — and was so sick with the stink that he brought up everything he had in his stomach. He told Eulenspiegel how badly the room had stunk of human filth.

Eulenspiegel began to laugh, saying, 'If that fellow didn't want to invite me to dinner, and be generous to me with his food, at least I've been more generous and true with him than he was with me. I've been generous to him with my food anyhow. If I'd been there, the place wouldn't have stunk so badly.' And within the hour he paid his innkeeper and rode off. He was a bit worried about what might happen.

Well, his innkeeper listened carefully to what he said — that he knew something about the smell — but the innkeeper still could not understand how Eulenspiegel could have managed it. It all puzzled him greatly. With Eulenspiegel out of the city, the innkeeper went looking about the house and found the bellows, quite coated with shit, and found the hole as well that Eulenspiegel had bored through the wall of the neighbour's house. The innkeeper found them within the hour, brought his neighbour over, and told him about it — how Eulenspiegel had done it and what he had said.

The rich man said, 'Dear neighbour, nobody's improved by

rogues and musicians. That's why I never want them in my house. If this nonsense emerged from your house, I can't do anything about it. I knew your guest was a clown. I could read it by his appearance. Better that this happened in your house than in mine. He might have done worse things to me.'

Eulenspiegel's innkeeper said, 'Dear host, you've noticed something all right, and that's the way it is. You've got to set up two lights for a clown.[1] And that's something I'll certainly have to do, since I've got to take in all kinds of people. I've got to take in clowns, along with the best people, if one comes along.'

With that they parted. Eulenspiegel was gone, and he did not come back.

77. *How Eulenspiegel, at Eisleben, frightened an innkeeper with a wolf he had promised to catch.*

At Eisleben lived an innkeeper who was arrogant, considered himself clever, and fancied himself an important householder.

Well, during the days of winter, after a great snow had fallen, Eulenspiegel arrived at his inn. Three merchants also came along from Saxony, travelling toward Nuremberg. They got to the inn in dead of night.

Well, the innkeeper was quite sharp-tongued and short in welcoming these three merchants. He said, 'By the devil, where are you coming from?'—because they had taken so long to get there and had arrived at his inn so late.

The merchants said, 'Mr Innkeeper, you really shouldn't be put out with us. We had quite an adventure along the way. A wolf gave us a lot of trouble. He attacked us in the snow on the moor. We had to fight him off. That's what kept us so long.'

When the innkeeper heard this, he simply sneered at them and said it was a complete disgrace that they had allowed a wolf to delay them. If he were alone and two wolves met him

---

[1] i.e., so you can spot him.

on the moor, he would simply pummel them and drive them off — they certainly could not frighten him. But these merchants had been three in number, and had let themselves be terrified by a single wolf. His taunting lasted all evening, till the innkeeper showed them to their beds, and Eulenspiegel sat nearby, listening to him.

When they went up to bed, the merchants and Eulenspiegel were placed in one room. The merchants immediately began to discuss how they might get even with the innkeeper for what he had done.

Eulenspiegel quickly said, 'Dear friends, it's clear to me that the innkeeper's a pompous boaster. If you'll listen to me, I'll pay him back so he'll never say a word to you about that wolf again.'

This delighted the merchants, and they promised him money and provisions.

Eulenspiegel now told them to keep on with their business trip, and on their way back, to stop off at the inn again. He would also be there, and then they would get even with the innkeeper. So it happened. The merchants got ready for their journey, paid their bill, paid Eulenspiegel's as well, and rode off.

But the innkeeper called sarcastically after them, 'You merchants, watch out that you don't run into a wolf on the meadow!'

The merchants said, 'Mr Innkeeper, thank you for warning us. If wolves eat us, we won't be back. If wolves eat you, we won't find you here again.' With that, they rode off.

Eulenspiegel now rode into the Harz Mountains to set traps for wolves. God gave him the good luck to catch one. He killed it and let it freeze stiff against the time when the merchants returned to the inn at Eisleben. Then he placed the wolf in a sack, and met the three merchants there, as they had agreed. But Eulenspiegel had brought his dead wolf without anybody's knowing about it.

During dinner that evening, the innkeeper kept teasing the merchants about the wolf. They said that so indeed it had gone with them and that wolf. Now, if it happened that the innkeeper met two wolves on the meadow, would he really be able to beat off one of them while he killed the other? The innkeeper boasted hugely that he would cut both wolves to pieces — and this sort of talk went on all evening, till they went to bed.

Well, Eulenspiegel kept quiet till he approached the merchants in their room. At that point Eulenspiegel said, 'Good friends, keep quiet and watch. What I'm going to do you're going to like too. Keep a light burning for me.'

Well, when the innkeeper and all his servants were in bed, Eulenspiegel crept softly out of their room. He took the dead wolf, which was frozen stiff, lugged it to the hearth, and planted it on sticks so it stood up properly. Then he prised open its mouth, and inserted two children's shoes into it. He now returned to the merchants in their room and yelled, 'Mr Innkeeper!' The innkeeper, who was not yet asleep, heard this and called back, asking what they wanted — whether a wolf was maybe nipping at them.

They replied, 'Ah, dear innkeeper, just send your maid or

boy to bring us something to drink! We can't stand this thirst!'

The innkeeper got angry, saying, 'That's the Saxon way, all right. They drink day and night!' He called out to his maid to get up and bring them something to drink in their room.

The maid got up and went to the fire, planning to light a lamp. She looked up — and looked the wolf right in the mouth. She was terrified, dropped the lamp and ran into the courtyard, imagining only that the wolf had already devoured the children.

Eulenspiegel and the merchants again called for something to drink. The innkeeper thought his maid must be asleep, so he called his servant boy. The boy got up and also tried to light a lamp. He too saw the wolf standing there. He at once thought it must have eaten the maid whole. He let the lamp fall and ran into the cellar.

Eulenspiegel and the merchants took note of these developments, and Eulenspiegel said, 'Keep quiet now. This game's about to get interesting.' Eulenspiegel and the merchants then called out for the third time: where were the maid and boy? — They weren't bringing anything to drink. The innkeeper had better come himself, and bring a light. They could not leave their room.

The innkeeper thought only that his boy must also have fallen asleep. He got up, thoroughly irate, and said, 'The devil serve these Saxons their drinks!' He too lit a lamp at the fire. But when he saw the wolf standing in front of him on the hearth, and saw the little shoes in its mouth, he began to scream. He shouted, 'Murder! Save me, dear friends!' He raced to the merchants' room, shrieking, 'Dear friends, come help me! A terrible animal is standing at the fire — and it's eaten my children, my maid, and my boy!'

The merchants were all too ready to accompany him. Eulenspiegel was too. They all went to the fire with the innkeeper. The boy emerged from the cellar. The maid came in from the garden. The innkeeper's wife brought his children out of their rooms. They were in fact all very alive. Eulenspiegel now walked over and poked the wolf with his foot. It lay there and lifted not a paw.

Eulenspiegel said, 'This is a dead wolf. Were you doing all that screaming over this? What sort of weak character are you? Can a dead wolf really attack you in your own house, and chase you and all your servants into corners? And it isn't so long since you were going to kill two live wolves out in open country. But you've only got words where some have courage.'

The innkeeper listened to him, realizing he had been tricked. He went back to his room, to bed, feeling ashamed of his vain words and that a dead wolf had so humiliated him and all his servants. The merchants laughed. Then they paid what they and Eulenspiegel had spent and rode off.

But after that the innkeeper no longer talked so much about his bravery.

78. How Eulenspiegel shitted on an innkeeper's table in Cologne, telling him he would come and find it.

Just after that, Eulenspiegel arrived at an inn in Cologne. He kept to himself for two or three days, and so went unrecognized. During those days, however, he noticed that his innkeeper was a cheat.

He now thought, 'Guests don't have it so good where their innkeeper's a cheat. You'd better look for another hotel.'

That evening his innkeeper revealed to Eulenspiegel that he already had another hotel. The innkeeper showed the other guests to bed, but not him.

Eulenspiegel at once said, 'What's this, Mr Innkeeper? I pay as much for my food as those whom you've shown to their beds — and I'm supposed to sleep on this bench?'

The innkeeper said, 'Look, here are a couple of sheets for you.' Whereupon he loosed a fart, with another on top of it, adding, 'Look, here's a pillow.' Then he loosed a third fart, and really began to stink, saying, 'See? There's a whole bed for you. Get by somehow till morning, and then pile these together for me again.'

Eulenspiegel kept quiet, but he thought, 'See? Of course you see. You've got to pay this cheat back with a trick.' But he stretched out on the bench for the night.

Well, the innkeeper had an elegant folding dinner-table. Eulenspiegel opened it, shitted into it, and folded it up again. The next morning he got up early, went to the innkeeper's door, and called out, 'Mr Innkeeper, I thank you for my overnight stay,' and with that let fall a huge shit, calling in to him, 'Those are the bed feathers. The pillows, sheets and blankets I've put together in a pile.'

The innkeeper said, 'Mr Guest, that's just fine. I'll look for the pile when I get up.'

Eulenspiegel said, 'Just look around. You'll find it.' With that, he left the house.

The innkeeper was to have quite a few guests for lunch, and he said, 'My guests shall eat at my pretty table.' But when he opened the table, he found himself attacked by a terrific stink. He discovered Eulenspiegel's excrement, and said, 'He pays according to one's labour all right: a fart paid for with a shit.' Then he had Eulenspiegel invited back, planning to test him further. Eulenspiegel came straight back, and they settled their fooling, so that from then on Eulenspiegel got into a good bed.

79. *How Eulenspiegel paid the innkeeper with the sound of his money.*

Eulenspiegel stayed quite a while at that inn in Cologne. Then it happened that the food was brought to the fire very late, so it was high noon before lunch was ready. Eulenspiegel felt annoyed that he had to go hungry so long. Well, the innkeeper could see that this bothered him, so he told Eulenspiegel that whoever could not wait till the food was ready could just eat whatever he had. Eulenspiegel went off to one end of the table to eat a roll, and then went to sit by the hearth, where he basted the roast till it was ready. Well, when the clock struck twelve, the table was laid, the food was served, and the innkeeper and his guests took their places — but Eulenspiegel stayed in the kitchen.

The innkeeper said, 'What's this? Don't you want to sit at the table?'

'No,' said Eulenspiegel. 'I don't want to eat. I got full from the smell of your roast.'

The innkeeper said nothing, and ate with his guests. When the meal was over, they paid the innkeeper. Then one left, another stayed behind, but Eulenspiegel remained sitting by the fire. The innkeeper came over with his tally board. He was irritated, and told Eulenspiegel to pay him two Cologne white-pennies for the meal.

Eulenspiegel said, 'Mr Innkeeper, are you the sort of fellow who takes money from someone who hasn't eaten his food?'

The innkeeper said acidly that he had better just pay the money. Even if Eulenspiegel had eaten nothing, he had still gotten full from the smell. He had been sitting near the roast and that was the same as if he had sat at the table and eaten the roast. The innkeeper would count that as a meal.

Eulenspiegel took out a Cologne white-penny and threw it onto the bench. 'Mr Innkeeper, do you hear that sound?'

The innkeeper said, 'I hear the sound all right.'

Eulenspiegel was fast with his penny and flipped it back into his purse. He said, 'The sound of that penny helps you exactly as much as the smell of your roast helped my stomach.'

The innkeeper was not a little peeved, as he wanted the white-penny, but Eulenspiegel refused to hand it over, and even threatened to bring the matter to court. The innkeeper gave in. He had no desire to go to court. He was afraid that Eulenspiegel might pay him back as he had with the folding table. The innkeeper let him go.

Well, Eulenspiegel left that place — letting the innkeeper honour his own bill — and left the Rhine. He then travelled back to the district of Saxony.

80. *How Eulenspiegel took his leave of Rostock.*

After playing that trick, Eulenspiegel rode quickly out of Rostock,[1] and came to an inn in a country town.

[1] This tale ought perhaps to follow other tales having to do with Rostock, such as 39 or 49. See Notes on the Tales.

There was little to eat in the house. There was nothing but poverty there, and the innkeeper had many children—whom Eulenspiegel did not enjoy being around.[2] Well, Eulenspiegel tied up his horse in the stable, went into the house, and walked over to the fire. But he found a cold hearth and a bare house. He saw at once that there was nothing but poverty in the place.

He said, 'Mr Innkeeper, you've got terrible neighbours.'

The innkeeper said, 'Yes, Mr Guest, so I do. They steal everything I've got in the house.'

Eulenspiegel began to laugh, thinking, 'The innkeeper here is like a guest.' He wanted to stay there, despite the children, whom he did not like because he saw that they went to do their business behind the door of the house, one child after the other.

Eulenspiegel told the innkeeper, 'Your children certainly

[2] See Tale 21.

have filthy habits! Don't you have some place other than behind your front door for them to do their business?'

The innkeeper said, 'Mr Guest, why let it bother you? It doesn't bother me. I'm leaving tomorrow.'

Eulenspiegel kept quiet. Later, when he felt the need, he shitted a huge filthy pile into the fireplace.

Well, the innkeeper came in while Eulenspiegel was about his business and said, 'The plague on you! Shitting in the fireplace? Isn't the courtyard big enough?'

Eulenspiegel said, 'Mr Innkeeper, why let it bother you? It doesn't bother me. I'm leaving today.' And he mounted his horse and rode out through the door.

The innkeeper called after him to stop and clean his shit out of the hearth.

Eulenspiegel said, 'Whoever's last sweeps out the house. That way my shit and your shit can be cleaned out together.'

81. *How Eulenspiegel killed a dog, paying an innkeeper with its skin, because the dog had eaten with him.*

It once happened that Eulenspiegel went to stay at a house in a village, and found the innkeeper's wife alone. She had a shaggy little dog that she loved a lot, and that was always lying in her lap when it had nothing to do.

Eulenspiegel sat by the fire and drank beer from a jug. The woman had accustomed her dog to getting a bowlful of beer whenever she was drinking, so the dog could drink too. Well, while Eulenspiegel sat and drank, the dog got up, rubbed itself against Eulenspiegel, and jumped right onto his neck.

The innkeeper sat watching this and said, 'Oh, give him a bit to drink in the bowl. That's what he wants.'

Eulenspiegel said, 'Certainly.'

The innkeeper went about her work, and Eulenspiegel drank and gave the dog some to drink in the bowl, sticking in a bit of meat too. Well, the dog became quite full, lay down by the fire, and stretched out there.

Eulenspiegel now told the woman, 'Let's figure out how much I owe you.' He went on, 'Dear innkeeper, if a guest ate your food, drank your beer, and had no money, would you maybe give the guest credit?'

It did not occur to the woman that he meant her dog, and she thought, 'He must mean himself.' She said, 'Mr Guest, there's no credit here. People either pay with money or provide collateral of some sort.'

Eulenspiegel said, 'Then for my part, I'm happy. Anybody else takes care of his own bill.'

The innkeeper went out. As soon as he could manage it, Eulenspiegel took her dog under his coat into the stable. There he skinned it, stuck the skin under his coat, and went back into the house, to the fire.

Eulenspiegel called the woman over to him and said, 'Let's settle up.'

The innkeeper totalled what he had spent, but Eulenspiegel paid for only half his meal. She asked who was supposed to pay for the other half. He had, after all, drunk his beer by himself.

Eulenspiegel said, 'No, I didn't drink it by myself. I had a guest who drank with me and who had no money — but he offered excellent collateral. He's going to pay the other half.'

The woman said, 'What guest? What sort of collateral have you got?'

Eulenspiegel said, 'It's his very best coat, which he was wearing.' He pulled out the dog's coat, saying, 'Here, dear innkeeper. This is the coat of the guest who drank with me.'

The woman was horrified. She realized at once that it was her dog's skin, got totally enraged, and said, 'Oh, that nothing good ever comes your way! How could you skin my dog!' She flew into a tantrum.

Eulenspiegel said, 'Innkeeper, the fault's entirely your own. Rage all you like. You told me yourself to take care of your dog, and I said, "The guest has no money." You didn't want to give him credit. You wanted money or collateral. Well, he had no money, and the beer had to be paid for. Obviously, he had to leave his coat as collateral. Accept it, please, for the beer he drank.'

The innkeeper became even crazier with rage, telling him to walk straight out of her house and never come back.

Eulenspiegel said, 'I'm not going to walk out of your house. I'm going to ride out of it.' He saddled his horse, rode out through the door, and said, 'Innkeeper, keep that as collateral till I get your money. I'm planning to come back, uninvited. If it then happens that I don't drink anything at your house, I won't have to pay for any beer.'

82. *How Eulenspiegel convinced the same innkeeper that Eulenspiegel was lying on the wheel.*

Now listen a bit to what Eulenspiegel did near Strassfurt.

There is a village nearby, and he took lodgings there. He dressed himself differently, went to his inn, and noticed there was a wheel standing in the house. He stretched out on it and wished the lady-innkeeper good day. Then he asked her whether she had ever heard of Till Eulenspiegel. She said that what she had heard about that scoundrel she would not like to hear repeated.

Eulenspiegel said, 'Woman, what's he done to you to turn you so against him? Because wherever he goes he doesn't leave without some sort of trick.'

She said, 'I found that out, all right. He was here and skinned my dog. Then he offered me its skin for the beer he drank.'

Eulenspiegel said, 'Woman, that wasn't nice.'

The woman said, 'He'll have his own surprises, I'm sure.'

He said, 'Woman, that's happening already. In fact, he's stretched on the wheel.'[1]

The innkeeper said, 'God be praised for that.'

Eulenspiegel said, 'I'm him! Adieu! I'm leaving!'

---

[1] The medieval punishment of strapping prisoners to a revolving wheel was commonly reserved for serious criminals, such as arsonists, thieves, and highwaymen; mere murderers were simply stabbed to death with a sword. See Notes on the Tales.

83. *How Eulenspiegel seated a lady-innkeeper in hot ashes on her bare arse.*

Nasty, angry gossip brings nasty rewards.

When Eulenspiegel left Rome,[1] he arrived at a village with a large inn. The innkeeper was not at home. Well, Eulenspiegel asked his wife whether she had ever met Eulenspiegel.

The woman said, 'No, I don't know him. But I've heard this much about him, that he's a perfect scoundrel.'

Eulenspiegel said, 'Dear Innkeeper, why do you say he's a scoundrel when you don't even know him?'

The woman said, 'What difference does it make that I don't know him? There's nothing ever said against the idea. People say he's a wicked fellow.'

---

[1] See Tale 34, which this tale ought perhaps to follow.

Eulenspiegel said, 'Dear woman, has he ever done anything wicked to you? You've just heard gossip that he's a scoundrel.'

The woman said, 'I'm just telling you what I've heard from the people who come and go here.'

Eulenspiegel kept quiet. But the next morning he got up early, raked aside the hot ashes, went straight up to her bed, lifted the lady-innkeeper right out of her sleep, set her bare arse into the hot ashes, and quite scorched her arse. He said, 'How's that, woman? Now you've got the right to say that Eulenspiegel's a scoundrel. You've encountered him now and even seen him. You'll remember him by this.'

The woman started screaming with pain. But Eulenspiegel left the house, and laughed, saying, 'That's how to finish one's trip to Rome.'

84. *How Eulenspiegel shitted in his bed and convinced his innkeeper that a priest had done it.*

Eulenspiegel played a wicked trick at Frankfurt-on-the-Oder. He went there with a priest. They both stayed at the same inn. That evening the innkeeper's wife treated them handsomely, offering them fish and venison.

When they were ready to sit down at the table, the woman seated the priest near the head of it. She also served the priest the best of what was in the serving-bowl, saying, 'Father, eat this for my sake.'

Eulenspiegel sat far down the table, looking the innkeeper and his wife firmly in the eye, but no one served him anything or asked him to eat. He had to pay just as much anyway, though.

When the meal was over and it was time to go to bed, Eulenspiegel and the priest were placed in a single room, and each found a fine bed ready for him to sleep on. Well, the next morning the priest was up early. He said his prayers, paid the innkeeper, and travelled on. Eulenspiegel remained lying there till it was about to strike nine. Then he shitted in the bed in which the priest had slept.

The innkeeper's wife soon asked her house-boy whether

the priest or other guest was up yet, or whether they had already reckoned up and paid.

The boy said, 'Yes. The priest was up early. He prayed, paid, and left. But I haven't seen the other fellow today.'

The woman was worried that Eulenspiegel might be ill, so she went into his room and asked him whether he did not want to get up.

He said, 'Yes, Mrs Innkeeper. I wasn't feeling terribly well — till now.'

In the meantime the woman tried to take the sheets off the priest's bed. As she opened it, she discovered a huge pile of excrement lying right in the middle of it.

'God save me!' she said. 'What's this here!'

'Yes, Mrs Innkeeper, that doesn't surprise me a bit,' said Eulenspiegel. 'Because last night that priest was served everything good and the very best that was brought to the table. There wasn't anything said all evening except, "Father, eat this." It surprises me that so much of what the priest ate stayed in him — that he didn't shit all over the room too.'

The woman was furious with the innocent priest and said that if he came back, he would be sent packing. But Eulenspiegel — that honest boy — she would gladly let stay on with her.

85. *How a Dutchman ate Eulenspiegel's baked apple, into which he had put saffron, off his plate.*

Eulenspiegel paid back a Dutchman, fairly and cleanly. It happened that merchants from Holland were once staying at an inn in Antwerp. Eulenspiegel, who was also staying there, felt a bit ill, so he did not order any meat, but just cooked boiled eggs for himself.

When the guests were sitting at the table, Eulenspiegel sat down at the table too, bringing his soft-boiled eggs with him. One of the Dutchmen took Eulenspiegel for a farmer and said, 'What's this, farmer? Don't you like the innkeeper's food. Do you have to have eggs cooked for you?' And with that he took both eggs, broke them open, poured them out, one after the other, placed the shells in front of Eulenspiegel, and said, 'There — lick the barrel. The yolk's gone.' The other guests laughed. Eulenspiegel laughed with them.

That evening Eulenspiegel bought a fine apple, which he hollowed out and filled with flies or gnats. Then he baked the apple slowly, peeled it, and sprinkled it on the outside with ginger. When everybody was sitting at the table that evening, Eulenspiegel brought his baked apple out on a plate and then turned away, as if he were reaching for more. As he turned his back, the Dutchman snatched his baked apple right off his plate, and gulped it down. Within an hour the Dutchman began to vomit, bringing up everything he had in his stomach and feeling so violently ill that the innkeeper and other guests thought he must have poisoned himself with the apple.

Eulenspiegel said, 'This is actually no poisoning at all. It's a cleansing of his stomach. A cleansed stomach receives its food easily. If he'd told me he was so eager to gulp down my apple, I'd have warned him. There weren't any gnats in my soft-boiled eggs, but there were plenty in my baked apple. He'll have to vomit them up again.'

With that the Dutchman came to himself and no longer felt quite so worried. But he said to Eulenspiegel, 'Eat and bake all you like! I wouldn't eat with you again, even if you had fieldfares!'

86. How Eulenspiegel made a woman break all her pots at the market in Bremen.

After Eulenspiegel played that trick, he went back to Bremen, to the Bishop[1] there. The Bishop had a lot of fun with Eulenspiegel, and liked him too, since he was always engaged in some roguish adventure which both made the Bishop laugh and led him to maintain Eulenspiegel's horse free of charge.

Eulenspiegel then suddenly acted as if he had wearied of clowning and preferred going to church. The Bishop scoffed at him for this, but he refused to be dissuaded, and went off

[1] See Tale 69 for a related story.

praying, till in the end the Bishop got pretty annoyed with
him.

Well, Eulenspiegel secretly made an arrangement with a
woman, a potter's wife, who sat selling pots in the market
place. He bought up all her pots, and agreed with her on
something she was to do when he waved or gave a signal.

Eulenspiegel then went home to the Bishop and pretended
that he had just been to church. The Bishop began to jeer at
him again, till finally Eulenspiegel said, 'Gracious Lord, come
to the market place with me. There's a potter's wife there who
sells clay pots. I'll make a bet with you. I won't speak to her
or wink at her—and without saying a word I'll make her get
up, grab a stick, and smash those clay pots to pieces.'

The Bishop said, 'That I'd like to see.' But first he offered
to bet him thirty guilders that the woman would never do it.
They shook hands on it, and the Bishop went to the market
place with Eulenspiegel.

Eulenspiegel pointed the woman out to him, and they went

across to the city hall. Eulenspiegel stayed close to the Bishop, but made signs to the woman, with words and gestures, as if he wanted her to do something. Finally he gave the woman the sign they had agreed on. She at once got up, took a stick, and smashed her clay pots to pieces. Everybody in the market place laughed.

When the Bishop got home again, he took Eulenspiegel aside. He asked Eulenspiegel to tell him how he had made the woman break her own pots. Only then would the Bishop give Eulenspiegel the thirty guilders he had lost on their bet.

Eulenspiegel said, 'Of course, Gracious Lord, with pleasure.' He told the Bishop how he had first paid for the pots and afterwards set it up with the woman. He had not used black magic after all. When Eulenspiegel told him everything, the Bishop laughed and gave him the thirty guilders. But Eulenspiegel had to promise to tell nobody about it: the Bishop would get him a fat ox if he kept his word. Eulenspiegel said, sure, he would be happy to keep quiet about the matter. Then he got his things together, and went travelling.

With Eulenspiegel gone, the Bishop called a meeting of his knights and servants. He told them he knew the trick by which he too could make the woman break all her pots. His knights and servants had no particular interest in seeing pots smashed, but they did want to learn the trick of the thing.

The Bishop said, 'If each of you gives me a good, fat ox for my kitchen, I'll teach the trick to all of you.'

It was just autumn, when oxen are fattest. Each of them thought, 'You can risk a few oxen to learn this trick — that can't do any harm.' So each knight and servant sent the Bishop a fat ox. They delivered them all together, and the Bishop received sixteen oxen. Well, each ox was worth four guilders, so the thirty guilders the Bishop had given Eulenspiegel were paid back twice over.

As the oxen were standing there, Eulenspiegel came riding by and said, 'Half this loot belongs to me.'

The Bishop told Eulenspiegel, 'Stick to what you've promised me. I'll treat you as I promised you. Just let the lords of the country earn their keep too.' And the Bishop gave him a fat ox. Eulenspiegel took it and thanked the Bishop.

The Bishop then collected his servants, drew himself up, and told them to listen to him. He would tell them all about the trick. He now told them everything—how Eulenspiegel had set it up in advance with the woman, and how he had paid for the pots. As the Bishop told them about it, his servants sat there feeling utterly betrayed, but not one dared say a word to the others. One fellow scratched his head, the next scratched the nape of his neck. They all felt miserable, as they were bitter about losing their oxen. In the end they had to accept things as they were, and they consoled themselves with the idea that the Bishop was after all a noble lord. If they had been forced to give him the oxen, well, the oxen were still around, and it had all been just a joke. Actually, they felt less annoyed about the oxen themselves than about having been such fools as to give away their oxen to learn this trick— which was pure nonsense—and that Eulenspiegel had gotten one ox.

87. *How a farmer taking plums to the market in Einbeck gave Eulenspiegel a ride in his cart, and how Eulenspiegel shitted on them.*

The Most Serene and High-Born princes of Brunswick once held racing, jousting, and tilting matches with many foreign princes, lords, knights, and servants, and their tenants as well, in the city of Einbeck.

Now, this happened during the summer, when plums and other fruits were getting ripe. Well, an honest, simple peasant was living at Oldenburg near Einbeck, who had an orchard of plum trees. He had a cartful of his plums picked, planning to drive it to Einbeck. Lots of people were arriving there, and he thought he could get rid of his plums better now than at other times.

When he got near the city, he came across Eulenspiegel, who was lying there in the shade, under a green tree. Well, Eulenspiegel had drunk so much at the lords' court that he could neither eat nor drink any more—and looked more dead than alive. As the honest man was driving by, Eulenspiegel called out as feebly as he could, 'Ah, good friend. Look, I've been lying here sick like this and without any help for three days and nights. If I lie here this way for one more day, I'm sure I'll die of hunger and thirst. For the sake of God, give me a lift into the city.'

The good man said, 'Ah, good friend. I'd be happy to do so, but I've got plums in my cart. If I put you on top of them you'll ruin them.'

Eulenspiegel said, 'Take me along. I'll manage in the front of the cart.'

The man was old. He strained life and limb in getting the rogue (who made himself as heavy as possible) into his cart. Then, on account of his ailing passenger, he drove more slowly.

When Eulenspiegel had been travelling a while, he pulled the straw off the plums, secretly lifted his behind, shitted on the poor man's plums, and pulled the straw back over them. When the farmer reached the city, Eulenspiegel cried, 'Stop! Stop! Help me out of the cart! I've got to stay outside here, at the gate.'

The good man helped the evil rogue out of his cart and drove to the market by the shortest route possible. When he got there, he unhitched his horse and rode it to his inn. In the meantime, many citizens were coming into the market place. Among them was one who was always first whenever something was brought for selling but who rarely bought anything. This fellow now came over, pulled the straw half off, and made his hands shitty. At that moment, the farmer returned from his inn. Eulenspiegel had changed his clothes and arrived there too, by another way. He said to the farmer, 'What've you brought to sell?'

'Plums,' said the farmer.

Eulenspiegel said, 'You've brought them like a rogue! These plums are shitty! You ought to be banned from the whole country with these plums!'

The man looked at him more closely, realized who he was, and said, 'There was a sick man lying outside the city — a man who looked just like this man standing here, except he had different clothes on. I drove him — for the sake of God — up to the gate. And that very rogue did this disgraceful thing to me.'

Eulenspiegel said, 'That rogue definitely deserves a beating.'

Well, the honest man had to drive his plums off to the slaughterers' graveyard, and was unable to sell them anywhere.

88. *How Eulenspiegel counted the monks into vespers at Marienthal.*

Now, the time came when Eulenspiegel had run around through every country. He was old and fed up and began to feel worried about dying. So he thought he might commit himself to a cloister, in his poverty, end his days well, and serve God for the rest of his life, because of his sins. If God took charge of him, he might not be lost.

With this in mind, he went to the Abbot of Marienthal and

asked him whether he would take him in as a brother: he would leave the cloister his entire estate. Knaves were acceptable to the Abbot too, and he said, 'You're still strong. I'll be happy to take you in, as you've asked. But you'll have to do something and have a job. As you can see, my brothers and I all have things to do, and each of us is assigned something.'

Eulenspiegel said, 'Yes, Father, that's fine.'

'All right then! Now — God knows — you don't like working. You'll be our porter. That way you can continue your easy life and have nothing to worry about — just getting food and beer from the cellar and opening and closing the gate.'

Eulenspiegel said, 'Worthy Lord, may God reward you for thinking so well of me, an old, sick man. I'll do everything you tell me and not do anything you forbid me.'

The Abbot said, 'Look, here's the key. You mustn't let everyone in. Let every third or fourth person in. For if lots of people are let in, they'll eat the cloister into poverty.'

Eulenspiegel said, 'Worthy Lord, I'll handle it properly.'

Well, of all who arrived there, whether they belonged to the cloister or not, Eulenspiegel always admitted only every fourth person, and no more. Complaints about this reached the Abbot, who said to Eulenspiegel, 'You're a perfect scoundrel! Can't you let in those who are surrendered to the cloister and belong here?'

'Father,' said Eulenspiegel, 'I've been letting in every fourth person and no more, as you told me. I've simply obeyed your orders.'

'You've done it like a rogue,' said the Abbot, who would have been delighted to get rid of him. He appointed a different gatekeeper, as it was clear to him that Eulenspiegel had no intention of giving up his old tricks. The Abbot now assigned him another job, saying, 'Look, you're to count the monks into vespers at night — and if you miss even one, you can just go on your way.'

Eulenspiegel said, 'Father, that's a tough job for me to handle. But if that's how it's got to be, I'll have to do it as best I can.'

And that night he ripped a number of steps out of the staircase.

Now, the Prior was a God-fearing old monk who was always first in coming to mass. He came quietly enough to the staircase, but as he tried to walk downstairs, he fell through and broke a leg. Well, he screamed horribly, so the other brothers ran out to see what was the matter with him — and they fell down the stairs, one after the other.

Eulenspiegel immediately said to the Abbot, 'Worthy Lord, have I done my duty? I've counted all the monks.' Eulenspiegel handed the Abbot the tally board, on which he had notched the monks off as they fell, one after the other.

The Abbot said, 'You've counted them like a damned rogue! Get out of my cloister and go to the devil where you please!'

So Eulenspiegel headed for Mölln. There he fell seriously ill, and a short time afterwards, he died.

89. *How Eulenspiegel fell ill at Mölln, how he shitted in the pharmacist's medical book, how he was brought to 'The Holy Ghost', and how he said a sweet word to his mother.*

Eulenspiegel became weak and quite ill as he went from Marienthal to Mölln. There he stayed with a pharmacist to get medicine. Now, the pharmacist was rather malicious and tricky, so he gave Eulenspiegel a strong laxative. When morning came, the laxative began to work, and Eulenspiegel got up to relieve himself. But the house was locked up everywhere. He was full of worry and need, so he went into the pharmacy, shitted into one of the books, and said, 'The medicine came from here. It ought to be returned here. That way the pharmacist doesn't lose anything. I can't pay for it anyway.'

When the pharmacist found out about this, he got furious with Eulenspiegel and no longer wanted him in his house. He had Eulenspiegel brought to the hospital (called The Holy Ghost). Eulenspiegel told the people who were taking him there, 'I've struggled hard and always prayed to God to let the Holy Ghost come into me. So now He sends me the opposite—that I come into the Holy Ghost. So He stays outside of me, and I enter Him.' The people laughed at his words and left him there. Indeed, a man dies as he has lived.

It became known to his mother that he was ill. She got ready in a hurry and came to see him, thinking to get some money from him, for she was an old, poor woman. When she arrived at his bedside, she began to wail, and said, 'My dear son, where are you sick?'

Eulenspiegel said, 'Dear mother, here between the bed-box and the wall.'

'Ah, dear son, say a sweet word to me.'

Eulenspiegel said, 'Dear mother, "honey"—that's a sweet word.'

His mother said, 'Ah, dear son, give me some sweet advice to remember you by.'

Eulenspiegel said, 'Yes, dear mother. When you want to do your business, turn your arse away from the wind. Then the stink won't get into your nose.'

His mother said, 'Dear son, give me some of your belongings.'

Eulenspiegel said, 'Dear mother, one should give to him who has nothing and take from him who has something. My possessions are hidden—where, nobody knows. If you find something that's mine, you may take it, for of my goods I leave you all that's crooked and straight.'

In the meantime Eulenspiegel was getting very ill, so the people urged him to confess and take communion. Eulenspiegel did so, for he knew very well that he would never get out of his sick bed.

90. *How Eulenspiegel was told to repent of his sins—so he repented of three sorts of tricks he had not played.*

Eulenspiegel had better feel repentance and sorrow for his sins during his illness. Then he could receive Holy Communion and die more sweetly—or so an old beguine told him.

Eulenspiegel replied, 'It won't happen that I'll die sweetly, for death is bitter. Also, why should I confess in secret what

I've done during my life? Lots of countries and people know what I've done. The man I've treated well will speak well of me, and the man to whom I've done something awful won't keep quiet because I'm repentant. I'm repentant about only three sorts of things, and I'm sorry that I didn't, and couldn't do them.'

The beguine said, 'Dear God, just be happy if it's something terrible you didn't do, and just be sorry for your sins.'

Eulenspiegel said, 'All I'm sorry for are those three things I didn't do — and never got to do.'

The beguine said, 'What are these things? Are they good or bad?'

Eulenspiegel said, 'There are just three things. The first is this. In the days of my youth, whenever I saw a man walking in the street, whose coat showed because it hung down below his cloak, I followed him, thinking his coat might trip him, because I wanted to lift it up. But whenever I got up to somebody like that, I saw that his coat was fashionably meant to be that long — so I got angry and would gladly have snipped his coat off, as much of it as hung out below his cloak. And I'm just sorry I never got to do that. The second thing is that whenever I saw somebody sitting or walking, who was picking his teeth with a knife, that I couldn't stick the knife through his throat. That makes me sorry too. The third thing is that I can't stitch up the arses of all the old women who are past their prime. That makes me sorry as well, since they're of no use to anybody on earth and just make the ground shitty where fruit grows.'

The beguine said, 'Oh, God save us! What're you saying! I hear you all right. If you were strong and had the power, you'd sew up my hole for me too — for I'm a woman of easily sixty.'

Eulenspiegel said, 'I'm sorry that hasn't been done.'

The beguine then said, 'Well, the devil protect you!' And she walked away from him and left him lying there.

Eulenspiegel said, 'There's no beguine who's really devout when she's angry. Then she's more spiteful than the devil.'

91. *How Eulenspiegal prepared his legacy — in which the priest covered his hands with shit.*

Be careful, all you religious and worldly people, that you do not dirty your hands on legacies, as happened with Eulenspiegel's legacy.

A priest was brought to Eulenspiegel to confess him. When the priest came to him, the priest thought, 'He's been an extraordinary person, so he must have gotten a lot of money together. It can't be otherwise. He must have a remarkable amount of money. You ought to be able to tease it out of him now, at his final end. Maybe there'll be some for you, too.'

Well, when Eulenspiegel began to confess to the priest and they began to talk, the priest said to him, in the middle of other things, 'Eulenspiegel, my dear son, reflect on your soul's holiness here at your end. You've been an amazing fellow and have committed many sins for which you should be sorry. But if you have a bit of money — I would give it to honor God and poor priests, such as I am. Thus would I advise you, for that money was strangely come by. And should you decide to do such a thing — to show me your money and entrust it to me — I shall certainly arrange that you arrive in God's grace. And should you wish to give me some too, I would thank you all the days of my life and read vigils and masses for you.'

Eulenspiegel said, 'Yes, my dear fellow, I'll think of you all right. Just come back this afternoon. I'll put a piece of silver right into your hands. That way you'll be sure of it.'

The priest was delighted, and came running back that afternoon. Well, while he was gone, Eulenspiegel got a jug, filled it half-full with human excrement, and strewed a bit of money on top, so the money covered the excrement.

When the priest returned, he said, 'My dear Eulenspiegel, here I am. If you would like to give me something now, as you promised, I am ready to receive it.'

Eulenspiegel said, 'Yes, dear Father. If you'll just grab modestly, and not be greedy, I'll let you make a grab into this jug. That way you'll remember me.'

The priest said, 'I'll do as you wish, taking as little as I can.'

Eulenspiegel opened the jug, saying 'Look, dear Father, the

jug's rather full of money. Just reach in and pull out a handful. But don't reach too far.'

The priest said, 'To be sure.' But he became pretty eager—driven by greed—and plunged right into the jug, thinking he would pull out a good handful, and shoving his hand deep inside. He now discovered something damp and soft under the money. He pulled his hand out again. His knuckles were covered with excrement. The priest said, 'Ah, what a terrible rogue you are! If you can trick me now, at your very end, when you're lying on your death-bed, those you tricked in the days of your youth have every right to complain.'

Eulenspiegel said, 'Dear Father, I warned you not to dig too deep. If your greed betrayed you and you ignored my warning, it's not my fault.'

The priest said, 'You're a rogue to end all rogues! If you could talk yourself out of the gallows at Lübeck, you'll be able to answer me all right.' He walked away, leaving Eulenspiegel lying there.

Eulenspiegel called after him to wait and take his money. The priest refused to listen.

92. *How Eulenspiegel divided his possessions into three parts—one for his friends, one for the Council of Mölln, and one for the priest there.*

As Eulenspiegel became more seriously ill, he made his last will and testament, dividing his possessions into three parts—one for his friends, one for the Council of Mölln, and one for the priest there—but with this stipulation: that when God finally took him and he went his way to death, that his corpse be buried in hallowed ground and his soul dispatched with vigils and masses according to Christian practice and custom. Then, after four weeks, they might together unlock the fine chest, well secured with expensive locks, that he showed them—if it was still locked—and divide among themselves what was in it and come to an agreement about his property.

All three parties took this cheerfully, and Eulenspiegel died. When everything had been done according to his will, and the

four weeks had slipped by, the Council, the parish priest, and
Eulenspiegel's friends came over and opened the chest to
divide the treasure he had left. But when it was opened they
found nothing in it but stones. Everybody looked at everybody else, and they began to get angry. The priest suspected
that since the Council had been taking care of the chest, they
had secretly removed the treasure and locked the chest up
again. The Council thought his friends had taken the treasure
during his illness and filled the chest with stones. His friends
thought the priest must secretly have carried off the treasure
when everybody left to let him confess Eulenspiegel. Well,
they parted unpleasantly.

The priest and the Council now decided to dig Eulenspiegel
up again. But when they began to dig, the grave stank so
badly that no one could remain there. So they filled in the
grave a second time.

Well, Eulenspiegel stayed buried, and in his memory a stone
was placed on his grave, which can still be seen in that spot.

93. *How Eulenspiegel died and how pigs knocked over his bier during the vigils, so he took a tumble.*

After Eulenspiegel had given up the ghost, people came to the hospital to mourn him. Well, they placed him on a bier made of wooden planks. The priests arrived to sing vigils and started singing.

The hospital sow now trotted in with her piglets, walked under the bier, and began to rub herself against it so Eulenspiegel fell off. The women and priests rushed over to chase the sow and piglets outside—but the sow got angry and refused to let herself be moved. In fact the sow and piglets tore madly through the hospital, leaping and racing over the priests, over the beguines, over the sick, over the healthy, and over the coffin in which Eulenspiegel was lying—causing the old beguines to scream and yell so much that the priests gave up their vigils and ran outside, letting the others finally chase the sow and piglets away.

The beguines now set about placing the tree of the dead[1] back on the bier. But it got placed incorrectly, with Eulenspiegel's belly facing the ground while his behind was turned upwards. Well, when the priests left, the beguines said they would bury him. The priests were happy to let them do so, but they would not come back. So the beguines picked up Eulenspiegel and carried him the wrong way around, lying on his belly because the tree was turned over, to the churchyard. There they set him down beside his grave.

The priests now came back anyway and considered what advice they ought to give on how to bury him — he could not simply lie down in his grave, like other Christians. Then they noticed that the tree was turned over and that he was lying on his belly. Well, they began to laugh and said, 'He's showing us himself that he wants to lie upside down. Well, that's how we'll do it.'

94. *How Eulenspiegel was buried, as he wanted to be buried not by religious or lay people but by beguines.*

Things went oddly at Eulenspiegel's burial. When everybody had gathered in the churchyard, around the tree of the dead in which Eulenspiegel was lying, and they set it on two ropes and tried to lower it into his grave, the rope at his feet snapped and the tree shot into the grave, leaving Eulenspiegel standing upright in his coffin.

Everybody who was standing there quickly agreed, 'Let him stand. As he was odd while he lived, he ought to be odd in death too.'

So they filled in the grave and left him standing up. They placed a stone over the grave, and on half of it carved an owl, with a mirror which the owl held in its claws. Over that they carved on the stone:

> Don't move this stone: let that be clear —
> Eulenspiegel's buried here.
> Anno domini MCCCL.

[1] This was an actual tree trunk, which had been dug out and to which the body was firmly strapped, that served as the coffin. See Notes on the Tales.

95. *How Eulenspiegel's epitaph and inscription were carved over his grave at Lüneburg.*

EPITAPH

Don't move this stone: let that be clear —
Eulenspiegel's buried here.

Printed by Johannes Grüninger in the
free city of Strassburg, on Saint
Adolph's Day, in the year
MCCCCCXV.[1]

---

[1] The 1519 edition has 'in the imperial city of Strassburg on St Margaret's Day'. For a discussion of the reference to Lüneburg in the title here, see Notes on the Tales.

NOTES ON THE TALES

TITLE PAGE The edition of 1515 reads *Ein kurzweilig lesen von Dyl/Ulenspiegel gebore uss dem land zu Brunsswick. Wie er sein leben volbracht hatt. xcvi seiner geschichten.* The edition of 1519 has *Dil* instead of *Dyl*, and *hat* instead of *hatt*. A literal translation would read *An amusing story of Dyl* (or *Dil*) *Eulenspiegel*, though the idea of the book as a compilation, collection, or even vintage of tales is implicit in the use of the word *lesen* here. (The rest of the subtitle reads *born in the country of Brunswick. How he spent his life. 96 of his tales*.) The earliest complete editions of the tales use the Low German 'Ulenspiegel'. The first appearance of the High German 'Eulenspiegel' occurs in Weygrand Han's edition (1557, 1563), published in Frankfurt. The familiarity, fame, and widespread use of 'Eulenspiegel', even before Han's publication of it, together with its universality today, argue its use in the present translation. Further discussion of Eulenspiegel's name and its possible meanings is to be found in the Introduction and in the note on Tale 1, below. The publisher Grüninger's assertion that the book presents 96 tales is incorrect; there are in fact 95. The error may result from a miscounting of the tales after Tale 41; the next tale is numbered 43, with this confusion running through the rest of the book.

FOREWORD The author's, or compiler's, Foreword presents a number of knotty problems, having to do with the date of composition, the author's references to himself, and the literary conventions present here. These are mentioned in the Introduction. The word 'countries' is to be understood as including various principalities in what is today Germany, as well as Poland, Denmark, and Italy (Rome, specifically), where Eulenspiegel's adventures also take place. The references to the tales of Pfaffe Amis and Pfaffe vom Kalenberg confirm them as influences on the Eulenspiegel stories.

1 The Elm (or Melbe, in the 1515 edition; the Melme, in the 1519 edition) is a forest in Saxony, extending from Ampleben to Schöppenstedt. Kneitlingen, Eulenspiegel's birthplace, is spelled Knetlingen in the 1515 edition, which frequently retains Low German forms. This village was described, in 1654, as still containing the house in which Eulenspiegel was born. The several

references in this tale to Eulenspiegel's parents, their names, and the name of his godfather are historically inconclusive. Most likely, they form part of the author's technique, one common among many authors, that allows him to lend authenticity to his hero's exploits by mentioning names recognizable to his audience. Thus a Frau Ulenspiegel, referred to in court documents of around 1355 as living in Brunswick, is not necessarily Eulenspiegel's mother; the family name 'Ulenspegel', while recorded in Brunswick in 1335, 1337, and 1355, is connected only much later—and then perhaps falsely—with the qualities of the hero (see also the more detailed account of Eulenspiegel's name in the Introduction); and Uetzen, the name of Eulenspiegel's godfather, which is mentioned only in the 1519 edition, and which shows up as an old family name in Ampleben in 1360, is nowhere connected with a 'Till von Uetzen'. The destruction of the castle at Ampleben, noted in this tale, is recorded as having occurred in 1425, during a skirmish between Brunswickers and the robber-baron Herwig von Uetzen. An Abbot Arnold Papenmeyer, from Brunswick and Altwick, perhaps alluded to in this tale, was in fact alive in 1500, the year in which N. claims to have done his writing; in the 1519 edition he is described as the Abbot of Saint Agidien. The custom of toasting an infant after baptism, with 'Kindelbier', was common in the fourteenth century. What was uncommon, and indeed unknown, is Eulenspiegel's triple baptism. At a minimum, it suggests his life to come, with its jests and absurdities. The end of Eulenspiegel's life (see Tales 93 and 94) presents a similar topsyturvydom.

2   Various editors argue that the last part of this tale, in which Eulenspiegel's father is described as moving his household to the principality of Magdeburg, properly belongs at the beginning of the tale that follows. The editions of 1515 and 1519 present this section as it appears here.

3   The possible influence of this episode on Friedrich Nietzsche's *Also sprach Zarathustra* (1883) should certainly be considered. In Zarathustra's well known encounter with a tightrope walker (Pt. I, 3–8), he watches as a jester suddenly joins the professional acrobat on his rope, high above assembled townspeople. The jester, who is also walking the rope, leaps over the professional rope-walker, terrifying him. He loses his balance and falls into the crowd. He dies in Zarathustra's arms. Zarathustra carries his body off to the gravediggers. On the way, he is accosted by a

man who rebukes him and describes him as one who 'talked like a jester'.

4 The reference to Helmstedt shoes ('helmstetesche Schuch') here has not been satisfactorily explained. It is possible that this phrase makes a now lost slangish reference to senseless and pointless activity of some sort.

5 Eulenspiegel's aphoristic statement here that 'anything a man decides on will take care of him all his life' ('wozu sich einer begibt, daz wurt ihm sein Lebtag gnug') seems to find an echo in Hermann Bote's *Köker* (ca. 1520): 'Wo sik ein jederman to hol, des wart eme sin levedage genoch'. It thus forms part of the 'evidence' that Bote may be the author of the Eulenspiegel stories. This issue is dealt with in the Introduction. The Saint Nicholas referred to here is Pope Nicholas I (d. 867), whose death-day falls on November 13; Saint Martin's Day, honoring Bishop Martin of Tours (316/7–397), falls on November 11. Pope Nicholas (not to be confused with Nicholas, the patron-saint of scholars, who was Bishop of Myra in Lycia and who died in 326) was devoted to fasting. Bishop Martin was known for his philanthropy, this extending even to his dividing his coat among the poor. Eulenspiegel's idea, therefore, is that one should fast with the fasting and eat with the generous.

6 The theme of this tale — the deception of a baker — also appears in Johannes Pauli's *Schimpf und Ernst* (561; edition of 1522).

7 The breakfast bread (*weckbrot*) mentioned here is actually, as can be seen, not a bread at all but a soup, or the breakfast itself. The modern German *Abendbrot*, literally 'evening bread', but actually 'supper', is comparable. The statement that the malicious householder sliced 'the fatty rind of the bread into a milk jug' is confusing (as bread has no fatty rind), and is perhaps meant to suggest that he had mixed pig-fat (or some other fat) in with the bread.

8 Compare with Wilhelm Busch's *Max und Moritz*, ch. 1.

9 Lindow observes that this tale appears in the poem *Salomon und Markolf* (1479; W. Hartmann ed., Halle, 1934, lines 1197f), and believes that its presence there is perhaps the result of its having been taken from an earlier edition of Eulenspiegel's adventures.

10 That Eulenspiegel hires himself out as a page-boy at a castle here seems to hark back to an earlier, definitely medieval stage in the

development of the Eulenspiegel legend, and perhaps in the composition of the tales; the same may be said of the word play on 'henep' and 'senep', which is apparently a residue of a Low German play on these words ('Hennep' and 'Sennep').

11   Büddenstedt is in Brunswick, between Schöningen and Helm-städt. The idea that the priest here comes to an agreement with the farmers to take Eulenspiegel on as a sacristan reflects a common North German custom in place well before the Reformation.

13   Easter passion plays, such as the one described here, commonly, and throughout Europe, mingled various Latin phrases, or tropes, with the vernacular of the audience. From the tenth century, such plays included a *Visitatio Sepulchri*, performed after Matins on Easter Sunday and allowed a greater dramatic freedom precisely because it was formally separated from the mass. A 'sepulchre', or some sort of structure (the meaning apparently varied from place to place; but see the woodcut accompanying this tale for one conception), was put up near the altar or in the transept. The drama at its simplest involved a question asked by the angel at the tomb of Christ, and a response by the three Marys as they visited the tomb on Easter morning. This part was in Latin. The angel asked, 'Quem quaeritis, mulieres?' (Whom are you seeking, women?) To this they replied, 'Jesum Nazarenum, crucifixum'. The angel then informed them of Christ's resurrection, and they, and presumably the audience, rejoiced. (The 1515 edition spells 'quaeritis' as shown.) The satire in this tale is clearly directed at the farmers' inability to understand the Latin, and perhaps at their ignorance more generally.

15   The Bruno of this tale is probably Burchard III, Archbishop of Magdeburg from 1307 to 1325. His predilection for fools, jesters, and entertainers is documented by his contemporaries. While Eulenspiegel plays the part of a medical doctor in this tale, the Bishop's 'doctor' is probably a learned man who had received a degree of some sort. He is in any case no physician.

16   Peine, between Brunswick and Hannover, dates from at least 1130. The 'naked bastard page-boys' present a puzzle. In the earliest editions of the tales one finds 'Bankressen', which may refer to the illegitimate children of the local nobility. The term may also mean 'miserably dressed castle-watchmen out of uni-form', 'lazy rascals lying about on benches', or simply 'bastards'. 'Coldville', from 'Koldingen', not far from Hanover, reflects the Low German word play on 'kold'.

17   A hospital fitting exactly the description of the hospital in this
     tale was established at Nuremberg in 1331.

18   'Half-City' is Halberstadt, with the word play intended. Eulen-
     spiegel's aphoristic reference is to Matthew 12, 13: 'For whoever
     hath, to him shall be given, and he shall have more abundance:
     but whosoever hath not, from him shall be taken away even that
     he hath'.

19   The first sentence of the 1515 edition of this tale speaks of a
     'weaver' as living nearby; the 1519 edition corrects this to 'baker'.
     There was apparently an inn in Brunswick called 'At the Wild
     Man'. Saint Nicholas Eve is December 5. Saint Nicholas is the
     patron saint of school children and sailors.

20   The Uelzen of this tale is a town south of Lüneburg.

21   Lindow (64) believes that the rather witty reflections on food,
     fate, and drink found here are more properly those of a court
     jester than a *Schalk* of Eulenspiegel's ilk. This tale, which in fact
     presents neither prank nor adventure, must therefore be an alien
     addition to a now 'lost' and earlier compilation of Eulenspiegel's
     tales. In fact, however, many tales offer quite similar 'witty'
     reflections, while others show Eulenspiegel playing the part of a
     court jester (cf., for instance, 23, 24, 25, and 38). On the enigma
     of the 'foolishness' of Eulenspiegel's reddish-gray horse, no clear
     facts are forthcoming. One possibility is that the pranksterish
     quality of the horse derived from its mottled appearance. Motley
     was of course a traditional and conventional part of the costume
     of professional medieval and Renaissance jesters and buffoons.

22   The 'Count of Anhalt' mentioned here is most likely Bernhard
     II of Anhalt, who acquired the title 'Prince of Anhalt' in 1318.
     Bernhard II was a descendant of the Bernburgers. A tower, still
     referred to as 'Eulenspiegel's', and thought to be over eleven
     hundred years old, still stands in Bernburg. An Eulenspiegel
     memorial was erected there in 1959.

23   The 1519 edition describes Eulenspiegel here as a 'Hofman', or
     'Gaukler', an entertainer who travelled from court to court. The
     1515 edition, whose terminology is a bit curious in this as in
     other places, terms him a 'koufman', or (in this instance) an
     entrepreneur. The Danish king here may be Christopher II, who
     died in 1332.

24 If there is any historical basis to this tale, the king involved may have been Casimir III (1330–1370).

25 Celle was founded by Otto of Lüneburg in 1292.

26 Johann Christoph Sachse, described by Goethe as the German Gil Blas, reported (in 1822) the existence of an 'Eulenspiegel stone', or memorial of some sort, near Lüneburg, commemorating Eulenspiegel's adventure here.

27 This tale makes an oblique reference to Flanders as an important centre of Renaissance painting in the fifteenth and sixteenth centuries (Eulenspiegel has apparently purchased various paintings there). The Landgrave's personal concern with alchemy is described in the 1519 edition, but not in that of 1515. As it is the Landgrave's gullibility that is being satirized, this new emphasis makes sense. Satirical treatments of quack alchemists are fairly frequent in late medieval and Renaissance literature (cf. Chaucer's 'The Canon's Yeoman's Tale' and Ben Jonson's *The Alchemist*), in which gullibility is likewise an issue. The Landgrave's gullible devotion to alchemy is here skilfully interwoven with two quite ancient folk-tale motifs whose use, in this adventure of Eulenspiegel's, is also to satirize gullibility. These are the motif of the invisible object as a test of legitimacy (cf., Hans Christian Anderson's 'The Emperor's New Clothes') and the magical object as a test of nobility (as, for instance, in the sword test which must be passed by a future king, such as King Arthur, before he can be accepted as a rightful or proper king: only the rightful and proper king will be able to draw the sword from the stone). Beliefs in such possibilities are plainly one target of Eulenspiegel's manipulations. The Landgrave's wife may be the Elizabeth who was the wife of Ludwig VI, Count of Thüringen, and the daughter of Andreas II, King of Hungary. She died in 1227. On the other hand, the ancestral line indicated by Eulenspiegel as he describes his 'painting' is a complete invention. Female fools, or jesters, such as the one referred to in this tale, make infrequent appearances in German literature straight into the eighteenth century; for the most part they are presented as mentally incompetent.

28 The University of Prague, mentioned here, was founded by Emperor Karl IV in 1348 as the first German university (quite a few universities, in Italy, France, Spain, and England, date from considerably earlier). John Wycliffe (1320?–1384), who taught at

Oxford and was an early translator of the Bible into English, along with his Lollard followers, represented a direct challenge to the Curia, canon lawyers, and the Roman Church, with its dependence upon, and advocacy of, Latin. Wycliffe is thus notable for his promotion of vernacular, or 'vulgar', literature, and belongs in a developing tradition of like-minded authors, such as Dante, Chaucer, and (shortly after the publication of the Eulenspiegel stories) Martin Luther. Preachers and professors at the University of Prague were deeply influenced by Wycliffe and the Lollards, and sought for the first time to turn Czech into a literary language. John Huss (1370–1415), who received a master of arts degree from the University of Prague in 1396, was himself influenced by Wycliffe's ideas.

29 Erfurt, noted here, was a university town from 1392 to 1816.

31 Saint Brendan of Ireland (484–577?), mentioned here, is, in legend at least, reputed to have discovered America long before the Norsemen. Geoffrey Ashe, in *Land to the West* (New York, 1962), examines the legend of Brendan through investigations of both Irish history and the medieval European versions of Brendan's possible voyage.

33 The incorrect price of 28 pennies for eating at 'the next table' is corrected to 18 in the 1519 edition.

34 The 'old saying' cited here is unknown in the form in which Eulenspiegel presents it, though variations were certainly familiar in pre-Reformation German-speaking areas, to wit, 'Wer nach Rom zeiht, sucht einen Schalk, beim zweiten Mal findet er ihn, beim dritten Mal bringt er ihn mit' [Whoever goes to Rome is looking for a rogue. On his second trip he finds the rogue, and on his third trip he brings the rogue along himself]. The 1515 edition terms the Basilica of St John in Lateran 'Latronen', which means 'thieves'. The 1519 edition changes, or corrects, this to 'lateran'. If this is not simply a printing error, its satirical sense may be compared with Eulenspiegel's possibly satirical apostrophe of the pope later in this tale as a 'Servant Among All Servants'. The latter is a translation of the conventional 'servus servorum Dei', and as Eulenspiegel uses it, bowing elaborately, at least ironic.

35 Various versions of this anti-Semitic tale appear in other contemporary jest-books, such as Heinrich Bebel's *Facetien*. What is more interesting than the bigoted satire of Jewish gullibility here,

however, is the fact that the Eulenspiegel stories, in their rapidly multiplying editions after 1519, were popular among Jews themselves. A transliteration of the tales, specifically intended for Jewish readers, and done into Hebrew letters, was published on October 11, 1600, by Benjamin Merks (Tannhausen and Augsburg), as *Wunderparlich und seltsame Historien Til Eulenspiegels* (a modern edition of this book, with transliteration into roman type, is John A. Howard, ed., Königshausen + Neumann publ., Würzburg & Bamberg, 1983). This book contains Tale 35 in full, though Eulenspiegel's reference to the Jews here as 'dogs' is eliminated. Virtually no effort is made in Merks' edition to alter the numerous Christian references in the Eulenspiegel stories. It has been argued that the name 'Alpha' in this tale is a variant of 'Kaiphas.'

37 Hoheneggelsen is fifteen kilometres northeast of Hildesheim. The bacon referred to here would have consisted of the meatless fat behind the ribs of the pig. It was both the cheapest and poorest tasting part of the animal. The commercial pig-slaughterers were those who slaughtered pigs for products other than food. The sudden entrance of a 'third man', who overhears the priest in this story as he speaks with his servant-girl, is left a mystery.

38 Both the editions of 1515 and 1519 give the location here as 'Ryssenburg', which makes no sense. Kissenbrück is a village south of Wolfenbüttel. The Duke of Brunswick mentioned here, may have been Henry the Strange, who died in 1322, or his son, Henry II.

41 Eulenspiegel's verses addressed to the wife here, as well as his little speech in prose directed at the maid, may have erotic implications. The wife with 'lots of white in her eye', who stands about looking at men all day instead of working, will want to go after them (this is a version of a contemporary popular saying). The 'beef' that the maid should 'guard against' is a *double-entendre*.

43 Stade, mentioned here, was founded ca. 1150.

44 Bootmakers should not be confused with shoemakers during this period (the late Middle Ages and the Renaissance). The two occupations were quite distinct. Eulenspiegel's target here is thus different from his target in tales dealing with shoemakers.

45 The 1515 edition has 'kalck' in the title here (the 1519 edition 'Talck', or tallow), no doubt a typographical error.

46 Einbeck, mentioned here, was famous for its beer in the Middle Ages.

48 Honegger's discovery of the previously printed fragment of the tales (see also the Introduction) cites Bernburg as the location of this tale.

49 Convocations of artisans, such as that of the tailors, which is described in this tale, were frequent throughout the North German towns belonging to the Hanseatic League. The league itself developed slowly during the High Middle Ages, as groups of merchants or Hansas, trading in foreign principalities, together with the towns and cities where they were located, began to cooperate for protection against competition and theft. The Hanseatic League dates formally from 1358. Despite its dissolution in the seventeenth century, Bremen, Hamburg, and Lübeck are still referred to as Hanseatic cities. Readers of Chaucer may recall the apropos and nearly contemporary description of the haberdasher, carpenter, weaver, dyer, and maker of tapestries in the General Prologue to *The Canterbury Tales*: they all belong to one 'solempne and . . . greet fraternitee', or parish guild, with each of them seeming 'a fair burgeys/To sitten in a yeldehalle on a deys' (ls. 364, 369–70).

50 Stendal, the site of this tale, was well known for its textiles and wool-weaving during the Middle Ages. The colloquialism 'blue Monday', alluded to here as a labour-free day for wool-weavers' apprentices, apparently has its origin in the dyeing practices of the wool-weavers in the fourteenth century. When woad (from *Isatis tinctoria*, powdered and fermented) was used to dye the wool blue, it was necessary to allow twenty-four hours, at a minimum, for the process: twelve hours in the dye-bath and twelve hours of oxygenation in the open air. On Sundays, the entire day was allotted to the dyeing process, and an equal amount of time — in other words, all of Monday — was given over to the necessary oxygenation. As long as woad remained in use, the apprentices, therefore, could take Mondays off. The widespread introduction of indigo, in the sixteenth century, put an end to this custom, though the term 'blue Monday' survives. The wool-weaver's admonition to Eulenspiegel to beat the wool 'a little higher' is a bit of wool-weaver's slang, which Eulenspiegel

of course takes literally. It refers to a taxing operation of beating the wool to induce its lightness and springiness, so that it is 'higher'.

51 Aschersleben, like Berlin (see Tale 53) and Leipzig (see Tale 54), was famous for its fur trade during the Middle Ages.

54 The humour of this tale depends on the absurd self-delusion of the furriers, in a city noted for its fur trade, Leipzig (see note on Tale 51, above), allowing them to mistake the skin of a rabbit for the whole animal. The motif of mistaking one animal for another is common in folk tales (see Thompson, 494, motif J1757: Rabbit thought to be cow). This tale appears in a quite similar form in Hermann Bote's *Schichtbuch*. There is perhaps an echo here as well of the popular expression 'eine Katze im Sack kaufen' (to buy a cat in a sack), and even of its English equivalent 'to buy a pig in a poke'.

55 The absence of punishment, or even the suggestion that legal recourse is possible, in cases such as occur in this tale, in which Eulenspiegel destroys property gratuitously, reflects the difficulty of punishing criminals for petty crimes during the Middle Ages. It may also reflect a secret delight in such nasty activities. The delight, surely, is unquestionable for the audience reading Eulenspiegel's adventures, and remains part of the pleasure of the audience to this day: it is part of the audience's enjoyment too of Eulenspiegel's skill in evading the consequences of his bad deeds. Far more likely, therefore, is that tales such as this offer a specifically literary pleasure, usually denied in life, of simply 'getting away with it', whatever the 'it' may be. The opportunities of enforcing laws against petty criminals, however, varied considerably from place to place, as is shown in Tale 56.

56 The name of the proprietor of the wine cellar near Lübeck's town hall, Lambrecht, who is specifically cited only in Tale 57, is untraceable. The description of Lübeck's 'justice', and indeed of the strictness of law enforcement in Lübeck, especially in cases of crimes of theft and against property, is accurate. The municipal code of laws, or town charter, of Lübeck dates from 1226, and became a model for similar charters of principalities in the Baltic area.

57 It is correct to say that the punishment of 'death on the gallows' for Eulenspiegel's rather trivial crime is harsh even for Lübeck. According to town statutes, capital punishment followed only

when the property stolen amounted to at least four shillings. In an amendment to these laws of 1294, however, it is established that a thief operating in the Ratskeller may be hanged if he is found to have stolen property worth more than eighteen pennies. Honegger speculates that the 'weak' request Eulenspiegel makes toward the end of this tale—that only the wine-tapster and skinner kiss his arse—may be the result of censorship in Strassburg after 1512. Eulenspiegel would more likely have asked the city council and the mayor to administer the humiliating kisses: a far more persuasive means of escape for him. The censor, who apparently existed, may have toned down Eulenspiegel's last wish to avoid 'complications' with the town council and mayor of the Hanseatic city of Lübeck. Eulenspiegel's last wish has been traced as well to an earlier source, the *Mensa philosophica* (1470).

58 The satire here is clearly interwoven with motifs to be found in much earlier folk literature, as is often the case with Eulenspiegel's adventures. The theme of the bottomless purse appears, in variant forms, in ancient Greek folk literature as 'the coin which keeps returning to the owner' and 'magic self-supplying tables' (Thompson, 280; Type 745, Motifs D1602.11, cf. N211, and D1472.7).

60 This tale appears in various versions in other jest collections, to wit, in *Les repues franches* and Montanus' *Wegkürzer*.

61 The opening sentence, in which the Erfurt of the previous tale is misplaced in Hessen, is perhaps a printer's error, or the result of one. The description of Dresden as located 'by the Bohemian Forest on the Elbe' harks back to a time when the Bohemian Forest was better known than Dresden itself.

62 In this, as in other tales in which Eulenspiegel manages a deception and a satire through eloquence, an echo of *maqama*, an Arab folk tale type, dating from the twelfth century, may perhaps be detected. In stories by al Hariri and al Hamadhani, tricksters who deceive through eloquence put in frequent appearances. Other historical references in this tale are, as is often the case, problematic. Frankfurt am Main became the site of the official election of Kaisers, according to an edict known as the 'Golden Bull', in 1356. The Count of Supplenburg, referred to here, may or may not be Lothar III, who was elected 'Roman King' in 1125. Spectacle-making originates in Venice in the thirteenth century, and is established as a recognized craft in

Nuremberg by 1482. Eulenspiegel's mention of Brabant, in Flanders, no doubt has to do with the fact that Brabant had become an important centre of spectacle-making by the fourteenth century. The Bishop of Trier, whom Eulenspiegel meets and entertains with his eloquence, may have been Archbishop Baldwin of Trier, who died in 1354.

63 The 'odd clothes' that Eulenspiegel is described as wearing in this tale remain unidentified. It is unlikely that they were the clothes of a fool or jester. In the woodcuts accompanying the 1515 and 1519 editions, Eulenspiegel never appears in jester's costume, not even in the sardonic woodcut on the title page. Honegger bases his view, that Eulenspiegel commonly appears in riding clothes typical of the late fifteenth century, on comparisons of the woodcuts in the editions of 1515 and 1519. Eulenspiegel appears more consistently as a jester in Melchior Sachse's 1532 edition (Erfurt) for the first time. The wife's sarcastic remark to her husband here, that he has perhaps hired Eulenspiegel only because he was afraid that their bread might be moulding, is to be understood as meaning that there was no one to eat it. The Father Heinrich Hamenstede, referred to in the tale, is perhaps an actual person, a chaplain at Volkersheim, near Bockenem (twenty kilometres southeast of Hildesheim). Hamenstede was the priest of Goslar from 1474 to 1509, when he died. The author's intention, in having Hamenstede driven under the gallows, is no doubt personally satirical.

64 'Black magic', or indeed any sort of magic, receives scant attention in the Eulenspiegel stories. In the subsequent editions (after 1519), this tale is often altered so that Eulenspiegel is allowed to manage his deception by 'natural' means.

65 The 'pipemaker' here is a maker of wind instruments, who has become a wandering musician.

67 Exports of English fabrics, such as that cited here, were well known in German-speaking areas even earlier than the fourteenth century. The motif of deception here, in perhaps its oldest written form, has been linked to India, and the *Panchatantra* (ca. 500 A.D.), which contains a story in which three con men trick a farmer into thinking that he has purchased a dog instead of a goat (on the *Panchatantra* see also Thompson, 69, and especially 376–78, in which the worldwide transmission of such motifs from India is discussed). The presence of Wends at a country fair

in Uelzen is appropriate. 'Wendland', an area distinguishable according to customs and language (and Slavic in the sources of both), extends through parts of east Saxony. The fact that the 'Scottish priest' described here is a wandering monk of some sort probably means that he was in fact a Benedictine and originally Irish.

68 The phrase here having to do with 'earth, ashes, and sand', which is meaningless, is perhaps the result of the omission of a line by the printer. Interestingly, this peculiarity occurs in both the 1515 and 1519 editions.

69 This particular prank takes various forms in jest-literature, appearing, for example, in Pauli's *Schimpf und Ernst*.

70 The episode with the twelve blind men forms the basis of Hans Sachs' Shrovetide play of 1553, *Eulenspiegel mit den Blinden*.

72 This tale, in which Eulenspiegel sows rogues in the street — with stones as seeds — may have satirical-political meanings. A broadside of 1606 presents the episode rather differently. Eulenspiegel sows decent citizens instead of rogues, and they rise in rebellion against local landowners. It is possible that in 1500 this tale may have had implications similar to that of the broadside. The Battle of Hemmingstedt, in 1500, saw the people of Ditmarschen, mentioned here, defending their freedom against the invading Dutch and Danish. The story as it appears in this and other early editions, however, cannot have had precisely these democratic undertones. Eulenspiegel unquestionably sows rogues, and the satire takes aim at those 'dishonest' citizens of the two cities in which he sows them — citizens who scarcely tolerate his mockery and in fact force him to perform his usual vanishing act.

73 The hops market mentioned here is reliably reported to have existed in 1353.

75 The white jam here may also be either a milk pudding or a cabbage stew.

76 Saint Martin's Day, 'when parties like this usually took place', falls on November 11; and in the Middle Ages was commonly followed by parties, dinners, and celebrations (see also the note on Tale 5).

78 This tale also appears in Heinrich Bebel's *Facetien* and in Johannes Pauli's *Schimpf und Ernst* (cf. note on Tale 6).

79 Variations on the theme of paying an innkeeper with the sound of his money appear in a good deal of folk literature. An extremely likely immediate source of this tale is the Italian *Le cento novelle antiche* (late thirteenth century).

80 Rostock is not in Saxony (where the previous tale occurs), a fact that suggests the misplacing of this episode. A nearly word-for-word repetition of the tale is to be found in Heinrich Bebel's *Facetien*. Eulenspiegel's remark at the end, 'Whoever's last sweeps out the house', echoes the adage 'Der Letzte muss die Zeche zahlen' [Whoever's last pays the bill].

81 According to Tale 82, the village cited here must be near Stassfurt. A misprint typical of the frequent differences between the editions of 1515 and 1519 occurs when Eulenspiegel says (in the 1519 edition), 'Ob ein Gast Euwer Kost Isset' [If a guest ate your food]. The 1515 edition absurdly repeats 'Gast'.

82 The symbolism of the wheel as a medieval torture instrument reserved for serious criminals is clear enough. Some scholars believe that Eulenspiegel's description of himself as lying stretched on the wheel indicates a self-conscious perception of a powerful sort. Certainly the tale hints, if delicately, at a sense of torment.

83 Familiar adages, such as the one with which this tale begins, are sprinkled throughout the tales (cf. Tales 16 and 18, for instance, which lead off with similar popular sayings). The last sentence here ('That's how to finish one's trip to Rome') is a clearly satirical remark directed against the Church.

84 This tale, like others (cf. the notes on Tales 69 and 78), appears in Pauli's *Schimpf und Ernst* (Lindow, 242); it is eliminated from subsequent editions.

85 The word play here, on 'Hochländer' and 'Holänder', is puzzling. The texts do not make it clear whether the reference is to a Dutchman or a Highlander. On grounds of proximity and credibility, and because a choice is clearly required in translation, I have opted for the Dutchman.

86 The Archbishop here may have been Burchard Grelle, who died in 1344, and whose character might indeed have led him to play the sort of trick described. The trick, at any rate, is quite in accord with the spirit of the times. Both the editions of 1515 and 1519 speaks of the Bishop as receiving three times the money (30

guilders) that he gives Eulenspiegel for revealing his little secret.
I have corrected the error.

87 The editions of 1515 and 1519 present Lübeck in the title here,
but Einbeck in the story. Tale 46, which also takes place near
Einbeck, ought perhaps to follow this one. We are told that the
'honest, simple peasant' who wishes to sell his plums was living
at Oldenburg near Einbeck, but no such place exists near
Einbeck. The three villages of Stadtoldendorf, Markoldendorf,
and Kleinoldendorf are close to Einbeck, however. N. may have
had one of these in mind, most likely Stadtoldendorf, where in
1328 an Otto von Oldenburg is mentioned. The peasant in this
story, some critics argue, is as much a sinner as Eulenspiegel,
who ruins his plums. The peasant wishes to sell them at too high
a price, or to engage in profiteering. He thus deserves what he
gets. This seems a weak argument in light of the 'punishment'
visited on him.

88 Marienthal, in the district of Helmstädt is a Cistercian abbey
founded ca. 1136. This may be the abbey described here, and
confused with Marienwohlde, a nunnery founded in 1412 and
located some two kilometres from Mölln—where (in Tale 89)
Eulenspiegel becomes ill and dies. This tale, at any rate, finds a
close parallel in *Bruder Rausch*, published in 1515 in Strassburg;
Lappenberg (282f) cites as well a poem of the fifteenth or
sixteenth century, with comparable behaviour.

89 The hospital 'The Holy Ghost' (*Domus Sancti Spiritus Molne*) is
mentioned in a Lübeck document of 1289.

90 The origin of the term 'beguines', which figures in this and
succeeding tales, is unknown. Dayton Phillips, in his interesting
study, *Beguines in Medieval Strassburg* (Stanford University
Press, 1941), 2, suggests that the word is derived 'from the Old
French word *beige* or *bege*, referring to the gray-brown color of
the penitent robe of undyed wool worn by "beguines"'. Phillips
believes that 'a person wearing such a robe came to be called
beguinus, through the addition of the Latin adjectival suffix -*inus*
to the adjective *bege*, and that this combination in German-
speaking provinces gave the *g* its hard sound'. Beguines, in any
case, is the name of certain laymen and laywomen who were first
organized in Belgium and France during the twelfth century.
While they devoted themselves primarily to charitable and
religious lives, they were nonetheless free to marry. For a good

history of the beguines in the Middle Ages, see Ernest W. McDonnell, *The Beguines and Beghards in Medieval Culture* (Rutgers University Press, 1954). Beguines were for the most part attached to specific clerical orders, or lived on designated streets. They were active in charities after 1311. Eulenspiegel's unpleasant remark about a beguine's losing her piety when she is angry is in fact a medieval commonplace. There indeed existed a contemporary fashion of letting one's coat hang below one's outer cloak, which Eulenspiegel mocks in this story, with the first of his last wishes. For the sake of clarity, I have inserted the word 'fashionably' into my translation here.

92 The custom of drawing up one's last will and testament in the manner described here was well in place by 1300. Such documents were registered and deposited with local city officials.

93 The practice of strapping a body into a hollowed-out tree perhaps dates from the Bronze Age.

94 The word 'wunderlich' is applied no less than three times to Eulenspiegel and his burial in this tale, as in the first sentence: 'Bei Ulenspiegels Begräbtnis gieng es wunderlich zu'. The word can mean 'strangely', as well as 'oddly', or even 'amazingly' and 'peculiarly'. Each offers a slightly different critical emphasis, or in this case, interpretation of the events and of Eulenspiegel's life. I have opted for the more conservative 'oddly', though all senses of the word are surely to be understood. Curiously enough, Ben Jonson, at his own request, was buried standing on his feet in Westminster Abbey. The parallel with Eulenspiegel's vertical position in his grave may not be accidental. Jonson mentions an 'Howleglass' in his *Masque of the Fortunate Isles* (1626). On Jonson's posture in death, see Marchette Chute, *Ben Jonson of Westminster* (New York, 1953), 347. An inscription on a gravestone at Mölln, while commemorating Eulenspiegel's death, may in fact have been erected only after the publication of the earliest editions of the *Volksbuch*.

95 This final tale, numbered 96 in the editions of 1515 and 1519 (but see the note on the title page, above, for the probable reasons for this error), presents a problem for the 'acrostic' of Hermann Bote's name that some scholars wish to establish. Obviously it does not continue the name with an expected additional letter. On the other hand, the tale is clearly numbered as an additional adventure, and is introduced in the same manner

as all the rest: 'Die. xCvi histo:i sagt wie Ulen/spiegels
EpithapCium onnd obergeschrifft zu Lünen/burg off sienem
grab gehowen stot' [*sic*]. The tale of course simply repeats,
though with the important modification of the illustrative woodcut, the motif of the previous tale. For this reason, a few readers
believe it possible that this tale marked the original final page of
the book, while others observe that the tale is not in fact a true
tale. If the tale is therefore omitted from consideration, it
becomes superfluous to investigate — as has often been done —
the mysterious identification of Lüneburg as Eulenspiegel's
burial site. Sichtermann favours this approach. The confusion is
compounded by suggestions that Lüneburg in the title here may
be the result of a mixup between Lüneburg and Lauenburg,
which is the name of the duchy in which Mölln is located. All of
this is sheer guesswork, to be sure, with the added disadvantage
that it seems to eliminate evidence on the basis that it does not
fit into an established hypothesis. What is perhaps more interesting, and certainly more consistent with the text itself, is a long-
previous speculation of Lappenberg. Lappenberg reports that a
Senator Albers of Lüneburg remembered (as recently as 1846)
having seen a gravestone, in the Church of Saint Mary at
Lüneburg, on which was carved an owl, but no mirror. As this
cemetery has since been torn up, no confirmation of Albers'
childhood memory is possible. Lappenberg himself believes that
the confusion between Mölln and Lüneburg is either a deliberate
final joke of the author's or a misprint (of the sort to be found
perhaps in Tale 64, in which the title gives us a location for the
tale that is at variance with the location given in the tale itself).
The idea that the insertion of Lüneburg may be N.'s final joke is
certainly tempting. Certainly too it is consistent with a text in
which both the author and his hero seem to remain, in various
important ways, not only jesting but invisible.

THE WORLD'S CLASSICS

A Select List

HANS ANDERSEN: Fairy Tales
Translated by L. W. Kingsland
Introduction by Naomi Lewis
Illustrated by Vilhelm Pedersen and Lorenz Frølich

ARTHUR J. ARBERRY (Transl.): The Koran

LUDOVICO ARIOSTO: Orlando Furioso
Translated by Guido Waldman

ARISTOTLE: The Nicomachean Ethics
Translated by David Ross

JANE AUSTEN: Emma
Edited by James Kinsley and David Lodge

Northanger Abbey, Lady Susan, The Watsons,
and Sanditon
Edited by John Davie

Persuasion
Edited by John Davie

WILLIAM BECKFORD: Vathek
Edited by Roger Lonsdale

KEITH BOSLEY (Transl.): The Kalevala

CHARLOTTE BRONTË: Jane Eyre
Edited by Margaret Smith

JOHN BUNYAN: The Pilgrim's Progress
Edited by N. H. Keeble

FRANCES HODGSON BURNETT: The Secret Garden
Edited by Dennis Butts

FANNY BURNEY: Cecilia
or Memoirs of an Heiress
Edited by Peter Sabor and Margaret Anne Doody

THOMAS CARLYLE: The French Revolution
Edited by K. J. Fielding and David Sorensen

TOBIAS SMOLLETT: The Expedition of Humphry Clinker
Edited by Lewis M. Knapp
Revised by Paul-Gabriel Boucé

ROBERT LOUIS STEVENSON:
Treasure Island
Edited by Emma Letley

ANTHONY TROLLOPE: The American Senator
Edited by John Halperin

GIORGIO VASARI: The Lives of the Artists
Translated and Edited by Julia Conaway Bondanella and Peter Bondanella

VIRGINIA WOOLF: Orlando
Edited by Rachel Bowlby

ÉMILE ZOLA: Nana
Translated and Edited by Douglas Parmée

A complete list of Oxford Paperbacks, including The World's Classics, OPUS, Past Masters, Oxford Authors, Oxford Shakespeare, and Oxford Paperback Reference, is available in the UK from the Arts and Reference Publicity Department (BH), Oxford University Press, Walton Street, Oxford OX2 6DP.

In the USA, complete lists are available from the Paperbacks Marketing Manager, Oxford University Press, 200 Madison Avenue, New York, NY 10016.

Oxford Paperbacks are available from all good bookshops. In case of difficulty, customers in the UK can order direct from Oxford University Press Bookshop, Freepost, 116 High Street, Oxford, OX1 4BR, enclosing full payment. Please add 10 per cent of published price for postage and packing.